EMT

D1286897

Dear Reader,

I live in Oregon, a continent away from Maine. But the Pine Tree State is a place that I love to visit. I was twenty-five the first time I visited the state—and fifty-two the last time.

It was that last trip that I drew from emotionally as I wrote *Tearoom in a Tempest.* My husband and I met kind, strong, no-nonsense people throughout our Maine visit, saw amazing scenery, and learned more about the state's history. Sweet memories from that trip inspired me to say "yes" to writing for the Tearoom Mysteries series.

But as much as I like Maine, it was the two main characters and cousins, Elaine and Jan, who truly captured my heart. I'm close in age now to the cousins, and they pulled me into their stories, as did their children and friends.

No matter what state we live in or the details of our lives, we face changes with each and every year. Jobs change. Children move—or return home. Some friendships fade. Others grow stronger. One generation passes on as another begins.

We adapt, move forward, and rely on friends and family to help us navigate the changes, but, as with Jan and Elaine, it's our faith that ultimately sustains us. No matter your state or stage of life, I hope that this story of Elaine and Jan encourages you to rely on God as you navigate the changes in your own life!

Leslie Gould

Tearoom Mysteries

TEAROOM
mysteries

Tearoom in a Tempest

LESLIE GOULD

Guideposts

New York

Tearoom Mysteries is a trademark of Guideposts

Published by Guideposts Books & Inspirational Media
110 William Street
New York, New York 10038
Guideposts.org

Copyright © 2017 by Guideposts. All rights reserved.

This book, or parts thereof, may not be reproduced, stored in a retrieval
system, or transmitted in any form or by any means, electronic, mechanical,
photocopying, recording or otherwise, without the written permission of the
publisher.

The characters and events in this book are fictional, and any resemblance to
actual persons or events is coincidental.

Acknowledgments

Every attempt has been made to credit the sources of copyrighted material used
in this book. If any such acknowledgment has been inadvertently omitted or
miscredited, receipt of such information would be appreciated.

Scripture references are from the following sources: *The Holy Bible,* King James
Version (KJV). *The Holy Bible, New International Version.* Copyright ©1973, 1978,
1984, 2011 by Biblica, Inc. Used by permission of Zondervan. All rights reserved
worldwide. www.zondervan.com

Cover and interior design by Müllerhaus
Cover illustration by Ross Jones, represented by Deborah Wolfe, Ltd.
Typeset by Aptara, Inc.

Printed and bound in the United States of America
10 9 8 7 6 5 4 3 2 1

CHAPTER ONE

A s Elaine Cook approached Tea for Two, her windshield wipers sped back and forth across the windshield, clearing a small path through the driving rain. She paused for a moment, gazing out on Chickadee Lake, where the waves rode high and choppy and the April rain bounced up and then back down against the still-frigid surface.

Fortunately Elaine had too many fun events planned in the next few days to give in to the gloom. She pulled in to the driveway, turned off the wipers, and then shut off the engine. Bracing herself against the sleety rain, she grabbed the paper bag of groceries, the plastic bag with printer ink and a new blank notebook, and her purse from the passenger seat, then climbed out of her red Chevy Malibu, kicked the door shut behind her, and then dashed toward the house.

The rain beat against her face as she sloshed through the mud puddles in her waterproof boots. Ahead was the Victorian house that she and her cousin Jan Blake had turned into a tearoom over two years ago.

Elaine had left their employee Rose Young in charge while she ran errands and Jan finished up the baking. Their other employee, Archie Bentham, had left with his wife, Gloria, and his sister, Geraldine, for a visit to England, where they were from. She and Jan had received a postcard the day before saying they were having a wonderful time, visiting museums where Archie and Geraldine's father's works of art were displayed. Elaine was thrilled for Archie, but it meant a little more planning on her part to coordinate schedules and keep the tearoom running smoothly.

Yes, there was a lot going on but no more than usual. Elaine was looking forward to spending the evening with her mother in Augusta, and then in three days, on Monday, her daughter, Sasha, would return to Maine from her time of training in Vermont, and stay until the Monday after Mother's Day. Sasha had combined her vacation days and a leave of absence from her job as a fitness trainer in Colorado for some time off.

As Elaine stepped into the house, the sound of spoons clinking against cups and the chatter of the customers greeted her. It was music to her ears and further lifted her spirits.

Rose smiled from the cash register as she rang up an order for an elderly woman. Elaine could see customers sitting at several of the tables covered with lace and linen and set with china. The tearoom appeared to be much busier than she'd anticipated it would be on a rainy Friday afternoon.

Rose nodded at Elaine's inquiring expression, making the wheat-colored bun atop her head wiggle a little. She motioned toward the dining room. "We've got a group in there too."

"Lovely," Elaine said. "I'll help you fill orders."

Rose smiled in appreciation.

Elaine made her way to the kitchen, put the groceries on the kitchen counter, hung up her coat, brushed her fingers through her short, damp hair, and then placed the ink and notebook on her desk in her office. After she rolled up the sleeves of her sweater, put on an apron, and scrubbed her hands, she began steeping a pot of Earl Grey tea and then placed two chocolate almond scones on a plate. Next she started a pot of orange spice tea and plated cranberry and white chocolate cookies.

Together, she and Rose quickly filled the orders. When Rose returned after delivering the next-to-last one, Elaine had a chance to ask where Jan was.

Rose, standing at the kitchen island, placed teacups on a tray. "She went with Bob to help friends with a cabin on the lake. A tree uprooted and fell across their garage and damaged their car. Bob was going to give them a ride into town. When he stopped by here, we weren't busy so I told Jan to ride along, that I'd be fine."

"What horrible weather to be out in." Elaine glanced out the kitchen window through the screened porch, hoping the rain had slowed. It hadn't, and the lake was churning even more. There wasn't a single boat on the water.

"More rain is predicted," Rose said. "I didn't think we'd have much business today, but almost everyone who's come in commented they just wanted a hot cup of tea to combat the dreariness. Mostly locals though," she added. "I think the tourists are staying away."

Elaine hoped it wasn't raining as hard in Augusta. For a moment she wondered if she shouldn't drive in the storm, but she planned to include Jan's granddaughter Avery in the outing and hated to cancel. Elaine was looking forward to taking the girl to visit her great-great-aunt, Elaine's mother. She didn't want to disappoint either one of them.

Rose interrupted Elaine's thoughts. "I almost forgot. A woman dropped off a package for you and Jan. She said she was remodeling her house and found something."

Elaine placed a pot of peppermint tea on Rose's tray. "Oh?"

"Yeah, it was kind of weird. She said she wanted the 'Pritchard cousins' to have what's inside."

"What *is* inside?" Elaine asked.

Rose shrugged. "I have no idea, and she didn't say. But the package is about the size of a small book." She nodded through the kitchen doorway toward the cash register cabinet as she lifted the tray and headed out to the floor. She called out over her shoulder, "The package is on the bottom shelf."

Curious, Elaine stepped to the counter and retrieved the parcel. She unwound the thick brown paper, revealing a small leather-bound book with the title *Evangeline: A Tale of Acadie* imprinted on the cover and the author's name, Henry Wadsworth Longfellow.

"Oh my," Elaine said out loud. Every Mainer knew Henry Wadsworth Longfellow. He was one of the state's most beloved authors. But why would someone gift the book to the "Pritchard cousins"? And who even remembered that she and Jan used to go by that designation? It was Jan's maiden name and also Elaine's mother's maiden name, but once Jan's parents died

4

there wasn't anyone with that last name left in the area. Not more than a handful of people would make the connection to Jan and Elaine, except perhaps Jan's cousin Lori, who lived in Portland.

Elaine opened the cover, which was in remarkably good condition. On the title page of the epic poem was the name of the publishing company, *Boston: Ticknor & Company,* and the year, *1847.* Then an autograph. *Henry W. Longfellow.* Her heart sped—could the signature possibly be genuine? It was surprisingly easy to read even though it was written in that ornate, old-fashioned script of so long ago.

She turned to the next page. Faintly at the top right-hand side was a name, written in pencil. She squinted. *Lena Foret.* She was sure of it. That was the name of her and Jan's Grandmother Pritchard—their Nana—before she married their grandfather.

Elaine wanted to hug the book to her chest, but she feared damaging it so she held it in front of her. Their grandmother wasn't born until 1901, so obviously the book would have been given to her years after it was published.

As she leafed through the pages, Elaine struggled to remember what she could about the story of Evangeline. She couldn't come up with much more than that it was about a girl, born in Nova Scotia, during the Great Upheaval of the Acadians, sometime in the 1700s.

Elaine reached the back of the book, where a piece of white paper was affixed to the last page with something written on it. The ink had faded and the script was old-fashioned with lots of swirls—and not easy to read the way the autograph had been. She could make out the letter *L*, a few words in the one paragraph—*recover* and *book* and *hurt*, and then a lone *T* at the end. What in the world could the note be about?

She closed the book and pulled out her cell phone from the pocket of her sweater and snapped a photo of the front, then the title page with the autograph, Lena Foret's name, and the note, and sent a quick text to Jan with the photos attached. Maybe Jan had some memory of the book since she'd been in the Maine area all those years while Elaine was traveling the world.

Rose stepped out of the dining room with the empty tray. "What is it?" she asked.

Elaine pointed to the counter. "A book." She glanced at Rose. "As you'd guessed. It appears that it belonged to our grandmother."

"Wow," Rose said. "That's really cool."

"Tell me again who dropped it off?"

Rose's face reddened. "She didn't give her name. And we were really busy right then, so I'm afraid I didn't think to ask."

"That's okay," Elaine said. "I understand. But you didn't recognize her?"

"No." Rose frowned. "She was probably around your age. Shoulder-length white hair. Slender." She shrugged. "I'm sorry."

As Rose retreated to the kitchen, Elaine thought about what to do. She didn't have much time today, but a quick visit next door at the Bookworm with the owner, Bristol Payson, was in order. Perhaps Bristol would at least be able to tell Elaine the best way to care for the book while she tried to figure out where it had come from.

CHAPTER TWO

Elaine made sure Rose was okay with taking and filling the orders. Then she put her raincoat back on, grabbed an umbrella from the stand at the front door, and slipped the book, which she'd secured in a plastic bag, under her arm.

She squinted through the rain as she walked, her sights set on the Bookworm. Beyond it were the Pine Tree Grill, the marina, and the Art Gallery, and across the street, Murphy's General Store, the library, and Gift Me, along with a few gorgeous old homes like her own. The stores were all open, but no pedestrians were out and only a few cars splashed through the sodden streets. Clutching the book to her side, Elaine hurried on to Bristol's shop.

After shaking out her umbrella and leaving it on the stoop, Elaine pushed open the door. She stepped into the Bookworm just as Katelyn Conrad, Bristol's employee, headed toward the door.

"Off work already?"

Katelyn grinned, her eyes lighting up behind her dark-framed glasses. "I've got a hot date with my honey tonight.

Bristol is letting me off early." Katelyn had started seeing her now-husband Frank as a result of a crossword puzzle mystery the cousins had solved, and Elaine and Jan always felt pleasantly responsible for the match.

"Where are you going?"

"A production of *All's Well That Ends Well*. At a small theater in Portland."

"Oh, lucky you," Elaine said. Katelyn was intelligent, thoughtful, and well read. It didn't surprise her at all that a hot date with her husband would include a Shakespeare play. "Don't let me keep you. Have fun!" Elaine stepped aside and swept her arm toward the door.

Katelyn grinned and waved as she hurried out.

Elaine continued on into the store. Bristol stood at the register, her dark-blonde hair pulled back in a ponytail. She held a book in her hand as she checked out a purchase by a young woman at the counter.

Elaine waved. Bristol smiled and said, "I'll be right with you, Elaine."

With a nod, Elaine scanned the store. A middle-aged woman stood at the magazine rack browsing through the *Cryptogram* magazines that Jan enjoyed so much, and an older man, probably in his early seventies, sat in the reading area with a book in one hand and one of Bristol's complimentary cups of coffee in the other. No one else was in the shop.

Elaine began browsing the books in the rack closest to the counter. All had a Maine theme—the sixty-five lighthouses located along the coast, the best hiking trails in the state, the forty-four National Historical Landmarks, the most beautiful back roads for day trips. Elaine perused the last one, thinking how fun it would be to explore them with Nathan Culver, her boyfriend.

As she thumbed through it, Bristol greeted her. Elaine closed the book and asked Bristol how she was doing.

"Great!" She looked around and lowered her voice. "I'm thankful for any business on a dreary day like this."

Elaine nodded in agreement.

"What brings you in?" Bristol asked.

"The strangest thing happened," Elaine answered as she put the book back in the rack. She'd buy it later.

She approached the counter, taking the copy of *Evangeline* out of the plastic bag. "Someone dropped this off at the tearoom." She placed it on the counter.

Bristol leaned toward it. *"Evangeline."*

"Yes, and it appears the printing date was 1847."

The man in the reading area turned toward them.

Elaine started to open the book.

"Wait," Bristol said, her blue eyes bright. "Let me grab a pair of archival gloves."

"All right." Elaine's face grew warm. She should have thought of that. As an antiques expert, Nathan certainly would have.

The man in the reading area stood as the front door chimed. Elaine automatically turned toward it, but whoever the customer was had already disappeared among the shelves of books.

Just as Bristol returned with the gloves, the older man started toward them. Bristol handed the gloves to Elaine, who slipped them on and opened the book to the title page.

Bristol whistled. "It's autographed."

"Yes," Elaine said.

By now the man was at the counter. He wore a tweed jacket and expensive leather shoes, and his thin hair was cut close to his head.

Elaine smiled at him and then turned back to Bristol. "My grandmother's name—she's Jan's grandmother too—is here." She flipped to that page. "And in the back is a note that's difficult to read." She turned to that page. "I can only make out a few words."

"Goodness, 1847," Bristol said. "It was first published that year."

"It doesn't say it was a first printing."

The elderly man spoke up. "Of course not. There was no way to know if there would be any subsequent printings, but there were. Within a decade, 36,000 copies had sold. It was a runaway best seller for its time." He stepped closer to Elaine and extended his hand. "Patrick Stark," he said. "I'm a docent at the Maine Historical Society. In fact, I'm in search of treasures just like this."

Elaine shook his hand. "Really?"

"I'm working on an exhibit," he explained, "called Maine Books. I recently found an 1859 copy of Nathaniel Hawthorne's *The Scarlet Letter* at a little shop in Augusta."

"Oh my," Elaine said. "That's quite a find." Nathaniel Hawthorne was another Maine treasure. The state had quite a few renowned authors to its credit.

"Yes." He smiled. "I stopped in here hoping for another one."

Bristol wrinkled her nose. "Sadly, we don't often get rare books here."

The man dipped his head a little and then said, "But what a coincidence that this book should arrive while I'm here."

Elaine chuckled to hide her discomfort. "This one isn't for sale, I'm afraid."

"Perhaps you'd consider loaning it." The man's tone was serious.

Elaine shook her head. "I'm sorry, but not at this point. Right now I simply want to find out where it came from, when my grandmother had it, and what the note in the back says. Beyond that, I have no idea what my cousin and I will decide to do with it."

"Well, it's a Maine treasure," Mr. Stark said, stepping within a couple of inches of Elaine. "Don't forget that. The people of our state would love to see this on display. If you reconsider, you can find me over at the Green Glade cottages."

Feeling uncomfortable with the man standing so close, Elaine reached for the plastic bag and glanced up a Bristol. "I'll take it home for now and bring it back later, when you're not so busy."

"No!" Bristol and the man both shouted in unison.

Stunned by the reaction of the two, Elaine slipped the book into the bag anyway. She couldn't help but feel they were overreacting.

"I have a professor friend I can call about it," Bristol quickly said. "At Bowdoin College. He's a premier expert on Longfellow."

"Dr. Day?" Mr. Stark asked.

Bristol nodded. "You know him?"

Mr. Stark answered, "Yes. As an acquaintance, from a talk he gave at the historical society. It's a great idea to contact him."

Elaine zipped the plastic bag and took off the gloves as Bristol opened a document on her computer.

"That plastic could harm the book," Mr. Stark said. "You really need an archival container to put it in."

Elaine ignored the man and picked up the book as Bristol reached for her landline and started to dial.

"Perhaps a plain cardboard box," the man said.

"It's raining outside."

"True," he said. "But plastic is harmful to paper and other fibers."

"I'll keep that in mind," Elaine said, wondering where she'd store the book when she reached home. She had no idea how to care for it. She'd have to ask Nathan for his advice.

"Hello," Bristol said to the phone. "Dr. Day? I'm so sorry to bother you on a Friday afternoon. I imagine you're ready to leave for the weekend."

Elaine clutched the book, aware that Patrick Stark still had his eyes on it, as Bristol quickly explained the situation and then listened to the professor's response.

"You would?" Bristol asked and then after another short pause, said, "Five o'clock will be great."

Elaine started to say that she was headed to Augusta, but Bristol was already saying goodbye.

Once she'd hung up, Elaine said, "That won't work. I'm leaving for my mother's—in just a few minutes."

"Oh dear," Bristol said. "He wanted to look at it immediately. Would you be willing to leave the book, just for the afternoon and evening? I'll lock it in my office."

Elaine hesitated.

"I can vouch for Dr. Day." Mr. Stark stepped back from Elaine, giving her a little more space. "He's well known and respected."

"He can verify the autograph, most likely. And perhaps he's seen the book before," Bristol said. "He may also have an idea of what it's worth."

Elaine exhaled.

"I don't blame you if you don't want to leave it," Bristol said. "But Dr. Day leaves tomorrow for an academic conference. Once he returns, you could take the book to Brunswick, to the college. But having him look at it today would save you a trip, and it could provide information much sooner."

That was true. And with Sasha visiting, Elaine wouldn't have much extra time. She glanced at Mr. Stark. He'd retreated a little more and seemed to have composed himself.

For a minute Elaine considered calling Jan, but she knew her cousin would trust her judgment on what to do.

"All right," she finally said. "I'll get it back from you in the morning." The front door chimed again. Elaine turned her head again, but whoever it was had already exited the building. A blur of a black coat hurried down the walkway.

Elaine turned back toward Bristol and held the book out to her. The bookstore owner took it and cradled it as if it were a newborn baby. "I promise I won't let anything happen to it."

She stepped out from around the counter. "In fact, I'm going to go lock it in my office right now."

"Thank you," Elaine said. "I appreciate your care, not that I think anyone would try to take the book or anything..."

"Oh, you'd be surprised," Mr. Stark said as Bristol opened the door to her office. "There are lots of people who would covet a find like this."

Elaine nearly laughed. Surely the man, who at first glance appeared normal but now seemed extremely odd and aggressive, was overestimating the interest of the general public. Only those with both historical and literary bents like his would be interested in such an item.

A moment later, Bristol locked the door to her office. Elaine thanked her, told Mr. Stark goodbye, and then headed out the door.

She'd concentrate on finding out who dropped it off and then where it originated, knowing that somewhere along its journey it belonged to Grandmother Pritchard—their Nana. The thought warmed Elaine's heart again. On Monday she'd take the book to the bank and put it her deposit box—just to be on the safe side. It seemed possible the book had been missing for years, and she certainly didn't want to be responsible for anything happening to it.

CHAPTER THREE

The farther Elaine drove from Lancaster, the more the rain slowed. By the time she reached the home of Jan's son, Brian, and his wife, Paula, it had entirely stopped. Avery was ready, dressed in black leggings, a long lime-green sweater, and a pair of black high-top Keds. Yes, she was definitely a young teenager now.

Elaine was thankful the girl still wanted to spend time with her older relatives, but she wouldn't be surprised if Avery would continue to march to the beat of a different drummer, so to speak. She was smart and did well in school, but she'd already had some problems with mean girls in her grade. Elaine knew how important it was for a child to have as much support as possible, and she was thankful her own mother, even in her late seventies, was interested in having a relationship with those from the youngest generation.

"I'll have her back in a couple of hours," Elaine told Paula.

As she drove to her mother's house, Elaine told Avery about the book showing up at the tearoom. Avery listened with rapt attention, her big eyes wide. When Elaine finished her story,

Avery said, "I know all about Henry Wadsworth Longfellow. We took a field trip to his old house in Portland in the fourth grade, with the Maine Historical Society."

Elaine smiled, remembering a trip there with Ben, Jared, and Sasha years ago. But then she thought of Mr. Stark and his odd behavior.

"I've never read *Evangeline* though," Avery said.

"You probably will in high school. I imagine now it might be"—she almost said *difficult.* Instead she chose to say—"a little archaic."

"Oh, I like that word," Avery said, settling back in the passenger seat. "Archaic. Still, I'd like to read the book," she said.

"Let's ask your great-great-aunt Virginia if she has a copy."

Avery seemed to like the idea.

When they reached the Millpond Senior Community, Elaine turned back toward the cottages and then parked in front of her mother's small bungalow. After retrieving the plate of shortbread cookies Jan had made for her from the backseat of the car, Elaine and Avery headed toward the house. Elaine's mother had insisted on fixing dinner, even though Elaine had protested, not wanting to burden her mother with extra work.

The door swung open before Elaine could knock. Her mother, dressed in a sapphire-blue pantsuit with a paisley scarf around her neck, greeted them with hugs. "Come in, come in," she said, sweeping her arm toward the short entry hall. She quickly took Elaine's raincoat and then Avery's jacket and hung them in the closet.

The scent of freshly baked bread filled the house. "I hope you didn't go to too much trouble," Elaine said.

"Not at all," her mother answered, leading the way into the open kitchen and dining area. "We're having soup and salad. It's all very simple." It was and it wasn't. The salad was fairly complicated with chard, broccoli, kale, carrots, parsley, olives, and fresh albacore in aioli, with Dijon dressing. Not exactly kid fare. The soup was a creamy butternut squash. And the homemade bread was crescent rolls. Elaine's mouth watered.

They sat down at the table, set with Virginia's beloved Desert Rose wedding china and silver. "Oh, Mom," Elaine said, "this is all so lovely!"

Avery expertly flicked the linen napkin over her lap. After a blessing, Virginia passed the salad to Avery.

For a moment Elaine wondered if the girl ate such food, but she dished up a large spoonful while Virginia ladled soup for all of them from the tureen in the middle of the table.

Avery took a bite of the salad and said, "Delicious."

Elaine could have hugged her.

Virginia gave the teen a smile and then held up a spear of broccoli and shared a story about how her brother, Avery's great-grandfather and Jan's father, didn't like broccoli and that their mother always made him take a no-thank-you helping anyway. She explained to Avery, "That would be your great-great-grandmother. Lena Foret Pritchard."

"Oh, the book!" Elaine blurted out.

Virginia put down the fork. "What in the world?"

"I already told Avery, but I forgot to tell you." She quickly explained about the copy of *Evangeline* with Virginia's mother's name in the front that had been brought to the tearoom. "And there was an odd, undecipherable note in the back. I took a photo—it's on my phone."

"Show it to me when we're done eating," Virginia said and then pursed her lips as she glanced toward Avery.

"Of course," Elaine said. Her mother valued good manners highly and definitely had an aversion to cell phones at the table.

"I don't recall Mama having a copy of *Evangeline*," Virginia said as she tapped the side of her head. "But I'm not surprised she did. Foret is a French surname and she did say once that we had Acadian ancestors."

"I remember you mentioning that before."

Virginia nodded. "In the northern part of the state."

"Did they migrate from Nova Scotia?"

Virginia nodded. "It seems they arrived in Maine, up north around the St. John River Valley, long before the Expulsion of the Acadians though." Elaine had never heard that before.

"As I said, I don't remember Mama having a copy but I have one. It was a gift from your father, when we were in college. Just a cheap paperback."

"How sweet," Elaine said. "Avery is interested in reading it."

"Oh really?" Virginia smiled. "I doubt very many students your age would want to, but you can certainly borrow my copy. In fact, you can have it." She turned toward Elaine. "Unless you want it, dear?"

Elaine shook her head. "I think it would be lovely for Avery to have it. If you're sure."

"Would you sign the book?" Avery asked. "And date it? Because I'll keep it for the rest of my life."

Virginia nodded as she passed the salad around again. "I'll find it and sign it after we're done eating."

Elaine couldn't help but be charmed by the interaction between the two, and note that another copy of *Evangeline* was being passed down to the next generation.

"In the meantime," Virginia said to Avery, "I'll tell you a little about the story. There's a girl named Evangeline." Virginia grinned. "But you probably guessed that."

Avery nodded.

"And the young man she loves, Gabriel. The Acadians, who were of French descent, are forced by the British to leave Canada in the mid-1700s and some ended up as far away as Louisiana. Evangeline and Gabriel became separated and she spent the rest of her life looking for him."

"She must have really loved him." Avery's eyes grew wide. "Did she find him?"

"I'm not going to tell you," Virginia teased. "Not if you plan to read the book."

Avery grinned again. "Maybe I'll listen to it—you know, like an audio book."

Virginia wrinkled her nose.

But Elaine said, "Good idea." Maybe she'd do the same.

"I'll read it too though, Aunt Virginia. I'm just thinking that listening to it might be helpful as I read."

Virginia smiled at her great-great-niece and then turned to Elaine. "I'm so curious about the copy that turned up at the tearoom. I hope you can find out where it came from, and I'd love to see it."

Elaine cringed, wishing she'd brought it to Augusta instead of leaving it at the Bookworm.

"You know, my mother was a big reader," Virginia said. "There was nothing she loved more than to sit down with a cup of tea and a book."

Elaine nodded in agreement, emotion welling in her chest. She remembered. It was one of her fondest memories of her grandmother. Jan's too. "I'll bring the book as soon as possible," she said.

As Virginia gave her a smile, Elaine's phone dinged.

"Oh dear," she said. "That was an emergency alert." As she pulled her phone from her purse, it began to ring. "I know this isn't polite," she said, "but excuse me." She stepped farther down the little hall. The warning was for a flash flood in Lancaster. And the call was from Nathan. She quickly answered it.

"Elaine," he said, "you should head on home now in case the flooding gets worse tonight. Bob and I are going to fill sandbags and then stack them along the foundation of the tearoom."

Her heart began to pound. "Oh no," she said. "I'm on my way. Thank you for your help!" What would she and Jan do without Nathan and Bob?

She quickly told her mother what was going on.

"Of course you need to go." Virginia lowered her voice. "Would Paula and Brian be all right if I take Avery home after we have dessert?" She nodded toward the rose-colored cut glass dessert cups filled with chocolate mousse. "We'll have that, along with the shortbread Jan sent."

"I'll call," Elaine said. Her mother still drove and the route to the Blake home was familiar to her. After explaining things

to Paula, she said it was fine and wished Elaine luck. "Thank
you. We're going to need it," Elaine answered. The lake hadn't
flooded in a hundred years. She feared what she might find
when she reached home.

ON THE DARK drive back, Elaine prayed out loud as the rain
started again, pelting the roof of her car. She asked God to
protect Tea for Two, but even more so to protect the people
of their small village. "Please keep everyone safe," she prayed.
"That's what's most important."

When she arrived in Lancaster, standing water covered
many of the streets. She drove through a couple of deeper puddles, slowing down to a crawl as she did. She knew, with the
force of gravity, the deluge would flow downhill and reach the
lake sooner or later—and then spill out into the surrounding
area. As she neared the lake, she could make out figures along
the shore with flashlights. Hopefully they were the authorities
and not thrill seekers.

She pulled into the driveway of Tea for Two and noticed
a glow of light coming from the back of the side yard. She
quickly turned off her engine and climbed out of the car,
pulling her hood onto her head as she did. The ground was
soggy and she hurried toward the back, stepping gingerly as
she did, thankful she still had her boots on. Jan stood at the
corner of the house, a flashlight in one hand and an umbrella
in the other. Both Nathan and Bob dropped sandbags along
the foundation.

"Oh, good. You made it," Jan said, looking over the rim of her glasses. "I was beginning to worry about you being out on this dark and stormy night."

Elaine slipped under the umbrella and put her arm around her cousin. "We had a good time with Avery. Once I had to leave early, Mom volunteered to take her home. It's not raining nearly as hard up there."

"I'm so glad that worked out." Jan moved the beam of the flashlight toward the wheelbarrow, where Nathan and Bob were each retrieving another sandbag. Nathan glanced up at Elaine and smiled under the hood of his yellow rain slicker, his blue eyes twinkling. "Hello there!" he called out.

"Hello, yourself!" Elaine yelled back over the roaring of the storm, mixed with the crash of the waves on the lake. "Thank you!" she added and gave him a thumbs-up.

He nodded, smiled, and then turned toward the foundation of the house. They had quite a wall of sandbags built.

"I got your text about the book," Jan said. "I have no idea who would have dropped it off—and I couldn't read the note either."

"Maybe when you see it in person you can." Elaine directed her attention back to the men and the sandbags. "So how are things here?"

"So far so good," Jan answered. "The guys are almost done—then they're going down to the marina to check on a boat that belongs to a friend of Bob's, who is out of town." She motioned toward the sweeping lawn that led down to the dock, and then to the right, toward the marina.

"It seems our drainage system is working. The sandbags are precautionary," Jan explained. "Sorry to say, things aren't going as well over at the Bookworm."

"What do you mean?"

"Their drainage system is a mess. It's flooding."

Elaine's mouth flew open.

Her cousin took a step backwards, pulling the umbrella with her and bumping it against Elaine's head. "What's the matter?" Jan asked.

"The book. I left it with Bristol!" Elaine stepped out from under the umbrella and took off toward the bookstore.

CHAPTER FOUR

The inside of the building was completely dark, indicating no one was still inside. The water around the building stood at least six inches deep, worse in some places, and Bristol's flowerbeds were submerged. Obviously the water had reached the building and was flooding inside.

Grateful anew that she had on her boots, Elaine sloshed toward the street. She took out her phone to call, but as she reached the sidewalk she could see a gathering of cars, people, and lights in the library parking lot across the street. Elaine squinted through the pouring rain, hoping to see Bristol's red Toyota among several SUVs and vans.

Elaine hurried across the street. "Bristol!" she called out. Three of the figures turned toward her.

The one in the middle waved. "I was just going to go look for Jan." It was Bristol, holding an umbrella.

Elaine hurried to her side. "I came back early. Jan just told me about the flooding," she said. "I'm so sorry."

Bristol exhaled, appearing exhausted. "It could have been a lot worse. We got most of the books out—just a few on the bottom shelves were damaged. We called everyone we could think of with a van or SUV. And Mark had the good sense to bring boxes and sheets of plastic so we were able to protect the books." Mark, Bristol's husband, stood beside her, flanked on the other side by Sarah Ryder, Pastor Mike's wife. Elaine told both of them a quick hello.

Bristol rubbed the side of her face with her wet hand. "I'll call my insurance agent as soon as I get home. Thank goodness I have flood coverage."

Elaine nodded in agreement. What a blessing, especially for a small business owner.

Bristol turned toward her car and motioned for Elaine to follow her. As they walked she said, "Dr. Day was impressed with your book. He said he's 99.9 percent sure the autograph is authentic." She didn't seem as tired as she relayed the information. "He didn't really come up with a value, but he'd like to speak to you as soon as he gets back from New York later this week."

"All right," Elaine said.

"I figured you'd want to have it back tonight."

Elaine nodded as they walked to the car. "But thank you for showing it to Dr. Day."

"Of course." Bristol opened the back door of her car. "I put it in here, along with all of the other books in my office. But I put yours right here, in this bag." She reached inside. But instead of grasping a book, she turned toward Elaine and said, "Could you hold the umbrella for me?"

Elaine took it and tried to hold it over Bristol as she searched. "It was right here. On top of the pile," she said. "I promise."

"Maybe it slid to the floor," Elaine said. The thought was alarming, but she could hardly hold it against Bristol. The poor thing had been through quite the ordeal.

"It's not," she said, popping back out of the car. "Mark!" she yelled. "Did you do something with Elaine's book?"

He jogged to his wife's side and together they searched the entire car. But it was nowhere to be found.

The mysterious copy of *Evangeline* seemed to have disappeared into the rain-soaked night.

CHAPTER FIVE

Jan followed Bob and Nathan down the dock of the marina, her umbrella in one hand and the flashlight in the other. That was the entire reason she'd come along—to be the bearer of their only source of light. Otherwise she'd be back in the tearoom right now, brewing tea for all of the helpers to drink after the work was done.

She slipped a little on the wet wood, even though she'd been stepping carefully, and let out a yelp.

Bob stopped and turned quickly. "You okay?"

She nodded, embarrassed that she'd cried out.

He stepped back to her and took her arm, his chocolate-brown eyes lively. "Let me escort you," he said, his voice kind.

She took his arm with a flourish and said, "Why, thank you, my dear."

Nathan shot them an amused glance and then said, "Which boat is it?"

"The one on the end."

Bob's friend was in Florida on a business trip, so when he got the flash flood alert, he called and asked if Bob would check on his boat. Bob told him he would as soon as he had the sandbagging done at the tearoom.

The level of the lake had risen even more and the waves had grown high and rough. Jan appreciated Bob's dedication to others, and Nathan's too. She and Elaine couldn't do better than the two men who walked along the dock with her right now.

"You said the last boat?" Nathan called out, his voice nearly lost in the howl of the wind and lashing rain.

"Yep!" Bob quickened his pace.

"We've got tr—" As Nathan started to run, his voice vanished in the storm.

"Uh-oh." Bob took off running too.

Jan quickened her step, holding the flashlight up higher as she did, trying to light the way.

At the end, the sails of a medium-sized boat lay against the choppy water away from the shore, while the bottom smacked up against the dock. One of the ropes that had tied it to the deck had snapped.

Bob reached for the rope that had broken and yelled at Jan to call John Tuttle, the owner of the marina. He pointed toward a sign nailed to the pole in front of her.

She started to dial.

Nathan grabbed the rope still tied to the dock, straining against the tug of the boat, and untied it. Next he pulled on it and the boat started to tilt upward.

At the same time, Bob grabbed a pole from the edge of the dock and dragged it through the water, bringing up the end of the broken rope dangling from the side of the boat. He couldn't quite reach it though. He stood and balanced on the edge of the dock, reaching as far as he could.

Jan pointed the flashlight right where he needed it as the call went through. "Be careful!" she said, just as a wave pulled the boat away from the dock.

In slow motion, Bob lost his balance and tumbled into the water, the pole still in his hand.

"Bob!" Jan screamed, running toward the edge as John Tuttle answered the call. "Bob Claybrook just fell into the lake, off your marina dock," Jan yelled into the phone. "And a boat is about ready to capsize."

"I'm on my way," John responded, surprisingly calm. "Call 9-1-1."

She ended the call to John and dialed again, shouting for Bob as she did. The choppy waves tossed the boat around and then smacked it back against the dock. She waved frantically at Nathan and yelled that Bob was in the water. Nathan quickly retied the boat and raced to where Bob had been.

There was no sign of him and no gap between the boat and the dock now. If he hadn't fallen in the water, she could have reached out and grabbed the rope. She didn't dare do it now, without knowing where he was.

Dear Lord, she prayed, *please keep him safe.* He was a Maine boy. He knew how to survive around water. If he hadn't hit his head when he fell in, he'd probably swum under the boat to get away from it.

A voice came on the line. "Lancaster, 9-1-1. What is your emergency?"

Nearly breathless, she said, "Bob Claybrook just fell into the lake, down at the marina. We need help, right now!"

"I'll send a trooper immediately. And a game warden. Please stay on the line."

Protecting her phone from the driving rain, Jan said she would and squatted down as a gust of wind pushed against the umbrella and shoved the boat away from the dock again.

"Bob!" Jan screamed, wondering if she should jump in after him. The wind whipped around again and the sailboat came skidding over the water back to the dock. As it did, Nathan reached and grabbed the rope. Jan wasn't sure it was the right thing to do, but hopefully Bob was on the other side by now.

"We need to secure this," Nathan said. "And then I'll go in after him."

Jan didn't know if that was a good idea either. The water was icy cold. No one could survive for long. But she nodded as her heart raced.

She slipped her phone into the pocket of her coat and put her umbrella down. Immediately the wind tossed it across the dock. She didn't bother to go after it. Nathan handed her the rope and she held on with all her might, while he picked up the other end, where it had torn apart. He quickly tied a couple of knots and resecured it to the cleat. Then he snapped the life ring from the pole and stepped to the opening between the sailboat and the dinghy moored next to it. He squinted as Jan shone the flashlight out into the inky waves.

"Bob!" she shouted again.

Something bobbed up, just past the sailboat. Was it a buoy? An arm reached upward to the dark sky. Jan fixed the flashlight on the figure. Her knees grew weak with relief. It was Bob!

She waved.

The figure started swimming toward the dock between the boats.

Nathan held on to the rope on the life ring and then flung the object out toward Bob. It fell short, but in a few strokes, Bob reached it. Nathan began to pull. Jan breathed a prayer of thanks as she steadied herself. The night could have turned into a horrible tragedy. Just then an emergency vehicle, its lights flashing, stopped above the marina.

Before Trooper Benson reached them, Nathan and Jan had helped Bob onto the deck. He'd managed to kick off his boots and wiggle out of his coat in the water. Both had been weighing him down. Thank goodness he'd grown up around cold Maine lakes and knew what to do.

Jan said, "We need to get you home," as she hugged Bob. Dan Benson stepped onto the dock, along with Elaine. John Tuttle was right behind them. The trooper quickly let the 9-1-1 operator know Bob was safely out of the water and Jack Weston, the game warden, wasn't needed.

"What happened?" Elaine gasped.

After a quick explanation, Bob told Dan Benson not to call an ambulance, that he'd go straight home and get warm. John grabbed two wool blankets from his office and Jan helped wrap them around Bob. John and Dan decided they would finish securing the sailboat, while Nathan took Bob home.

Jan hugged Bob again when they reached Nathan's car. She still felt weak-kneed over what had happened. She couldn't imagine losing Bob—tonight had been a close call. Too close. She could burst into tears at the thought, but that wouldn't do anyone any good. "Get going," she said to him instead. "Call me when you get a chance."

Elaine told Nathan goodbye, and then the two women started toward the home.

As they walked into the wind, the rain pelted their faces. Jan's umbrella had completely disappeared—it was probably on the other side of the lake by now. "How did you know we'd had an accident?" Jan asked Elaine.

"Dan Benson was interviewing me when he got the call. You'd said you were headed to the marina—I was afraid it was Bob or Nathan."

Jan nodded. That made sense. Actually, it didn't. "Wait," she said. "Why was Dan interviewing you?"

"Oh," Elaine answered. "Bristol no longer has the book. I reported its disappearance as a possible crime—just in case. I mean hopefully it's in somebody's van or SUV. But Bristol swore she put it in her car and now it's nowhere to be found. I even dusted the door handle for fingerprints with my kit."

"Wouldn't the rain wash them away?"

"No," Elaine said. "I was able to lift the prints—two sets. Dan's going to run them."

"Goodness." Jan shivered. "What a crazy night."

THE NEXT MORNING, after Jan started a pot of English breakfast tea, she fed Earl Grey. The cat, purring loudly until he tucked into his food, seemed to have weathered the storm just fine, safe in his shelter on their porch.

Then Jan started in on her baking. The day had barely dawned. A streak of gray light came through the kitchen window but the rain continued, and Chickadee Lake still churned. As Jan mixed the ingredients for the salted caramel chocolate pecan bars she was making—Bob loved those flavors and she planned to set aside a few for him—she couldn't stop thinking about him, even more than usual.

Elaine stepped into the kitchen and when the phone rang, she quickly answered it. Jan was sure, from Elaine's side of the conversation, that it was Bristol and the book hadn't been found.

Elaine finally hung up the phone. "Poor Bristol. All of the books are now in her living room and dining room, but she can't find the copy of *Evangeline* anywhere. She feels horrible."

"It's a little suspicious." Jan spread the shortbread crust on the greased bottom of the metal baking pan.

"Definitely," Elaine answered. "Oh," she said, "I didn't tell you about Dr. Day." She filled Jan in on those details and then added, "Bristol said just now that she'd consult with Dr. Day about how much the book is worth. In the meantime, she encouraged us to do some research."

Jan shrugged. "Unless we can find it, I'm not sure what the point would be."

Elaine headed to her little office off the kitchen as she spoke and then returned with her laptop. "Hopefully it will still turn up." She placed her laptop on the island and opened it. "Have you heard from Bob this morning?"

"Yeah, he's fine," Jan replied. "He was laughing about it when he called. I was so relieved he survived that I didn't get all the details last night. He said he dove deep once he fell in and realized the boat was coming toward him. He knew he had to get on the lake side of it. He still had the pole in his hand, the one he'd been using to try to fish the rope out of the water, so he pushed off from the boat with that and managed to get on the other side of it."

"Was he scared?" Elaine asked as she clicked away.

Jan shook her head a little as she sprinkled the pecans over the crust. "He didn't seem to be. And he said he warmed up after a hot bath. All's well that ends well, right?"

Elaine whistled.

Jan couldn't help but chuckle a little. "To be honest, I was terrified." She met her cousin's gaze. "What would I do if something had happened to him?"

"Don't think about it now," Elaine said. "Thank goodness he's fine."

Jan nodded. Both she and Elaine had found love again after being widowed. Bob's near miss made her more grateful than ever for the way he'd blessed her life.

She turned back to her work and Elaine hovered over her laptop, concentrating on what she was reading just as her cell phone rang.

She dug it out of her pocket. "It's Trooper Benson." She answered it with a cheery "Hello, Dan."

Elaine listened for a minute and then said, "So both of their prints are in the identification system?"

Again there was a pause and then Elaine said, "Thank you for getting right back to me."

"What's up?" Jan asked as Elaine ended the call.

"The prints belong to Bristol and Mark—from a background check for volunteer work."

"Maybe the thief wore gloves."

"I was thinking the same thing. It's a very real possibility." Elaine began looking at her computer again.

"What have you found?" Jan asked as she sprinkled chocolate over the nuts.

"A copy of *Evangeline* for $3,000 on eBay—with an 1860 copyright and it's not autographed."

Jan dropped a piece of chocolate on the floor and bent down to pick it up. "You don't say."

Elaine nodded. "That's a lot more than I expected."

"Me too, but aside from any monetary value, it was Nana's book," Jan said. "That makes its sentimental value important too." She was grateful to whoever dropped it off—even if she didn't understand why they'd do it.

"That's right." Elaine smiled up at her cousin. "But now I understand why Bristol and that Mr. Stark were so excited about it."

Jan dumped butter into a saucepan. "Who's Mr. Stark?"

"The man who was at the Bookworm yesterday. He volunteers at the Maine Historical Society. He was practically salivating over the book yesterday."

"Did you see him last night?" Jan asked. "After the flood?"

"No. He said he was staying at Green Glade though. I can check with Macy."

Jan hesitated for a moment but then asked, her voice low even though no one else was in the house, "I hate to ask this, but do you think he took it?"

Elaine winced. "He certainly was enthusiastic about the book, but that would be too obvious, right? He was one of only a handful of people who even knew about it."

Jan nodded. "You should write him down as a suspect then, just in case—any chance he was wearing gloves when you saw him yesterday?"

Elaine smiled. "He was in the Bookworm the whole time, and I don't remember seeing any in his pocket. But I agree I should write him down. I'll be right back." She returned with her new notebook and a pen. "Okay, I'm writing down Mr. Patrick Stark." She scribbled away as Jan stirred the butter.

Elaine looked up. "We have one suspect."

Jan added vanilla and salt to her mixture. "Well, technically Bristol and Mark could both be suspects."

Elaine shook her head. "Technically you're right, but both of us know they'd never do such a thing."

Jan agreed. "How about the mystery woman who dropped it off?"

"But why would she steal it back?"

Jan smiled wryly. "Maybe someone told her how much it was worth."

Elaine nodded and jotted something down in her note-book. "So who would have dropped it off? Who would have had Nana's book?"

Jan spread caramel over the nuts and chocolate as Elaine asked, "Do we have any long-lost relatives who would have ended up with it?"

"You would think it would have either gone to my dad or your mom, and I don't remember Dad having it," Jan said, popping the bars into the oven. "But then again, he wasn't a big reader. And I went through all of his things after he died. I think I would have remembered an old book like that."

"Do you think he would have given it away, at some point?"

"I suppose it's possible," Jan replied. "Although I don't think Mom would have let him."

"So any distant relatives who might have ended up with it? Anyone from Nana's family?"

"Hmm." Jan thought for a moment and then said, "The Foret side was relatively small, and I don't know of anyone from that side who's still in the area."

Jan began mixing up an oatmeal crust for the raspberry bars she was making next. She'd always loved their grandmother's maiden name. *Foret.* "Fo-*reh.*" They'd lost touch with their French heritage and language centuries ago, but the name had lasted until their grandmother married Grandfather Pritchard. Perhaps she'd look into some French pastries to make in honor of Nana's family.

Jan vaguely remembered that their grandmother had a brother, but she'd never met him or knew anything about him. She didn't think he'd had any children.

Elaine interrupted her thoughts. "Rose said she didn't recognize the woman who brought the book in. What if she's a distant relative we've never met?"

"But how would a distant relative ever get the book?"

"Good point. We really need to find out who our mystery woman is." Elaine twirled the pen in her hand. "So we have one suspect with a name and one suspect without a name. Anything else?"

Jan wiped her hand on her apron. "What about this Dr. Day?"

"It seems he was long gone by the time the flood happened—he had a flight to catch this morning."

"Maybe you should put him on the list anyway," Jan said. "And we should find out who helped move the books last night. Did Bristol say if she mentioned the book to any of them?"

Elaine shook her head. "But I'll ask her."

Jan's eyebrows shot up. "It seems to me we have all sorts of possible suspects. We're going to need a list of everyone who was at the Bookworm last night."

Elaine nodded and spun the pen a few more times as Rose stepped into the kitchen.

The first thing she said was, "I heard about the missing book."

Rose had stopped in the kitchen doorway, a concerned expression on her face. "I'm so sorry."

"We're hoping it'll still turn up," Elaine said, her voice calm.

"How'd you find out that it's missing?" Jan asked Rose.

"I stopped by Murphy's on the way here. Macy was in there picking up creamer for her guests. She helped Bristol last night."

"Oh?" Elaine appeared concerned.

Jan shook her head gently. "Macy wouldn't have taken it."

Elaine wrinkled her nose. "I agree, but crazier things have happened..."

"The woman does have eyes in the back of her head though," Jan said. "We definitely should ask her who else was there. She wouldn't have been as stressed as Bristol—she's apt to remember more." She sighed. "And you should probably add her to the list too, just in case."

Elaine nodded and made another note in her notebook. "I'll ask her about Patrick Stark, while I'm at it, since he's staying at her cottages."

"Good idea." Jan turned toward Rose. "Can you tell us what the woman who dropped the book off looked like? We're hoping we can locate her and determine where the book came from."

"Like I told Elaine, she's around your age," Rose answered. Jan and Elaine were both in their midfifties. "Shoulder-length white hair," Rose added. "Petite. Delicate features. She wore a pair of jeans and a raincoat. I think she had a flannel shirt on under the coat. She looked like she was dressed in work clothes, as if she'd just been busy remodeling her house, like she said."

"Did she sound as if she was from Maine?" Jan asked.

Rose shook her head. "More southern, actually. It's not like she had a pronounced southern drawl or anything, but she spoke a little like that. She's definitely not from around here."

Jan exhaled. How could someone who was not even from the area link the name *Lena Foret* to the Pritchard cousins, a term no one had used to describe her and Elaine for thirty years, at least?

Who in the world could this mystery woman be?

CHAPTER SIX

That afternoon, in a drizzle of rain, Elaine walked over to the Bookworm with a small box of Jan's miniature maple croissants, a thermos of jasmine tea, paper cups, paper plates, forks, and napkins, all arranged in a picnic basket. Bookcases, covered in tarps, sat outside the shop under the eaves of the building where the ground was dry. The Closed sign hung in the door.

Elaine peered through the window. Bristol and Mark, wearing wading boots, pulled up carpet that was obviously waterlogged, judging by how hard they had to pull. But at least the water was no longer inches deep on the floor. Elaine knocked but when neither turned their head, she tried the door. It was unlocked. She pushed it and stepped inside.

A pump hummed in the background. No wonder they couldn't hear her knock.

"Hello!" she called out.

Bristol, stooped over and rolling carpet, turned toward her. "Oh, hi!" she responded loudly.

"I hope you're ready for a break," Elaine said. "I brought some treats."

Mark grinned.

Elaine sloshed over the carpet to the counter and placed the basket on it. As Mark and Bristol finished rolling the section against the far wall, Elaine unpacked the goodies.

Soon they headed toward her. When they reached the counter, they pulled their gloves off.

"How are you doing?" Elaine asked.

Bristol blew a stray strand of hair that had fallen out of her ponytail and across her face. "Surviving," she answered. "But a little overwhelmed with all the work it's going to take to get back in business."

Elaine gave her a sympathetic smile and handed her a couple of maple croissants on a plate. Then she handed a plate to Mark. The two thanked her profusely and dug in as Elaine poured them cups of tea. As they ate and drank, they updated Elaine on their progress, saying a Dumpster would be delivered soon for the ruined carpet.

"Then, once all of the water is out, we'll set up fans and a dehumidifier to help dry everything out." Mark's expression fell. "We're going to have to tear out part of the drywall too."

"Oh dear," Elaine said. "That sounds like a lot of work."

Mark nodded. "And once that's all done and the place is all dried out, we'll put down a new subfloor and have the new carpet installed."

"Our insurance agent will be here soon," Bristol said. "I mentioned the book to him but will give him the full story when he stops by." She glanced at Mark. "As you've probably surmised, it still hasn't turned up." She directed her attention back to Elaine. "I hate to even think this, but it seems more and more probable that it was stolen."

Elaine exhaled. "Any chance it could have fallen in a puddle? And been mistaken as trash? Or even washed out to the lake?"

Bristol shook her head. "I distinctly remember putting it into the car. I was very purposeful in caring for it."

Elaine smiled at her friend, hoping to reassure her that she wasn't angry about the missing book. "Hopefully it will still turn up, stuffed in a box in your living room. In the meantime, just in case, can you think of any more information from last night that might prove helpful?"

Bristol wrapped both of her hands around her cup. "I can't think of anything else."

"How about who all was helping?"

"Pastor Mike and Sarah."

"Yes, I saw Sarah," Elaine said.

Bristol nodded and went on. "Kit Edmonds was there for a while too." She sighed. "The thing is, I'm not sure if I was even aware of everyone that was helping. It was such a whirlwind for an hour or so."

"Of course," Elaine said. "Rose said that she heard Macy was helping too."

Bristol nodded. "For a short time." She took a sip of tea and then said, "She might remember who was around better than I do."

Elaine nodded. "I thought I'd ask her." Macy loved the Bookworm and spent a fair amount of time there when business was slow at the Green Glade. She was also a member of the Bookworm Book Club, which gave her another connection to the business. It was no wonder she'd rushed over to the bookstore once she heard it was flooding.

"It was all so chaotic," Bristol said. "From the time it was obvious the water was coming into the building until we had all the books out is a blur. Except for retrieving your copy of *Evangeline*. I was so careful about all of that." She gave Elaine an apologetic look.

Elaine put her hand on her friend's arm. "I know. Please know we don't blame you. Not at all."

After refilling both Mark and Bristol's cups and pushing the platter of maple croissants, the plates, and the napkins to the middle of the counter, Elaine placed the empty thermos back into the basket.

"Thank you so much," Mark said, after draining his cup. "We really appreciate it."

"My pleasure," Elaine said. She felt for the couple with all of the cleanup ahead of them, along with how bad Bristol felt about the book.

As Elaine picked up the basket, the door dinged and a man walked in.

"Hello!" Bristol called out. "Are you from the insurance company?"

The man nodded. "Bob Olson. Let's take a look at the damage."

"I'll show you around," Bristol said. "But first I want to introduce you to Elaine Cook. She's the woman I was talking about, the owner of the copy of the rare book that I mentioned."

The man extended his hand and Elaine shook it. "Nice to meet you," he said.

"Likewise," Elaine answered.

Bristol explained what had happened with the book up until the point it disappeared.

The man seemed annoyed by the story. "Did you write a receipt for the book?"

Bristol shook her head. "I didn't buy it. I was only holding it until Dr. Day could look at it."

"Is there any sort of proof it was actually here?" the man asked.

"I took photos of it before I dropped it by . . . " Elaine realized how foolish she sounded as she spoke. The photos proved nothing.

The man opened his notebook. "I'll record the missing book, but let's assume it will show up once you sort through everything. It's probably been misplaced."

Bristol pursed her lips but didn't say anything more.

"Now show me the damage," Mr. Olson said.

Elaine waved to Bristol and said, "We'll talk soon."

Both Mark and Bristol waved back, and Elaine headed toward the door, saying a prayer that the book would show up. Or that those in authority would take the case seriously. So far, neither the law nor the insurance agent seemed too worried about it.

She also said a prayer that the insurance settlement would cover all of Bristol's expenses. Elaine couldn't imagine how much it would cost to repair the bookstore—but she knew it was going to be a lot.

AFTER ELAINE LEFT the Bookworm, she walked along the lakeshore. The rain continued as a steady drizzle but the storm from the night before had abated. She stopped at Tea for Two and put her basket on the front porch and then continued on past Sylvia's Closet, A Little Something, and Kate's Diner. All were open for business, though Elaine doubted they had many customers. She knew Tea for Two had only three when she left.

She turned onto Cottage Road, past the I Scream Ice Cream stand, which wasn't open until the summer tourist season kicked off, and on down the drive toward Green Glade, on the lake side of the road. Elaine opened the office door and stepped inside, squinting a little in the dim light. The butter-colored room was made cozy by a crackling fire in the stone fireplace, and forest-green curtains framed the grayish light coming in through the windows.

There was no sign of Macy though, so Elaine rang the bell on the counter. A minute later, Macy opened the door from her private office, a book in her hand. Her straight gray hair was pulled back in two clips and she appeared tired. "Elaine," Macy said. "What brings you out on another dreary day?"

"I was hoping I could ask you about last night."

Macy tilted her head a little. "Does this have anything to do with your missing book?"

Elaine nodded. "I heard you helped Bristol clear out the bookstore. I wondered if you saw anything that might help us figure out what happened to the book."

Macy sighed and motioned toward the club chairs flanking the fireplace. "Might as well sit down." She placed her book on the counter. "I can make fresh coffee if you want."

"Please," Elaine said. A jolt of caffeine would do her good. She sat down in a chair while Macy started a pot brewing.

A young couple came into the office. Macy greeted them and asked what they needed.

"We decided to check out today," the man said. "And head back to Portland."

"We were hoping to do some kayaking," the woman said, "but the lake is so choppy."

"And the rain so relentless," the man added.

Macy grimaced. "I'll go ahead and check you out." She began the paperwork as the couple looked at their smartphones.

As Macy put the papers on the counter, she said, "I can offer you a discount for another visit later in the spring. Or even in the early summer."

The woman smiled at the man and nodded.

"Great," he said. "We'd like that. The accommodations were fine. It's just the weather..."

After Macy finished, the couple left.

"What a great idea to offer them a future discount," Elaine said.

"*Hmph.*" Macy stepped back to the coffee machine. "I don't understand why they didn't just curl up with a good book for

46

the weekend. It's almost as if they think I should be able to control the weather and the waves."

"I know what you mean," Elaine said. "Watching the lake in a storm is delightful. Of course the flooding—not so much. How high did the lake rise over here?"

"Not enough to flood. It was close but our drainage system worked, thankfully."

The conversation shifted to the night before as Macy poured coffee into two mugs and handed one to Elaine. Then she settled in the other chair.

Macy took a sip of coffee and then said, "I did help Bristol for a short time. None of the businesses on the lake have flooded in years. So I hurried right over."

"Could you name some of the people who helped move the books out?"

"Well, Pastor Mike and Sarah."

Elaine nodded.

Macy leaned toward Elaine. "My understanding is Bristol asked them to come help."

"Yes," Elaine said and then smiled. Macy seemed to be happy—or at least as happy as Macy *could* be—to have Elaine stop by.

"Anyone who seemed suspicious?"

Macy held her mug in midair as she shook her head. "No, I didn't see anything alarming last night. But you never know who might be hiding something," she added darkly.

Elaine decided to change the subject. Maybe if she came back to asking questions about the evacuation of the bookstore in a few minutes, Macy would remember more.

"Did you have many other guests this weekend?" Elaine asked.

Macy shrugged. "Some. I'm not at full occupancy but I can't complain, even with that couple leaving. We're still off season."

"I met one of your guests yesterday. A Mr. Stark."

Macy's eyes narrowed. "What a character he is."

Elaine nodded.

"I really do have the most interesting guests," Macy bragged, and took a sip of coffee.

"Did he help at the bookstore, by any chance?"

Macy stopped sipping. "Come to think of it, he did help for a while. In fact he was the one who told me about the bookstore flooding."

"Really?"

"Yes. He came barging in here and asked if I had any extra space where Bristol could store books."

"Oh my," Elaine said.

"Of course I don't, but you know how much I love that bookstore. I couldn't help but go over and see for myself."

Elaine guessed Macy actually did have some extra space somewhere in the big old house she lived in, all alone.

"But then I had a call from one of my guests. It was a younger couple whose heater wasn't working." Macy leaned closer, her hand wrapped around her mug of coffee, and lowered her voice. "Of course it was. They just didn't know how to use it." She rolled her eyes. "Millennials." She leaned back again. "Anyway, I got that started for them, but by then the rain was absolutely torrential and I decided not to go back out."

"Did Mr. Stark come back with you?"

Macy shook her head. "No."

"Do you have any idea how long he stayed?"

She shook her head again. "No," she repeated. "I didn't see him again last night."

"Do you think I could speak with him?"

"Well," Macy said, "he was supposed to stay another night, but he checked out this morning, which seemed a little odd. He seemed excited to be here the whole weekend."

"What did he say when he checked out?"

Macy harrumphed. "Nothing. He left a note on the counter, telling me to charge his card that I have on file. *Poof,* he was gone just like that."

"Just like that," Elaine repeated, anxious to get back and tell Jan about Mr. Stark. He definitely belonged in the "suspect" column. "How did you know the book was missing?"

"Who said that I did?"

"Rose said she saw you at Murphy's this morning and that you'd mentioned it."

Macy looked thoughtful. "Des Murphy told me."

"Do you know who told him?"

"He said one of my guests, who stopped by the store this morning on his way out of town. A man who walked with a cane."

"Patrick Stark," Elaine said.

Macy shrugged. "Seems that way. No one else who walks with a cane stayed at Green Glade this weekend. It had to have been him."

On Sunday morning, their day off, Elaine and Jan awoke to another day of rain. But it wasn't pouring.

"Shall we walk or drive to church?" Jan asked as they ate their breakfast. "Bob said he'd meet me there."

"Walk," Elaine said. "The fresh air will do us good and the rain won't hurt us." Nathan had an auction north of Waterville and wouldn't be attending church today.

A half hour later, with umbrellas over their heads, the cousins hurried up Pine Ridge Road to Lancaster Community Church. The white steeple rose above the village, as if beckoning them to the service. The gutter, along the sidewalk, was nearly full of storm water as it flowed toward the lake. Gravity and civic planning was doing its job. Elaine hoped the lake could keep absorbing more.

"We should probably check with someone about the drainage around the tearoom," she said to Jan. "Just in case the rain continues."

"Good idea." Jan's blue eyes lit up. "Maybe the Department of Public Works would have some information. We can go tomorrow afternoon. And one of us should stop by Town Hall and find out about recent building permits. Perhaps whoever dropped the book by recently applied for one—to do her remodeling."

"Great idea," Elaine said.

They trudged along, up the steep hill, past the parsonage. Pastor Mike stood at the door greeting the members as they hurried up the steps and into the building. Music invited them into the sanctuary and then, as Jan and Elaine slid into their usual pew, the bell began to toll.

"Bob's ringing it today," Jan whispered.

"Lovely," Elaine answered. The bronze bell had been cast by Paul Revere and then transported to Lancaster by a freight wagon. Elaine loved the history of the area. It was a delight to live in a place where she had such deep roots.

As the bell stopped ringing, Pastor Mike started up the center aisle. Before he reached the pulpit, Bob slipped into the pew beside Jan. Elaine caught her cousin giving him a loving smile. She couldn't imagine Jan's relief that Bob had survived his fall into the lake. As widows, both Jan and Elaine knew the pain of losing someone. That hadn't been the case this time, and Elaine was profoundly grateful.

The congregation rose to sing "Blessed Redeemer." No light came through the stained-glass window of Jesus holding a lamb that overlooked the pulpit. In fact the glass had a gray tinge to it from the lack of sun.

Elaine longed for blue sky and warmer days, but that would come with time.

When it came time for the sermon, Pastor Mike smiled and said he'd chosen the passage from Matthew 7, on building a house on rocks instead of sand, as the passage for the sermon. "I chose it a couple of weeks ago," he said. "Before I knew the rains were going to literally cause floods here in Lancaster."

He gazed out over the congregation. "Bristol, we know you didn't build your business on sand—and yet it still flooded. Sometimes we do all we can to make wise decisions, and yet things still go wrong in the physical realm. Jesus was talking about the spiritual realm, however, and that's what I'll address today."

As Pastor Mike spoke the rain continued to fall and the day grew even darker. "Jesus was a carpenter. He knew the importance of a solid foundation. The point of the story isn't whether bad things will happen or not—it's whether you'll collapse spiritually or stand firm in your faith."

Elaine couldn't help but think of bad times in her life. The worst had been when Ben died. She'd never dreamt she'd be a widow at such a young age. The healing process took time, but God had been faithful. Pastor Mike's sermon reinforced everything she'd been learning in the last couple of years.

At the end of the sermon, he led them in singing "On Christ the Solid Rock I Stand." All other ground certainly was sinking sand.

When the service was over, after chatting with those around her, Elaine approached Sarah, the pastor's wife, and asked if she'd seen anything suspicious while moving books from the Bookworm to the library parking lot the night before.

"I heard about your missing book. Macy told me at Murphy's yesterday morning. I'm so sorry. What a travesty," Sarah flipped her long braid over her shoulder. "You know how much Macy likes books. She's worried about it, though she probably wouldn't admit it to you. Obviously, the book is an heirloom. You've done a good job keeping it a secret."

"Well, we were just given it on Friday," Elaine explained. "It'd only been in our possession for a few hours. A woman we can't identify—yet—dropped it off."

"I see." Sarah frowned. "Well, I carefully rethought everything I saw. I don't remember anything out of the ordinary except that the store was flooding and we were rushing to save all of those books." She patted Elaine on the shoulder. "But I'll let you know if anything comes to mind."

Elaine thanked her and found Kit, who taught school in town, on her way out of the church. Kit hadn't heard about the book, so Elaine quickly filled her in. Kit offered her condolences and said, "I didn't see anything odd—just lots and lots of books. No really old ones though."

Jan left with Bob, and Elaine walked down the hill by herself. The rain had picked up and the gray skies seemed to mirror Elaine's feelings of discouragement. Surely someone knew something about the book. But who?

CHAPTER SEVEN

On Monday morning the rain slowed to a drizzle, and it finally stopped around noon. Jan worked in the kitchen, while Rose handled the customers just fine, although Jan did venture out with one order, a plate of lemon tarts and a pot of Earl Grey tea. The guests in the west parlor, two women who appeared to be in their early seventies, were passing through on their way north. As Jan placed the tray on their table, they nearly overwhelmed her with compliments.

"What an absolutely charming setting," the one with short gray hair said. "You have a gem of a tearoom. We're going to tell all of our friends back in New Hampshire."

"It would be worth the trip," the other woman, who sported a dark, curly hairdo, said. "The décor. The classical music." Strains of Bach filled the room.

The woman picked up her fork and took a bite of the tart. "And oh! the goodies," she gushed. "This is perfect. Just the right tartness and the crust is amazing."

The other woman took a sip of tea and then said, "And this Earl Grey is too. Clearly you know your teas."

"You're too kind," Jan said. "But thank you. We've tried hard to create a soothing atmosphere, where people feel pampered."

The first woman took another bite of tart and nodded her head vigorously. Once she'd swallowed, she said, "You've certainly accomplished that. We're headed up to visit our niece in Howland. We'll tell everyone between here and there about your tearoom. And back home too."

Jan thanked them sincerely—there was no better advertising than word of mouth—and then retreated back to the kitchen.

Elaine had decided to do some gardening. Eventually, they would purchase petunias and impatiens, but for now they had bought some flats of geraniums and needed to get them in the pots on the front porch and deck.

Plus, Jan thought, the flowerbeds needed to be weeded for the perennials that would soon flower too.

Jan glanced out the window as she beat egg whites for a meringue. Rays of sunshine pierced the clouds. She spotted Elaine on the deck, the hood of her rain jacket off of her head for the moment.

At three o'clock, Elaine came in and washed up, and then met with a bride-to-be and her mother about an upcoming bridal tea while Jan and Rose served the last of the customers.

After the bride and mother left, just after the tearoom closed, Elaine explained to Jan that the girl, Anna, was looking to book a tea for Saturday in two weeks. "Her original venue didn't work out," Elaine said. "I told her we could accommodate her. She wants a French theme."

"Perfect," Jan said, thinking about complementary pastries, and also about their family's long-ago French heritage. It would be a good reason to make some petits fours and that sort of thing.

"The bride is a French literature major. And the party all plans to dress for the occasion." Elaine paused for a moment and then said, "I thought about that French bleu tea that I read about recently, as the bride told me what she wanted. It's a green tea, so it would add to what we already have—the *vanille* and the *noir* with a hint of chocolate. I'm going to go order some of the *bleu*."

"Perfect," Jan replied, looking forward to the party.

Elaine slipped into her office and then came back out a few minutes later. "Should we go by and see what information Public Works has about our drainage system? Now would be a good time if so."

"I was thinking the same thing," Jan said. "I know you need to get ready for Sasha, so afterward why don't you drop me off, and I'll see what I can find as far as building permits go." She glanced out the window to see foreboding skies above. *Better grab an umbrella, just in case.*

The Department of Public Works was on the edge of town in a two-story brick building. The facility maintained the streets and operated the water and sewer lines in Lancaster, along with overseeing the drainage systems. It was one of those very necessary bureaucracies that went unnoticed—until something bad happened to your neighbor's property and you began to worry about your own.

The respite from the rain was all too short-lived. Just as they reached the door of the Department of Public Works, the skies opened up again, and the cousins scurried inside. Jan recognized the woman at the counter as the daughter of the Public Works manager.

"Patty, so nice to see you," Jan said as she approached.

The girl gave her a questioning look.

"We went to high school with your father," Jan said.

"Oh." She smiled, first at Jan and then at Elaine.

The two introduced themselves to the young woman, and then Jan added, "Your dad would've have known us as the Pritchard cousins."

The young woman nodded. "He's not here right now, but I'll let him know." She smiled again and then asked, "What can I do to help you two?"

Jan explained the situation over at the Bookworm.

Patty nodded as if she were familiar with the state of affairs at the bookstore.

"So now we're wondering about our property and how old the drainage system is."

Patty turned to the computer in front of her to open a program. "Hopefully the information is in the electronic record. If not, we'll have to search in the back…" The girl seemed to know what she was doing.

"We had friends sandbag the back of the house for us on Friday night and so far so good," Jan explained. "The lake isn't actually flooding although it's close to it—it's just that the water table is so high that we're afraid, since the Bookworm flooded, our property might too."

"What's the exact address?" Patty asked.

Jan rattled off the numbers.

Patty stared at the screen for a moment longer and then said, "Just what I thought."

"What's that?" Jan asked, hoping for good news.

"The drainage system was all updated by the previous owners, just over six years ago."

"Whew," Elaine said.

Jan felt just as relieved. She wasn't sure where the money would come from if their house flooded the way Bristol's business had.

Just as Jan began to thank Patty, two men carrying a chandelier came through the wide doors separating the lobby from the rest of the building.

"Oh my," Elaine said. "Look at that."

It was a large crystal chandelier with five tiers of teardrops and an ornate top. "It's gorgeous," Jan said.

Patty stepped out from the counter. "Put it in the corner over there," she instructed. The men headed toward the far corner of the lobby.

"What's happening to it?" Jan asked.

"We're getting rid of it."

"Oh my," Elaine said. "Whyever for?"

"It's been in a back room for years."

"Was it original to this building?"

Patty shrugged. "I doubt it, but no one knows for sure. We need the space for storage though. It's been sitting on a table back there. Dad told me to do whatever it took to get rid of it."

Jan had imagined the chandelier hanging in a back room from the ceiling—not sitting on a table. "It hasn't been in use?"

Patty shook her head. "We don't even know if it works. At this point we just want to get rid of it."

"Any chance we could take it off your hands?" Jan asked, surprised at her boldness. "That way it would stay in Lancaster. We could do some research and try to find out where it came from."

Patty crossed her arms. "What do you think, guys?" she asked the two men.

They both shrugged and one said, "Fine by me, and I'm sure your dad would agree. I can haul it over in my truck after work if you'd like."

"Perfect," Jan said, clapping her hands together. She could tell by the look on Elaine's face that she was just as thrilled.

A few minutes later Elaine dropped Jan, and her umbrella, off at Town Hall. Jan hurried up the steps, closed her umbrella, and quickly dashed through the front door. Building records were public and located down in the basement in the Code Enforcement office. Jan took the stairs. It was four thirty. She hoped the office stayed open until five.

She reached the door just as the clerk was coming out. Jan explained her situation and the clerk, a man in his thirties she didn't recognize, said he'd help as best he could. He opened the door for her, and then followed her in. "People can apply for the permits in person or online," he explained. "But, of course, we have a record of everything. Business was slow through the winter but it's picking up now."

Fearing perhaps the woman wasn't doing enough remodeling to warrant a permit, Jan asked for details about what a permit was required for.

"An owner or authorized agent who intends to construct, enlarge, alter, repair, move, demolish, or change a residential building or erect, install, enlarge, alter, repair, remove, convert, or replace"—he stopped and took a breath—"an electrical, gas, mechanical, or plumbing system needs to apply to a building code official and obtain the required permit first."

Jan smiled. The man knew his job, and his memorization skills were superb.

"In case of an emergency, a repair or replacement can be made without first applying if an application is submitted within three business days. Of course, there are some exceptions."

Jan nodded. It hadn't been that long ago that she and Elaine had their kitchen remodeled.

He began scanning through a logbook. "Female, right?"

Jan nodded.

"But you don't have any idea of what her name is?"

"That's right. Just that she's probably in her fifties."

He frowned a little. "We don't record people's ages." He flipped back a page. "So far all of the owners and contractors seem to be men. He turned back another page. "Here's a possibility. Abigail Samson. Outside of town, off the highway to Augusta."

"Do you have information for her?"

"Yes, an address," he answered. He took out a yellow sticky pad, wrote something down, and then pulled the top sheet off. "Here you go."

Jan read the address and the name. "Thank you." She slipped the sticky note into her coat pocket and hurried back up the steps to the lobby and back out into the rain. She walked the short distance home as fast as she could, dodging mud puddles as she did. Granted, it was a Monday before tourist season even started, but Jan had never seen the town so dead. Even in winter, more people were out in the snow, enjoying the sunshine, than were out on this dreary afternoon. As she hurried by the Bookworm, she couldn't help but notice the Dumpster in the driveway.

Perhaps if the previous owners hadn't updated the tearoom drain system, she and Elaine would be carting out flooring and drywall too.

Just as Jan neared Tea for Two, a pickup backed out of the driveway. The driver was the man from the Department of Public Works who'd volunteered to drop off the chandelier. Jan gave him a big wave and called out, "Thank you!"

He gave her a thumbs-up and turned left on Main Street. Jan hurried into the house, stashing her umbrella by the front door. "Elaine!" she called out, wondering where her cousin had the man leave the chandelier.

"Back here!" Elaine's voice came from the dining room.

Jan hung up her coat and then stepped quickly through the west parlor and into the dining room—where she found her cousin and the chandelier. A thick quilt covered the antique cherry table and the chandelier rested on top of it. The light coming down from the existing ceiling fixture now seemed awfully plain. It was a sad contrast to the light from the windows that refracted off the chandelier crystals, sending prisms of light bouncing around the room.

Jan put her hand to her chest. "It's beautiful!"

Elaine nodded in agreement. "I left a message for Bill Bridges to see if he can install it for us."

"Great," Jan replied.

"Isn't it?" Elaine asked. "I've had time to do a little research. It's called a wedding cake chandelier."

"Well," Jan said, "then that makes it even more perfect."

"I hope it will work in here—and that Bill can install it before the bridal tea that's coming up. Wouldn't that be perfect to use it as a selling point for wedding events?"

Jan agreed and then asked Elaine if she'd heard from Sasha.

"She should arrive any minute," Elaine replied. "Everything's all ready. I have the linens changed in the guest room and the fridge stocked with healthy food."

"Great!" One of the benefits for Jan of being in business with Elaine—and sharing a house—was getting to know her cousin's children better. She appreciated Sasha and loved having her visit. Sasha often cross-country skied at Sugarloaf in Maine both for competitions and training, but she'd decided to try Vermont for a change of scenery.

"I'm guessing we won't need to use this room for a while," Elaine said. "What do you think?"

"That you're right." Jan touched one of the crystals on the chandelier. "Probably not until the bridal tea."

Elaine nodded, just as someone yelled, "Anybody home?"

"Sasha's here," Elaine said as she started toward the parlor. Jan followed her. When she reached the entrance hall, mother and daughter were hugging. Sasha always had a glow to her, probably from her workouts and clean eating.

Over her mother's shoulder, Sasha smiled at Jan, her blue eyes sparkling, and then hugged her next. "What have you two been up to since I left?" she asked as she pulled away, her nutmeg ponytail swaying a little.

"Well." A smile crept over Elaine's face.

"Mom? What's up now?"

"Two things. I'll show one of them and then tell you about the second." Elaine sidestepped. "Come into my parlor," she said, leading the way in a playful manner. "And then on into the dining room."

Sasha glanced at Jan over her shoulder. Jan nodded and waved her forward. Sasha smiled and hurried after her mother.

As they entered the dining room, Sasha gasped. "Where in the world did you get this?"

"The Department of Public Works," Elaine answered.

"What was it doing there?"

"We don't know," Jan said. "But hopefully we can find out."

"Wow!" Sasha took out her phone and took a photo of the chandelier. "This is going on Instagram." She clicked a couple more pictures and then pressed a few more buttons on her phone to post her photos online.

As she finished she looked from her mother to Jan. "So what *else* is up?"

Elaine quickly explained the story behind the book. "We're actively trying to solve that mystery," Elaine concluded, "as soon as possible."

"Speaking of, I have a lead," Jan said. "From a building permit."

"Great!" Elaine and Sasha exclaimed in unison. Sasha seemed to genuinely love helping her mom with her mysteries, which pleased Elaine to no end.

"A woman by the name of Abigail Samson, off the highway on the way to Augusta."

"Do you have an address?" Elaine asked.

"Yep!"

"*Ooh!* Let's go," Sasha said.

"It's almost suppertime," Elaine said with a laugh. "We shouldn't intrude."

Sasha appeared disappointed. "It's only 5:15. We'll be there by 5:30."

"What do you think?" Elaine asked Jan.

She shrugged. "It will only take a minute. I wouldn't mind if someone stopped by here at this time of day."

Elaine broke out into a grin. "I'll drive. Let's go!"

CHAPTER EIGHT

They arrived at an old farmhouse with a Dumpster out front and a large blue tarp draped over a section of the side of the building. A mud-caked truck with the hood up sat in the driveway.

"Have you seen this place before?" Elaine asked Jan as she turned off the engine of her car.

Jan shook her head. "Never. I don't know if anyone in the family ever owned it."

As the three women started toward the front porch, a man, probably just over six feet tall, burst out of the front door with a wrench in his right hand. He wore a hoodie with *Army* across the front, a pair of black jeans, and work boots. His short dark hair and the way he carried himself spoke "military" as clearly as the word across his chest.

"Hello!" Elaine called out.

He bounded down the steps as he said "Ma'am" to Elaine and then nodded toward Jan and Sasha. He appeared to be both clean-cut and impeccably mannered, not to mention in possession of a gorgeous smile that spread across his chiseled face. "How can I help the three of you?"

"We're looking for Abigail Samson," Jan said. "We have a question for her about a book."

His bright smile faded. "That Longfellow book?"

"Yes, the copy of *Evangeline*," Elaine said, feeling elated that they'd found the right place but wondering at his sudden change in disposition. "Someone dropped it off at our tearoom on Friday."

"She didn't." He crossed his arms as he clutched the wrench tightly.

"What do you mean?" Elaine asked, feeling confused.

"Nothing," he muttered. "Go on with what you were going to say."

Elaine's face grew warm. "Well, someone dropped it off at our tearoom on Friday, like I said. The woman told our employee Rose that she found the book while doing a remodel. We wanted to discover who gave us the copy of *Evangeline*, so my cousin did some sleuthing and found out that an Abigail Samson was doing a remodel at this house. Do you think she could be the person we're looking for?"

"Without a doubt." His eyes softened just a little. "Abigail is my mother."

"I see," Elaine answered. That made sense. He appeared to be in his late twenties or early thirties.

"So now you know who gave you the book," he added.

"Yes," Jan said. "But it gets a little more complicated. The book was stolen that night."

"Stolen?" Was that a smirk on his face?

66

"Yes."

The expression disappeared quickly. "Forgive me," he said. "I'm sorry for your troubles. Honestly." He uncrossed his arms and extended his hand, saying, "And forgive me for my rudeness. I'm Brody. Brody Samson."

Each of the women shook his hand and then Elaine said, "Thank you for your service."

He glanced down at his sweatshirt and then back at Elaine with a hint of a smile. "I forgot I was wearing a billboard."

"It's not just that," Elaine said. "Other things give it away. Your hair. The way you carry yourself."

He cocked his head.

"My husband was in the army for thirty years." Elaine glanced back at Sasha. "It was our life for all that time."

"Well then," Brody said. "Thank you to both of you for your service too. I'm convinced it's harder on family members than on us soldiers."

"That's what my husband always said too, but I know it's not true." Elaine shook her head, thinking of some of the dangerous situations Ben had found himself in. "Where are you stationed?"

Brody inhaled sharply. "Fort Bragg, presently, ma'am."

"Oh my, we were there in '97." She couldn't help but smile. "Of course you were in elementary school then."

"That's right." He smiled again. "Fifth grade." So he was a few years older than Sasha.

"We lived in Southern Pines—do you remember, Sasha?"

Sasha nodded. "Second grade. I'll never forget it. Dad was around more that year than most."

67

"That's true," Elaine said. Even though they moved with him from assignment to assignment, he was gone often with extra travel to meetings, trainings, and then deployments. She knew it was hard on the kids at times.

Brody placed his free hand to his chest as he spoke. "Please thank your husband for his service too."

Elaine quelled a gasp. It had been quite a while since anyone assumed Ben was still alive. "Thank you," she said. "But he passed away a couple of years ago."

"Oh, I'm so sorry." Brody made eye contact with Elaine. Then he looked past her to Sasha. "And for you too."

"Thank you," they both said, in unison. Elaine wasn't sure what to think of Brody. There was a lot to like about him, but she had a niggling suspicion that he knew more about the book than he was letting on.

"Could I leave my phone number?" Elaine asked. "I'd like to speak with your mother about where exactly she found the book."

Brody patted the pocket of his sweatshirt, as if looking for his phone, as an older-model sedan pulled up next to Elaine's.

"Mom's here." Brody's voice had a hint of harshness to it instead of the relief Elaine expected.

A petite woman with shoulder-length white hair but a youthful face climbed out of the car. "Hello!" she called out.

"Mom," Brody said, "these ladies are from the tearoom, where you took the book."

"How nice!" She smiled broadly and stepped toward them. "I'm Abigail. Abigail Samson." She did have a hint of a southern drawl to her speech.

"I'm so pleased to meet you," Jan said, shaking the woman's hand and then introducing herself.

Sasha did the same and then Elaine.

"You'll never believe it," Brody said, "but the book was stolen."

"What?" Abigail's hand flew to her mouth.

Elaine nodded. "We're so glad we found you, because we feel horrible about the book going missing. I took it over to the Bookworm, right next door…" As Elaine finished explaining what happened, the rain started again and Abigail invited all of them into the house.

"Oh no," Elaine said. "We don't want to impose. Especially at this time of day."

"Nonsense," Abigail said. "Y'all come in. I insist."

Brody raised his eyebrows at his mother and then held up his wrench. "I'll just put the hood of my truck down and then come on in too."

"Brody is on leave," Abigail said, "and graciously offered to help me here. Unfortunately his truck broke down yesterday, and now he needs to work on that too."

"That's too bad," Elaine said, following the woman up the steps with Jan right behind her. When she reached the porch, however, she realized that Sasha still stood by the driveway.

As Brody reached his truck, Sasha asked, "What's wrong with it?"

"Hopefully just the starter," he said. "Although it may need a new alternator too." He eased the hood down and then dropped it. "She's been a great truck—but I'm afraid it's time to start thinking about replacing her."

"Oh, she doesn't look that old..."

Elaine didn't hear the rest of the conversation because she'd stepped inside the house. The interior had high ceilings with box molding. Along the outside living room wall were built-in bookshelves. The furniture in the room was covered with clear plastic. Elaine peered into the dining room, where the blue tarp covered the outside wall, and the patter of rain now fell on it. It appeared some sort of built-in had been there but now it was a construction site.

Abigail offered to take their coats.

"No, that's all right," Elaine said. "We shouldn't stay long."

The woman smiled and said, "It's fine, really." She stepped toward the couch and pulled back the plastic, sending a fine layer of sawdust to the bare floor. "Sit down," she said. "Please."

Elaine and Jan both complied as Sasha came in with Brody. Abigail uncovered a smaller couch and a chair and motioned to the young people to take a seat as she asked, "Who in the world would take the book, do you think?"

"We're not sure," Jan said. "But we thought if we could gather more details from you and why you brought the book to us, we might be able to figure it out."

"Well," Abigail said, motioning toward the dining room, "I found it in the window seat framing in the dining room. There was dry rot all around the area and we ended up having to rip out the lathe and plaster and all of the wood too. The book was wrapped in plastic and placed between the framing."

"Wow," Sasha said. "But how did you connect the name in the front to Mom and Jan?"

"I called the previous owners, a Mr. and Mrs. Baker, thinking the book belonged to them. But they didn't know what I was talking about. When I read the name in the front, they said the owner of the book was the grandmother of the Pritchard cousins, the women who owned Tea for Two, so I took it over there."

"But why didn't you keep it?" Elaine asked. "It appears it may be worth a bit of money. And by law, it belonged to you."

Brody shifted his gaze toward his mother, a tense expression on his face.

His mother ignored him. "I just couldn't keep it," Abigail said. "I knew there would be some family members somewhere that would be so happy to have the book."

"Well, thank you," Elaine said, leaning forward. "You're right. And we're very grateful."

Abigail smiled. "I'd want someone to do the same for me—you know, the Golden Rule and all of that."

Elaine nodded and thanked her again.

"I lived in Virginia most of my life, except for a few years during my twenties, north of Richmond. Not too far from my grandparents' old home," Abigail explained. "I imagined what if someone had found a book in their old house. Or a photo. Or something of sentimental value, like that."

"Well, we're thankful," Jan said. "Do you think Mr. and Mrs. Baker would mind if you gave us their phone number? We can find out through the country records who they bought the house from, but it would be quicker to find out through them."

"Oh, I'm sure they wouldn't mind," Abigail said. "They're the nicest people." She pulled her phone from the pocket of her sweater. "I only have the one number—I have no idea if it's a cell or landline. The house closed back in January, but they wanted me to have their number in case anything came up."

Jan took out a pen and notebook from her purse, and as Abigail rattled off the number, wrote it down. Then Abigail rattled off her own number. "Call me anytime," she said. "Let me know if you think of any more questions."

"We will," Jan said.

"Thank you so much," Elaine said. "You've been so helpful. I can't tell you how much we appreciate it."

"I'll be praying that you find the book," Abigail said. "So let me know when you do."

Elaine felt a rush of warmth for the woman. Abigail was a genuinely nice person...although she wasn't as sure about her son. "We will let you know," Elaine said. "Definitely."

Elaine turned to Brody and said, "You have a wonderful mother. She's very kind."

He sighed. "Too kind, let me assure you."

"Brody," Abigail said. "That's not true."

He just shook his head and gave her a resigned look, as if he didn't agree with her but doubted it would do any good. Then he opened his mouth as if to say something but then appeared to change his mind.

"What is it?" Elaine asked.

Brody nodded toward where the window seat was. "That dry rot? It's added a thousand dollars to the remodel."

"Brody..." Abigail's voice was calm but she sounded annoyed.

"The leak in the bathroom? Another thousand. The furnace that needs to be replaced? Another five thousand."

"That's enough," Abigail said, her voice was stern now.

"She's always put others before herself and it's gotten her nowhere."

"It's gotten me here," Abigail said.

"With all of these extra—"

"Stop." Abigail glared at her son. "This is my business."

Brody shook his head a little and then said, "You're right. I'm sorry, but I don't have the money to bail you out."

"And I'd never expect you too." Abigail's eyes softened and she smiled a little at her son. "I know you worry about me, but please don't. Everything will work out—God will provide. He always does."

Elaine felt uncomfortable to have witnessed their conversation. Abigail should have kept the book—and sold it. It couldn't help now, since it was missing. It all felt so complicated. Elaine started to thank her again when Sasha asked Abigail, "What brought you to Maine?"

"I needed a new start," Abigail said. "My mother died last year and left me enough money to buy this place, although I didn't anticipate all of the extra repairs that would need to be done. But it was time for a change, for a new home, so I'll just trust..." Her voice trailed off.

Elaine decided to focus on the positive. "Well, Lancaster is a wonderful place. I certainly found a home here again, coming back after being away for over thirty years."

"That's good to hear," Abigail said.

"How do you like the area so far?" Elaine asked.

"Oh, I love it!" Abigail enthused. "My husband was in the navy years ago and we were stationed at NAS Brunswick when

Brody was little. I've always loved it up here. Everything seems so wild and fresh and genuine. Strong people with strong morals that match the rugged countryside. People who pretty much mind their own business yet would do anything to help when it's needed."

Elaine smiled. That pretty much summed up Mainers.

"I've always wanted to move back," Abigail added. "I know I'll always be seen as 'from away,' but it's worth it to me to have a fresh start. I have a job lined up in Augusta as a nurse's aide. I'll start in a few weeks."

Elaine smiled but then concern grew for Abigail. Perhaps she was a widow too. "What happened to your husband, if you don't mind my asking?"

Abigail sighed. "I don't mind you asking. Nothing happened to him except that he ended up being"—she gave her son a quick glance—"well, let's just say *unreliable*. I stuck with him far too long but finally decided to leave a few years ago. I've been trying to put my life back together ever since."

"I'm so sorry," Elaine said.

Abigail thanked her. "I'm far better off now than I was for those thirty years, believe me." She laughed a little.

Brody shifted in his seat. It seemed the new topic was making him uncomfortable, but that was understandable.

Jan turned toward the young man. "How about you? What do you think of Maine?"

He frowned. "I barely remember when we lived here before, except for the mountains of snow. Maybe that had an influence on me because I'm not really a cold-weather person. I like Virginia. And North Carolina. A warmer climate definitely appeals to me." He grinned. "I'd love to get stationed in Hawaii sometime."

"Yep, we lived there too," Sasha said. "I was only little but it was wonderful."

Brody smiled again. "That's my kind of place."

"I ski," Sasha said, "so I might not be as thrilled with it now."

"What kind of skiing?" Abigail asked.

"Cross-country. I do biathlons."

"With the shooting?" Brody asked.

"Exactly. I used to target shoot with my dad. And we'd ski when we came back here to visit, at Sugarloaf. By the time I was a teen, I started competing."

"Cool." Brody looked at Sasha with what appeared to be respect.

Her face reddened a little and then Sasha said, "We should get going. We didn't want to intrude—and here we are. Intruding."

"No, I'm so glad y'all stopped by," Abigail said. "It's been a pleasure, truly."

"Likewise," Sasha said as Elaine and Jan nodded in agreement.

Brody even nodded, as if agreeing too, but he still had his eyes on Sasha.

After a round of farewells, Brody held open the front door and Elaine, Jan, and Sasha stepped out into another downpour. "It doesn't usually rain this much!" Elaine called out to Abigail as they all laughed.

Once they were in the car and Elaine started it, she said, "I'm adding Brody to the list."

"What list?" Sasha asked.

Elaine hesitated as she backed out of the driveway but then said, "The suspect list."

"Mom! How could you suspect him? He's so cute!"

Jan burst out laughing. "Sasha, you just met him."

"Exactly. And what's not to like? He's gorgeous. He's a soldier. He's protective of his mother. And he was nothing but kind to us. Why would you put him on your list?"

"Just a hunch." Elaine pulled onto the road. "He wasn't happy about Abigail giving the book away."

"But he seemed surprised that she actually had—although it appeared she'd mentioned the idea to him," Jan said.

Elaine said, "He could have faked his surprise, right?"

Jan shrugged.

"He's a soldier," Elaine said. "He could have easily snuck around outside the Bookworm and taken the book back."

"But how would he have known it was there?" Sasha asked, with a hint of disgust in her voice.

"That," Elaine said, as she turned onto the highway toward Lancaster, "is exactly what we need to find out."

CHAPTER NINE

As soon as they arrived back at Tea for Two, Elaine helped Sasha carry her suitcase up to the guest room. As Sasha settled in, Elaine called the number for the Bakers that Abigail had given her. The call went to voice mail and Elaine left a message and her number, asking that one of them call her back as soon as possible.

That evening Bob and Nathan stopped by, and they all discussed the events of the last few days over a supper of broccoli cheddar soup that Elaine had prepared earlier in the day and whole-wheat biscuits that Sasha quickly mixed up and baked.

They sat in the kitchen to eat because the chandelier covered the dining room table. Elaine finished the update by saying that she'd left a voice mail for the previous owners of the house Abigail was remodeling. "I hope they'll get back to me soon."

"If not, let me know, and I can ask around," Bob said. "We have mutual friends. I heard they were planning to go to Arizona."

"Oh?"

Bob nodded as he pushed his empty bowl toward the center of the table. "But most likely just for the winter—I'm thinking perhaps they were going to join the flock of snowbirds from here."

Elaine puzzled over the situation for a moment and then said, "Abigail didn't know if the number was for a cell or a landline. They could be here in Maine or in Arizona or anywhere."

"I'll call my buddy," Bob said. "And ask him what he knows."

Before Elaine could tell him she'd rather he wait a day or two, Bob had retrieved his cell from his pocket and stepped out onto the back porch. Earl Grey meowed hopefully, and Bob stooped to scratch the cat's ears with his free hand.

Sasha yawned as she began collecting the plates and bowls.

Elaine said, "You must be exhausted after your trip today."

Sasha yawned again. "I'll go to bed after I help with the dishes, but I'll stick around until the job is done," Sasha teased, shooting Jan a sassy grin.

As Jan and Sasha started on the dishes, Elaine and Nathan put the food away. Soon Elaine was lost in thought over Abigail Samson, the house she was remodeling, the book, and her son, Brody.

Sasha had seemed impressed with the young man, but Elaine wasn't sure if she should be.

"Sasha, how did your training go in Vermont?" Nathan asked.

"Good. The skiing was great for the first two weeks but turned to mush a few days ago. I figured I could run as easily here." She grinned. "With better meals."

"Not to mention company," Jan joked.

Sasha grinned again. "That's absolutely true. One of the guys who was there training…" Her voice trailed off. "I'll try to phrase this nicely…"

"Doesn't sound good," Elaine said.

"He was mostly a bore." Sasha shuddered. "But a few times he joined me on the trails. I was glad when the rain started."

"I'm sorry," Elaine said.

"Yeah, well." She sighed. "There just aren't that many good guys out there."

"Have you thought about one of those dating apps?" Jan asked.

"Yeah, actually, I have. I'm not getting any younger. I figure I have a year or two left to compete, and then I really would like to settle down. With the right guy, of course." Sasha grabbed the dishcloth and headed back to the table. "Do you two know how lucky you are? Do you know how much I hope to find a younger version of Dad? Or even"—she grinned at Nathan—"of the two old guys who are hanging around here all the time?"

"Hey." Bob stood in the doorway to the back porch. "Who are you calling old?"

Just then Earl Grey slipped into the kitchen.

"Oh no you don't." Jan dove toward the door.

Bob stepped backward and his hands flew up, his right one holding his cell phone. "Old and in trouble."

Jan grabbed the cat and laughed. "Not you—as far as being in trouble. I can't do anything about you being old though." She cuddled Earl Grey. "I think he's tired of the rain too."

"Aren't we all?" Bob asked, still holding up his cell. "So, my buddy said the Bakers moved to Arizona for the winter. He imagines they'll be back in Maine soon though. They bought a condo in Portland."

"They're probably waiting for the rain to stop before they come back," Elaine quipped. "Did you ask him about the best phone number to reach them?"

Bob nodded. "They only have one—a cell phone number. I'm assuming that's what the new owner gave you."

"Probably," Elaine said. "I'll have to wait until they return my call." Perhaps they were on their way back to Maine right now. In the meantime, she and Jan would keep pursuing the other leads.

THE NEXT MORNING Sasha left for a long run while Jan saw to the baking and Elaine readied the tearoom for customers. Rose had the day off and was spending it with her boyfriend, Brent, and his daughter, Emma, cruising secondhand stores in Augusta. Elaine was certain she'd be able to handle the serving on her own, with Jan's help. Business had been slow the day before and she guessed it would be again today too.

The dark sky released a constant drizzle throughout the morning. A couple of people came in, including Bristol, not long after they opened.

"How's it going over there?" Elaine asked.

"Slow," Bristol said. "It turns out *all* of the drywall needs to be taken out."

"Oh dear," Elaine said. "Any thoughts on your drainage system?"

"Yes," Bristol said. "We've come up with a temporary fix to get us through the next few weeks, but the whole thing needs to be redone. Otherwise, all of the repairs to the building could be pointless."

Elaine explained what they'd found out from the Department of Public Works.

"I'm so glad that yours was updated," Bristol said.

Elaine nodded. "I'm just sorry yours wasn't too."

Bristol shrugged but her expression was serious. "It's been so long since this area flooded. I didn't give it another thought." Her face grew even more serious, and she lowered her voice. "I'm not sure how we're going to come up with the money for the new drainage system though. Not when I won't have any income coming in until the insurance claim is settled and all the repairs are made."

Elaine reached out for her friend's hand and squeezed it. "I'll be praying for you to find the funding."

"Thank you." Bristol gave Elaine a rueful smile. "You haven't by any chance heard anything about your book?"

Elaine shook her head and then explained that they had found the woman who dropped it off at the tearoom, but speaking with her hadn't solved the puzzle.

Bristol thanked her for the update. "Even though we haven't settled with the insurance company, I heard back from the insurance adjuster about the missing book. He said it would be a separate claim from the flood."

"That makes sense," Elaine said.

Bristol nodded. "I'll keep you posted."

Elaine sent along an almond scone with Bristol as she said goodbye. As she watched her go, she said a prayer that Bristol would figure out the funding for the work that needed to be done.

But then, a few minutes later, as Elaine explained the situation to Jan, she wondered out loud if there was anything the two of them could do to help.

"Like a fund-raiser?" Jan asked.

"Yes, perhaps a tea and books party? Something like that?"

"It sounds as if she'll need the money right away," Jan said. "Right?"

Elaine nodded. "Maybe we could do a raffle, that sort of thing? And involve other businesses."

Jan pulled a tray of cakes out of the oven that she was experimenting with for the bridal tea. "Let's think about the idea and see what we can come up with."

Elaine agreed and then slipped into her office to call Patrick Stark—at least she hoped it was him. She'd found a number the night before online for a Patrick Stark who lived in Portland. She dialed and when she reached his voice mail, she left a message asking him to return her call.

She held her phone in her hand for a long moment, not sure whether to make the next phone call or not. Finally she decided to and Googled the Maine Historical Society. She clicked on the *contact us* button and then the phone number. When the receptionist answered, Elaine said she was looking for a volunteer named Patrick Stark.

"That name isn't familiar," the woman said. "But I'll transfer you to our volunteer coordinator."

Elaine thanked her. A moment later, another woman answered. Elaine explained whom she was calling for. "Oh, he just started with us a couple of weeks ago," the woman said.

Elaine was surprised to hear that. Mr. Stark had sounded as if he'd been volunteering at the historical society for years. "He said he was collecting books for an exhibit called Maine Books," Elaine said.

"Really?" The woman sounded genuinely surprised. "I haven't heard anything about that. Besides, he's volunteering in the library. He doesn't have anything to do with planning exhibits. Perhaps you misunderstood him."

Elaine shook her head, even though the woman couldn't see her. "I didn't," she said. "He was very clear about the exhibit. In fact he was admiring an old book that I brought into the bookstore where he was shopping. Later that night the book went missing. I wanted to speak with him about it."

The woman's gasp was audible. "And you think he took it?"

"Not necessarily," Elaine said. Even though he was certainly a suspect, she wasn't going to divulge that to a stranger. "I'd like to speak with him about that night. I'd like to ask if he saw anything suspicious. If he has any information that can help me figure out what happened to the book."

The woman's voice softened. "Of course. He volunteers on Fridays. You could speak to him then."

Elaine thanked the woman and disconnected the call. Rose would be working in the tearoom on Friday. Hopefully

Sasha would be willing to go to Portland with Elaine and ask Mr. Stark a few questions.

SASHA ARRIVED BACK at the tearoom soaked to the bone from the rain.

"How was your run?" Elaine asked as water dripped onto the kitchen floor.

"Great!"

Sasha's skin that showed—mostly her face, wrists, and her ankles between where her running tights ended and her socks began—was bright red.

She unzipped her jacket and hung it up, and then kicked off her shoes. "I'll tell you all about it as soon as I get showered and changed."

Sasha ran up the stairs in her stocking feet. Elaine had never been an athlete, not compared to her daughter. She enjoyed skiing and hiking, but she'd never been competitive.

Elaine delivered an order of English afternoon tea and walnut cake, the special of the day, to a middle-aged couple in the east parlor, seated near the fireplace. They'd already shared that they were from Portland and looking for a summer cottage to purchase in the area.

As Elaine served their food, the woman said, "Honestly, your little tearoom is one of the reasons we're looking at Lancaster."

"Oh?" Elaine didn't recognize the couple but that certainly didn't mean they hadn't come in before.

The woman nodded as she poured the tea. "We came last summer. A charming man with an English accent waited on us. He wore a cutaway suit with a teal vest."

Elaine grinned. "That's Archie."

"Is he here today?" the woman asked.

"No. In fact he's in England for a few weeks."

The woman's hand went to her bosom. "How wonderful for him, though I'm sorry to miss him. I'm a bit of an Anglophile. I hope he's back next time we visit."

Elaine nodded. "I'm sure he will be. And I know he'd love to tell you about his trip." She picked up the tray. "Let me know if there's anything else I can get you."

The couple thanked her and as Elaine headed back to the kitchen—first stopping to deliver menus to another couple who had just been seated, then removing plates from a table of four who had finished their scones and tea—Sasha, dressed in a dry running outfit, came downstairs. "Come back into the kitchen," Elaine said. "And let's have a cup of tea."

She convinced Jan to join them.

As they settled around the table, steaming cups of Darjeeling in their hands, Sasha leaned forward and said, "You'll never guess who I ran into while running around the lake."

Elaine couldn't come up with a single guess, but Jan said, "Macy!"

"Ha ha," Sasha responded.

"Pastor Mike?" Jan grinned.

Sasha shook her head.

"Tell us," Elaine said.

Sasha leaned back. "Brody."

"Oh?" Jan smiled.

Sasha nodded, a pleased look on her face.

Was Elaine the only one who found him suspicious?

"By coincidence, we both went out on a long run at the same time and literally almost collided when he was returning from the other side of the lake. He decided to join me and run the entire route a second time. It's been a while since I've enjoyed a run so much."

"Because of Brody?" Elaine couldn't hide the confusion in her voice.

"Not because I saw him. Because we ran together. It was nice to have someone to push me." Sasha took a sip of her tea.

Elaine hadn't seen her daughter so lit up in a while. And it wasn't that she'd seen her miserable anytime recently.

"In fact, he's coming by any minute. He's been working out at a gym in Augusta," Sasha said. "I'm going with him."

"Oh," Elaine answered, just as a knock came on the back door.

"That's probably him," Sasha said. "He had an errand to run before picking me up. I'll go see." She slipped out onto the screened porch.

Jan grinned. "Imagine that," she said. "Wasn't Sasha just saying last night that she never met any decent guys? This can't be a coincidence."

Elaine frowned, trying to figure out why she reacted negatively to Brody.

Sasha came in through the back door. "Come on in."

Brody whistled. "My mom said this place was gorgeous. And she was right."

"Yeah, Mom and Jan have done an amazing job…" Sasha led the way farther into the kitchen. Brody wore rainproof workout gear, which explained why he hadn't needed to change clothes as Sasha had.

"Hello," Brody said, greeting both Jan and Elaine. "You two have quite the setup here."

"Thank you." Elaine smiled, trying her best to be cordial. "We're really pleased how everything's turned out."

"Just yesterday, they found an amazing chandelier that they plan to hang in the dining room," Sasha said. "I'll show you."

"Nice to see you again," Jan said.

Brody nodded and told both of the women goodbye.

"I'll be back in a couple of hours," Sasha said, waving over her shoulder as she led the way to the dining room.

Elaine could hear Sasha and Brody's muffled voices for a few more minutes. Then the front door opened and closed and they were gone.

"I think it's exciting." Jan grinned. "This could definitely be a silver lining to the whole book mystery."

Elaine forced herself not to frown. "Let's not put the cart in front of the horse." It was an expression their Nana used to say.

Jan stopped grinning. "You're not thrilled about Sasha spending time with Brody."

"We don't know much about him," Elaine said. "Let's see what happens." As she finished her tea and headed to go check on the couple in the east parlor, the front door opened. She hurried out of the kitchen, eager to be distracted by more customers.

It wasn't until after the tearoom closed that Sasha returned. She practically bounced into the kitchen where Elaine was unloading the dishwasher.

"I had the best time," she said, before Elaine could even ask. "Brody showed *me,* the fitness trainer, some new stretches to strengthen my Achilles tendons. And also some tricks to get more out of my weight training. I'll use both of those with my clients when I go back to work. And then we went out for a late lunch to a cute little café not far from the capitol."

"Great," Elaine said, deciding she'd better bring up the trip to Portland on Friday before Sasha made plans to spend the day with Brody. She quickly explained her phone call.

"I'm definitely in," Sasha said, then smiled. She leaned against the counter and met Elaine's gaze. "Hey, Brody feels horrible about the book. He said he felt as if he didn't come across as very sympathetic yesterday." Sasha gazed out the window to the lake. Elaine followed her daughter's eyes. It was raining again and the drops were sending circles over the water. "He did say he hadn't wanted his mom to give the book away."

"Oh? Did he want it?"

Sasha smiled at Elaine again. "No. He'd heard of Longfellow before, of course, but not that specific book. I don't think he's anti-literature or anything, but he doesn't have a lot of time to read."

Elaine cocked her head.

"He wanted his mom to sell the book," Sasha said. "He Googled it and found the same listing you did, the one worth three thousand dollars."

"Hmm," Elaine said. She wasn't sure if that made him less of a suspect or more.

"Yeah, he feels like his mom is always putting others before herself."

"That's what the Bible teaches us to do," Elaine said.

"Of course. Brody knows that too. It's just that his mom does it to her detriment. He says, over and over, that she's helped others when she should have been saving her money for retirement or getting her car fixed or buying a new one."

"Oh, I see," Elaine said. That wasn't a problem a lot of people had.

"Anyway, do you mind if I go out to dinner with Brody tonight?"

"That's fine," Elaine said, doing her best to keep her voice in check.

"Just at the Pine Tree Grill," Sasha added. "We didn't want to drive back into Augusta. I won't be late." She started toward the doorway. "And then we're going to run again tomorrow." She raised her eyebrows. "So it's a good thing you booked me for Friday."

Elaine gave Sasha a smile, but she didn't feel it in her heart. On the one hand, it seemed Brody really cared about his mother. That was a good thing. On the other hand, it seemed he was pretty adamant about her keeping the book. That was understandable. She'd bought the house. The book was absolutely her property. The question was, to what ends might have Brody gone to get the book back?

CHAPTER TEN

The next morning, long before Sasha and even Jan were up, Elaine sat in her office, the wind pelting raindrops against the window. She exhaled, trying to brace herself for another waterlogged day, as she checked the Internet for their copy of *Evangeline*. If someone took it for its monetary value, they'd have to sell it somewhere. She doubted the thief would be naïve enough to post it on the Internet, but she couldn't be sure.

There was no new posting but the copy for three thousand didn't pop up. She went back to her Internet history and found the site. When she clicked on it, a sold sign spread across the item.

By the looks of it, their copy could sell for that much or more. Or it could have.

She closed down the tab, fed Earl Grey, and then started a pot of English breakfast tea and a pan of oatmeal for breakfast. She'd been in bed by the time Sasha came home the night before. Elaine couldn't have imagined Sasha and Brody could stay at the Pine Tree Grill for three hours, but it seemed they had, talking the evening away over dinner and then pie and coffee.

Sasha had stopped by Elaine's room on the way to the spare bedroom to say good night. She didn't say much about her evening, but she had a dreamy look in her bright blue eyes.

Once the oatmeal was done, Elaine turned the burner off and stirred it, gazing out through the back porch to the lake. It wasn't often she was up before Jan, but she awoke at 4:30 and couldn't go back to sleep. Now it was 5 a.m. and the first hint of light was glimmering over the lake. The rain had stopped, at least momentarily, but the clouds would surely keep the sunrise from showing its brilliant colors.

As Elaine ate her oatmeal and then savored each sip of her tea, she thought about Brody Samson again and said a prayer that God would protect Sasha from getting hurt.

But why was she even worried this man might harm her daughter? Or that he would steal a book? Didn't she trust Sasha's judgment?

Was there another reason he caused her alarm?

Was it that he was in the army? Was she afraid that Sasha might become an army spouse and move even farther away from Maine? She sighed as she pushed her half-empty bowl away. It was true that she hoped Sasha would leave Colorado and move to Maine, permanently. She hoped the same thing for Jared and his family too, but it seemed more likely Sasha would. It would be a lot harder for Jared and his wife, Corrie, and their children, Lucy and Micah, to leave Ohio and resettle in Maine.

She sighed. She probably did feel a little threatened at the thought of Sasha falling for a military man, which seemed a little hypocritical on her part.

Elaine grimaced, wondering if her parents had felt the same way when she started dating Ben. But perhaps not. Maybe they didn't realize how far away Elaine's family would end up and how seldom they'd be able to come home. Of course, when Ben joined the army, the signs were that the Cold War was coming to an end and it didn't seem there were any wars on the horizon.

But as it turned out, there had had been one conflict after another. First there had been Desert Storm. Then Bosnia. Then 9/11 and the wars in Afghanistan and Iraq, which had been constants throughout Sasha and Jared's middle school and teenage years. Another deployment was always a possibility—and quite often a reality—for Ben. Perhaps that's what she was afraid of. Sasha had gone through all of that as a child. How would she handle it again as an adult?

She stood and picked up her bowl. Who was putting the cart before the horse now? She chastised herself for borrowing trouble and then dumped the rest of her cereal in the compost and rinsed her bowl as Jan came into the kitchen.

"You're up early," Jan said.

"Hi. I couldn't sleep."

"Are you worried? Thinking about Sasha and her big date last night?"

Elaine put her bowl in the dishwasher. "A little. Sorry, I'm just out of sorts. I think I'll go for a quick walk. The fresh air will do me good."

Jan, in a sympathetic voice, told her to take her time.

Elaine grabbed her coat and slipped out the door to the back porch. She stopped for a minute to pet Earl Grey, then stepped on out into the cool morning. She glanced to the east as the sun rose over the horizon. The clouds had actually parted just enough for hues of pink and orange to splash across the sky.

She'd hoped Sasha would use one of the online dating apps—and specify someone who lived in Maine. She longed to have her close. It was hard enough having Jared and his family so far away. What if Sasha ended up in North Carolina? Or Germany? Or Korea?

Elaine tried to clear her thoughts as she passed the marina and then the art gallery before turning onto Cottage Road and heading toward the boat launch and swimming area. A flock of geese flew overhead, honking at each other.

Elaine patted her phone in her pocket and contemplated calling Nathan, but on the chance he was still asleep she decided not to. Besides, what would he say? *There's no reason to worry about Sasha getting involved with a soldier—not yet anyway.*

Trying to put those thoughts aside, again, she went through her mental to-do list. Rose had another day off, so Elaine would be on her own as far as serving—unless Sasha wanted to help.

She wanted to call Bill Bridges again about the chandelier. He hadn't returned the call she left on Monday, which wasn't like him.

Her thoughts fell on Friday and the trip into Portland with Sasha. She'd call her mother too and see if they could have breakfast with her in Augusta. And then she'd call Dr. Sean Day at Bowdoin College. He'd be back from New York on Friday and she hoped she and Sasha could stop and talk with him on the way home from Portland. She wanted to hear about his trip to the Bookworm the day the copy of *Evangeline* was stolen, what time he'd left, and if he had any idea who might want to buy a rare copy of the book. Surely there were online groups for that sort of thing, maybe ones she couldn't find with a simple search. Perhaps the thief would have no need to post it online for the general public. Hopefully, Patrick Stark would be at the museum on Friday, and she'd get a clear answer from him, or at least an inkling of whether he was involved in the theft or not.

Then, besides having a chance to quiz the professor, she'd enjoy stopping at Bowdoin. It was a beautiful college with towering trees and stately buildings and homes. She thought of Bristol's son, Greg, who attended the college. He had been doing much better there after getting into some trouble about a year ago, and he would be graduating soon.

When Elaine approached the swimming area, she stepped down to the beach. Across Chickadee Lake, the sun made its way over the hill, bathing the town in light. Her gaze shifted to Tea for Two. A heron had perched on the lawn. Even though a low cloud hung over the top of the house, she could make out the planters of pink geraniums on the deck and the potted petunias. Gratitude filled her.

She had so much to be thankful for. She turned and headed back to Cottage Road. Ten minutes later, by the time she returned, her head had cleared.

IT WASN'T UNTIL later in the morning that Bill called Elaine back. He apologized for the delay, saying he'd been on a tight deadline but could hang the chandelier soon. "I'm looking forward to seeing what you've got," he said.

Elaine thanked him and said they were eagerly awaiting having the piece hanging in the dining room of Tea for Two.

As Elaine and Jan readied an order together, Jan mentioned that the evening before, Bob had recommended a handwriting expert who could help them with the note that was in the back of the book. "I haven't had a chance to call her yet though," Jan said.

Elaine volunteered to do it, and Jan pulled the slip of paper from her back pocket. *Sally* was scrolled across it in Bob's handwriting with a phone number. "She's located in California so don't call until lunchtime."

Finally, around noon, during the usual lull in customers, Elaine made the phone call. First she explained her relationship to Bob, that he was dating her cousin. The woman's voice warmed. "Bob is a good friend of my dad's—they go way back to college."

Elaine guessed Sally was in her twenties, young to be an expert. After explaining the situation with the autograph and note, Elaine added that she only had photographs of the note.

The woman asked Elaine to e-mail the images to her, and she'd see what she could do over her lunch break. After getting the e-mail address, she asked Sally how much she charged.

"Oh, I'm happy to do it," she said. "I have fond memories of Bob from when we visited Maine when I was little. Tell him hello for me."

After thanking her profusely, Elaine hung up and then e-mailed the images on her phone.

Just after the tearoom closed, as Elaine was wiping down the tables, her phone rang. It was Sally's number. Elaine dropped the cloth on the table and answered quickly, wondering if the woman had information for her already.

After they'd greeted each other, Sally said, "Let's start with the autograph. This wouldn't hold up in court or anything because it's a photograph and blurry at that, but from what I could see, comparing it to legitimate signatures, I'd say chances are it's genuine."

"Great," Elaine said. She'd never doubted it was genuine but it was good to have it confirmed. Of course, if they never found the book it wouldn't matter—not to them anyway.

"As far as the note, don't you love that old handwriting?" She chuckled. "It's like a secret code and this person had it down to an art. Anyway, this is what I came up with: *L. If you ever recover this book, I want you to know how much you've hurt me. I'll never forgive you for what you've done. T.*"

"Wow," Elaine said. "Could you repeat that?" She dug a pen from her apron pocket and her pad too.

Sally said it again, slower this time.

Once Elaine had it written down, Sally asked if she had any idea who "L" and "T" were.

"We're pretty sure our grandmother—Lena—is 'L.' But I don't know who 'T' could be," Elaine answered. "Although she did have a brother named Tim, but I've never heard about any drama between them."

"Well, you'll have to let me know what you find out," Sally said. "And I hope you find the book."

"We do too." Elaine put her pen back in her pocket. "Do you mind if I ask what your background is? I find your job so fascinating."

"It is," Sally said. "I'll give you the short story. I got a bachelor's degree in history and then apprenticed under a forensic document expert. I also spent a lot of time in the California Historical Society Library pouring over old documents and figuring out different writing styles. That came in handy today."

"So you're no longer an apprentice?"

"That's right. I work for a state lab here in Oakland. We work with the state police, mainly, but handle other cases too."

"Fascinating," Elaine said. "Thank you so much." As she hung up, she thought of how many people it took to catch a thief. She was very grateful for the expertise of others.

An hour later, after cleaning up the tearoom for the day, Elaine sat on the window seat in the east parlor, sipping a cup of coconut oolong tea. Sasha had gone for an afternoon run with Brody, and the constant drizzle had stopped for a few minutes.

When the front door opened she realized she hadn't locked it. She started to stand, but Nathan appeared in the doorway.

"Hello there," he said as he stepped into the parlor.

"Nathan!" She stood, careful not to spill the tea. "What are you doing here?"

"I had a break in my schedule," he said, stepping toward her. "I've been missing you."

She smiled up at him as he put his hands on her shoulders and bent his head toward hers and kissed her on the mouth.

"Aww," she said as they pulled away. "I've been missing you too. I've been wanting to show you the chandelier I told you about."

Nathan followed her through the west parlor and whistled as they stepped into the dining room. "What a find," he said, circling the table, looking at the chandelier from every angle.

"Any thoughts about it?"

"Well, you're right, it's a wedding cake design. I'd say mid-nineteenth century, designed for gas, not electricity, but obviously adapted since then." Nathan leaned closer to the chandelier, lifting up a row of crystals. "Those bulbs look like originals but they must be replicas." The bulbs were little and mostly covered by the crystal teardrops. He smiled, his eyes nearly as sparkly as the chandelier. "This is such a great addition to the house."

Elaine agreed. "Do you have time for a cup of tea? And a lemon scone?"

"Sounds great," he answered.

They headed back into the east parlor, and Elaine grabbed a cup from the cabinet on the far wall. She poured the tea, and handed the cup to Nathan. "Back in a flash," she said.

When she returned with the scones, Nathan had pulled a table up to the window seat and was sitting looking out onto Main Street.

"Hey," he said. "Who's the dude in the army sweats running this way? With Sasha."

"Brody. Remember? I told you about him."

"That's right. His mother brought the book by."

"Yep."

"But why is he with Sasha?"

"Well..." She hadn't told him about that. "They've been running together every day." And going out to dinner...And into Augusta to work out...Elaine placed her teacup on the table.

"He's coming in with her," Nathan said.

The front door opened and Sasha's laugh rang out through the house.

Elaine couldn't help but smile.

"How about a glass of water?" Sasha asked.

"Thanks," Brody answered. "That would be great."

"Hey!" Elaine called out. "We're in here."

Sasha stepped into the parlor, followed by Brody. She waved at her mom and then said, "Hi, Nathan. How are you?"

He stepped forward and gave her a hug, and then she quickly introduced Brody.

"Army, huh?" Nathan asked as he shook the young man's hand. "How long have you been in?"

"Six years. I joined right after I graduated from college."

"What rank?"

"Captain," Brody answered. "Special Forces."

Elaine hadn't heard that yet and wondered if Sasha knew. By the smile on her face, she did.

Nathan cocked his head. "Can you be any more specific than that?"

"Green Berets." Brody's face had grown red, and not from the run. Perhaps he didn't like to talk about himself or draw attention to the fact that he was one of the most elite of all soldiers.

"Impressive. How many deployments have you been on?"

"Three," Brody answered. "One to Iraq and two to Afghanistan."

Sasha excused herself as the two men talked and headed toward the kitchen.

It was obvious Nathan was impressed with Brody. "You probably can't talk much about your deployments then, right?"

"No, sir," Brody answered. "But there's not much that's very interesting either."

"Oh, I doubt that," Nathan said, his voice full of respect.

"Will you join us?" Elaine asked. She'd brought double the amount of scones that she and Nathan would eat. "We can all sit around the table."

"Yes, ma'am," Brody said.

Elaine and Nathan moved the table out from the window seat and Brody quickly pulled chairs around it as Sasha returned with two tall glasses of water.

After they'd all sat down, Nathan asked Brody what was next for him.

"I have some time off," he said. "So I'm helping my mom renovate the house she bought."

"Then what?" Nathan asked.

"I'll meet back up with my unit, down at Fort Bragg."

"Do you have another deployment coming up?" Elaine asked.

"Well, we definitely have some tough training ahead of us," Brody answered, turning his head toward Sasha. "Although I'd say our run today was tough."

"It was just what I needed," Sasha said. "I'm really happy with my training this week. I definitely feel as if I've hit a new level."

"Tomorrow or Friday we're going to go to the shooting range."

"Yeah, I'm looking forward to that."

"Sasha..." Elaine met her daughter's eyes.

Her expression must have given away her question.

"Oops, that's right. Friday won't work. Sorry." She turned toward Brody. "Mom and I are going to Portland."

"No worries," he said. "Tomorrow works just fine."

After he finished his glass of water, without touching the scone, Brody said he needed to go. "I told Mom I'd be home by six."

After a round of goodbyes, Sasha walked him to the door and then Elaine could hear her footsteps on the staircase.

"Nice guy," Nathan said.

Elaine wasn't sure how much to say. Brody *was* a nice guy. Still, she felt uneasy about him. They didn't know for sure he hadn't taken the book. And just now, when she'd asked him about whether he had a deployment coming up, he hadn't answered directly.

Nathan reached across the table and took Elaine's hand. "What's the matter?" he asked.

She shook her head. "It's nothing," she answered.

"You've hoped Sasha would settle down with someone from around here."

"But he's not from around here. His mother moved here is all. He's from Virginia originally, and he's stationed in North

Carolina. We have no idea what's next for him. He could end up anywhere in the world."

"Well, they've just met. Right? Time will tell."

Elaine nodded, trying to figure out again why she was upset. It wouldn't be surprising if Sasha fell for a soldier. Her dad, whom Sasha adored, had been in the army for thirty years. He'd retired as colonel. Being a soldier was a large part of Ben's character—loyalty, honor, duty, respect, integrity. Even though she hadn't known Brody long, she could see those in him too. That's why she couldn't figure out what kept bothering her about the young man.

CHAPTER ELEVEN

The next morning, as Jan finished up the baking and Rose and Elaine served the handful of customers, Sasha stepped into the kitchen. She wore jeans, stylish boots, and a black turtleneck sweater.

Jan grinned at the girl. "I haven't seen you in anything but running tights all week. Where in the world are you off to?"

Sasha glanced down at her jeans and then back up at Jan. "The shooting range."

"With?"

"Guess." Sasha shot her a sassy smile as she opened the fridge.

"Want a chocolate chip scone before you go?"

The refrigerator door muffled her voice. "No, thank you. I made a green smoothie yesterday and saved half of it for today."

Sasha had already been out on a long run that morning, although it seemed Brody hadn't gone with her. Jan couldn't help but feel happy for Sasha. Perhaps Brody was just a friend for her to have during her time in Lancaster—but maybe it would turn into more. Sasha and Brody had a lot in common.

Their disciplined training regimens. Army life—Sasha as an army kid and Brody as a soldier. An interest in healthy eating. And the Samsons, both Brody and Abigail, seemed to be people of faith. That was important too.

Sasha pulled out a glass with a plastic lid on it, and then leaned against the counter and started drinking the green mixture.

"Sure you don't want a scone?" Jan teased.

"Believe me, more than anything." Sasha held up the glass. "But I've got to get my vitamins, minerals, and fiber—but no sugar."

Jan nodded. "Well, I certainly admire your dedication."

"Thank you." Sasha took another drink and then swallowed. "I figure this might be my last big push of training. I'm not getting any younger."

"Oh, I doubt you've even reached your prime," Jan said. "You have no idea how young you really are."

Sasha's eyes grew serious. "In some ways, yes. Right? But in other ways, I'm not sure. I'd really like to find the right guy and settle down." Her voice grew serious too. "I'd like to have children before too long. I grew up with the idea that I could have 'everything,' but I don't even know what that means anymore. And the truth is, I don't even know if I want 'everything' any longer."

Jan patted Sasha's shoulder. "It will all work out. You'll see." She truly believed that.

Sasha smiled. "I know. I just wish I knew exactly how."

A man's voice reverberated in the entryway with a hearty "Hello!"

"Hi there," Jan heard Elaine respond from one of the parlors.

Rose traipsed into the kitchen. "There's a way handsome guy out there, and I'm guessing he's looking for you, Sasha."

"Thanks." Sasha quickly swallowed the rest of the smoothie, rinsed out the glass, and put it in the dishwasher.

She gave Jan a quick hug. "Thank you for listening."

"Anytime," Jan responded.

Before Sasha reached the kitchen door, Brody came in sight and waved at Jan. He wore jeans and boots too, along with a fitted jacket. "Good morning," he said.

"Same to you." Jan wiped her hands on her apron. "You two have fun."

"We will," Brody answered. He certainly was a handsome young man with his chiseled features, dark hair, and light-brown eyes.

Both Sasha and Brody told Jan goodbye and headed back to the entryway.

A minute later Rose returned to the kitchen. "Ooh la la!" she said. "Is Sasha serious about that guy?"

"I don't know," Jan answered. "They just met a few days ago, but I think they'd make a great couple."

"You can say that again."

Jan started cleaning up as Rose placed tea bags in a pot.

A minute later, Elaine came into the kitchen. Rose commented on Brody and then said, "So do you think they're serious?"

Elaine frowned. "They only met on Monday, guys."

Three days ago. Jan knew a lot could happen in a relation-ship in a short time. She couldn't help but smile. Love was an amazing thing.

"You don't seem that happy about their relationship," Rose said.

Elaine frowned again. "I guess I don't know yet. I'm not happy or unhappy about it." She shrugged. "We'll have to wait and see what happens."

Rose placed the teapot and two cups on a tray. "My predic-tion is that good things will come from this." Rose picked up the tray and, as she headed out of the kitchen, added, "Did you see the way he looked at her? He's a keeper for sure."

When Elaine didn't respond, Jan hesitated for a moment but then asked, "Is everything okay?"

Elaine stepped to the counter and pulled a teapot from the shelf, speaking as she did. "Everything is fine."

"Are you concerned about Brody?"

Elaine turned toward her cousin. "You know what? I am. Nearly everything about him seems too good to be true— and we still don't know if he took the book. And I didn't like how he avoided answering me when I asked him about his next assignment."

"I hear you. But I sincerely doubt he took the book," Jan said. "Why would he pursue a relationship with Sasha if he did?"

Elaine seemed to consider that for a moment. "I guess time will tell as far as that goes, but why wouldn't he answer my ques-tion about his next assignment?"

"You're the army wife," Jan answered. "Maybe he can't. Maybe it's top secret."

Elaine sighed. "He didn't have to be specific. He could have said it was stateside or overseas. That's allowed."

Jan didn't respond. To her way of thinking, the truth was that, along with being Special Forces, he seemed pretty special himself. She was happy for Sasha, and she couldn't figure out exactly why Elaine wasn't. Except that she knew Elaine wanted Sasha to settle down in Maine. Jan understood that—all of her own children lived close by. She'd hate it if they were thousands of miles away.

IN THE EARLY afternoon, Jan checked with Elaine to see if the Bakers had called her back.

"No," Elaine said. "I haven't heard a word from them."

"I thought I'd go to the county recorder and do some research, track the deeds to Abigail's house, that sort of thing."

"Good idea," Elaine said.

"And as long as I'm in Augusta, I'll stop by and see the grandkids."

"Doubly good idea!" Elaine grinned. Jan knew Elaine missed her own grandkids, so far away in Ohio. She was thankful that Elaine had come to love Jan's grandchildren almost as much as her own.

A half hour later, Jan parked on the street not far from the Kennebec Courthouse on State Street. The Greek Revival–style building was getting close to two hundred years old and was one that Jan had always admired.

She headed up the stairs, through the wide double doors, and up to the second floor, to the records office. The clerk quickly found the Bakers' deed. Ernest Baker and his wife had bought the property from a man named Ronald Good Jr. in 1985. It had belonged to him since 1979, when he'd inherited it from his father, Ronald Good Sr. The elder Good and his wife, Donna, had bought it in 1963 from a Donald Smith, who'd owned the property since 1937. Smith had inherited it from his grandfather, who'd inherited the property from his father in 1902.

Jan jotted down all the names on the deeds, although none of them were familiar.

She thanked the clerk and decided she would walk down the street to the library to research the names on the list.

As she stepped through the front doors of the courthouse, raindrops landed on her face and she quickly extracted her umbrella from her bag and popped it open. She couldn't say that she missed living in Augusta, but it was nice to be back. And somehow comforting that the rain was falling on both the capital city and Lancaster. The good people of her new village weren't alone in their dreary spring weather.

A computer was open in the library, so Jan worked through her list, backwards. She couldn't determine that any descendants of Donald and Mary Smith were still alive. She did confirm that Ronald Good Sr. had died in 1979. Next she Googled Ronald Good Jr. An auto body shop with a Waterville address popped up on the screen. She quickly jotted the phone number down.

Once she was back in her car, she took out her cell phone and dialed the number. A woman answered with a cheerful hello. When Jan asked to speak with Ronald Good, the woman said, "I'm so sorry, he's not available."

Jan explained that she wanted to speak with him about a house that he'd owned years ago, outside of Lancaster.

"I can take a message," the woman said.

"Perfect," Jan answered, rattling off her phone number. "Tell him I'm looking forward to his call."

"Will do," the woman said, followed by a cheery, "Have a nice day!"

Jan hung up the phone, hoping Ronald Good Jr. could shine some light on the mystery of the book.

In the meantime, she would enjoy time with her grandchildren, first with Avery and Kelly and then with the twins, Max and Riley. She'd brought treats for all of them—cream puffs for Kelly, and the new chocolate pecan salted caramel bars she'd made again just that morning. Bob had loved them and she guessed her grandchildren would too.

"Can you stay for dinner?" Paula asked as she took Jan's coat upon her arrival.

"That would be lovely," Jan answered. "But I promised Amy I'd stop by and see the twins too."

"How about if I invite them over for dinner too? We have plenty."

"That would be great!" Jan responded.

Kelly appeared, her brown eyes twinkling when she saw the cream puffs. She thanked Jan and took the plate and then held them close to her chest, as if they were a precious treasure.

Pleased, Jan asked, "Where's Avery?"

"In her room, reading." Kelly rolled her eyes.

"Kelly," Paula chastised as she picked up her phone.

Kelly had that preteen tone to her voice. "That's all Avery does lately. She doesn't want to play any video games or even watch TV. It's just read, read, read."

Paula shook her head a little. "Don't forget homework and cello practice. She gets that done too. I'm sorry she's not spending time with you, sweetie, but reading is good. What if you ask her to go for a walk? That would be good for both of you."

Kelly sighed, dramatically. "A walk? In this rain?"

"Put on your raincoats or take an umbrella."

Kelly appeared to be concentrating on not rolling her eyes. She stepped to the hallway, still holding the plate, and hollered, "Avery! Grandma's here! She brought cream puffs!"

"Don't yell," Paula said, her voice low and calm. "Give me the cream puffs and go knock on her door."

Jan did her best to not even smile, but she found the entire interaction amusing.

After Paula put the cream puffs on the kitchen counter, she dialed Amy. During the quick conversation, it was obvious Jan's older daughter and family would be joining them. Next, Paula said she'd call Tara too and see if she and her boyfriend, Jack Weston, could join them.

"Great idea!" Jan hoped her youngest and her steady boyfriend could join them too.

Thankfully, Tara said yes, and Jan had a wonderful time with all three of her kids, her grandchildren, daughter-in-law, son-in-law, and likely future son-in-law. The twins were as entertaining as ever, showing Jan some gymnastics moves they'd learned from Avery. After dinner, Kelly passed the cream puffs around. Avery, who'd been quiet, said she needed to get back to her reading.

"What book?" Jan asked.

"*Evangeline.* Aunt Virginia gave it to me."

"Really? How do you like it?"

"It took me a while to get into it," Avery said. "But I like it now. Evangeline is really strong and she never gives up."

"Just like you, sweetie," Jan said, giving her granddaughter a hug.

Kelly grabbed Candy Land from the bookcase and asked the twins if they wanted to play.

"Want to join them?" Jan asked Avery, nodding toward the table where they'd landed.

Avery hesitated. "Not really, but I think I should."

"That's my girl," Jan said.

Jan left soon after, checking her phone to see if she'd missed a call from Ronald Good. She hadn't. She'd hoped that he would call right away.

As Jan pulled out of Brian and Paula's driveway, she thought about Virginia giving Avery the copy of *Evangeline.* Elaine and her whole family blessed Jan, over and over. And she knew Elaine felt the same about Jan's family. Starting Tea for Two had been a dream come true, but the relationships that had deepened because of the business were far more important. And it was more than just family. It was the relationships with the other business owners in Lancaster and the townspeople too. And Elaine's relationship with Nathan and Jan's with Bob.

So much good had come and would continue to come from their endeavors, Jan was sure.

As she drove home, the wind picked up, blowing the rain sideways. The drum of the drops hitting the car grew louder. As she concentrated on the road, darkness fell, and her thoughts returned to the missing book and Ronald Good. Hopefully he'd call—first thing in the morning.

CHAPTER TWELVE

On Friday morning, after Rose arrived, Elaine and Sasha left for Augusta. They would have breakfast with Virginia, visit the historical society, and then make a stop to a place from Sasha's childhood—but Elaine wouldn't tell her where. That was a surprise.

"I hope the surprise is indoors or at least in a covered area," Sasha said, over the swish of the windshield wipers.

Elaine pursed her lips together and said, "Let's hope for the best." She'd hate to just drive by the "surprise" and not stop and take a good look.

Sasha asked if Elaine had any more information about the book, and Elaine gave her an update about what Jan found out the day before.

"But there's no new information, right?" Sasha asked.

"No, but we're hoping there will be soon." There had to be a break in the case sooner or later. Elaine couldn't imagine how far the book might have traveled by now though. If it had left the area, it would be even harder to get back.

They chatted for a little while longer and then Sasha said, "I'm really enjoying spending time with Brody."

"I thought you were," Elaine said.

"But you're not crazy about me doing so, right?"

Elaine tensed. Was she that obvious? Jan had sensed it too. "No, I think it's fine." She smiled at her daughter and then focused back on the road.

"What don't you like about him, then? Come on, Mom. I know there's something."

Elaine smiled at her daughter and hesitated for a moment. "I don't know him. How could I not like him?"

"I know when you're suspicious of someone," Sasha said. "But there's no way Brody took that book. Why would he? He makes a good income. And he's a man of integrity."

"All right," Elaine responded. "That's fair." She was beginning to agree that Brody hadn't taken the book, only because there was no evidence against him and plenty in his favor. But she wasn't certain he was a man of integrity.

Sasha crossed her arms. "So what is it?"

"I guess...I'm worried about you having a long-distance relationship, about where he might be stationed next."

"He's going back to Fort Bragg."

"And usually, when a soldier has time off, there's a reason."

"What do you mean?"

"Well, maybe he had that much time accumulated and wanted to spend it helping his mom. But sometimes it's because they have a deployment coming up."

"He hasn't said anything about a deployment."

Elaine slowed for a curve. "Have you asked him?"

"No. Why would I?"

Elaine didn't answer. She shouldn't have voiced her concerns. "He appears to be a fine young man," Elaine finally said. "Ignore my motherly paranoia." She tried to sound light-hearted but her attempt fell flat.

"I don't get it," Sasha said. "You were an army wife all those years. There were times you and dad had a long-distance relationship."

"We were married," Elaine said.

"Yeah, but my point is you made it work."

"I get that. I'm sorry, Sasha, I shouldn't have said anything."

Sasha kept her arms crossed until the outskirts of Augusta. It wasn't until Elaine pulled into the parking lot of the restaurant where they were meeting Virginia that she seemed to relax a little.

When they entered the restaurant, Sasha spotted her grandmother first across the room in the downtown diner. She waved and led the way. The two hugged and then Elaine took a turn hugging her mother.

"Isn't this lovely," Virginia said as she settled back down onto her chair. "Two of my favorite people."

Sasha brought her grandmother up to date about her training time in Vermont, her drive back to Maine, and her training schedule for the week, leaving out any mention of Brody. Of course Elaine wasn't going to fill in any holes. It was up to Sasha to share what she wanted.

The waitress took their orders, and then the conversation shifted to the book. Elaine had told her mother in a phone conversation earlier in the week about the copy of *Evangeline* being stolen and then later about the trip to Portland, to speak with Patrick Stark. Now Virginia asked for an update. Elaine explained that Jan had gone through the recorded deeds for the house, all the way back to the early 1900s, long before Nana would have had the book.

"Who owned the house?" Virginia asked.

"No one we'd ever heard of." She mentioned the Smith family, Donald and Mary by name. "They sold it to a Ronald Good Sr., who left it to his son..."

Virginia's face grew pale.

Elaine continued, "... Ronald Good Jr."

Virginia's mouth dropped.

"Mom," Elaine said, "what in the world is wrong?"

Sasha reached out and took her grandmother's hand.

She closed her mouth. "Forgive me," she said. "I'm shocked, is all."

"What is it?"

"Ronald Good Sr. was my cousin."

"A distant cousin?"

"No, my first cousin. Good was Gladys's married name— Gladys, my mother's sister. Ronald Sr. was her son, and Ronald Jr. her grandson."

Elaine couldn't find her voice for a moment. Finally she managed to ask, "Why have I never heard of them?"

Virginia picked up her cup of coffee. "That, dear, is a complicated story."

The account did turn out to be complicated, but also sad. Elaine's grandmother, Lena, had a sister, Gladys, whom they seldom saw. "Mother said Gladys had her own life and that was why we never saw her and her family," Virginia said, a sad expression on her face. "I have no idea what exactly that meant or if there was more to the story than that—it was all very odd. When Gladys died, Mother went to the funeral but didn't tell me about it until afterward. I'm guessing it was one of those weird family things. So, in a nutshell, that's why you haven't met Ron—Junior or Senior."

Virginia's face brightened a little. "But enough of that! I've been thinking about the copy of *Evangeline* that you had for such a short time. I imagine her great-grandparents, as Acadian descendants, would have been very interested in the story. Longfellow graduated from Bowdoin College and then taught there for a while. Perhaps he signed the book sometime during that time."

Sasha took out her phone. "I'll Google him." She squinted for a moment. "*Evangeline* was published in 1847 and he retired from teaching in 1854, but he was a professor at Harvard by then." She scrolled down. "*Hmm,*" she said. "He wrote 'Paul Revere's Ride' and *The Song of Hiawatha* too."

"Yes, he really was an American treasure. We Mainers are very proud of him."

"I can see why," Sasha said. "I'm going to order his books." She tapped on her phone a few times. "I can get *Evangeline* for $5.99." She grinned at her grandmother. "What a deal, huh?"

Virginia smiled back. "I imagine when it was first printed in 1847 that it cost…a nickel? Maybe a quarter? What do you think, dear?" she asked Elaine.

"I have no idea." She wrinkled her brow. "But I imagine you're probably close."

"Oh, I almost forgot," Virginia said. "I have a box of photos and whatnot that belonged to my mother. I thought, given your current mystery, you and Jan would enjoy going through them together." She smiled at her granddaughter. "And Sasha too."

As the waitress approached with their tray of food, Elaine thanked her mother. She was happy that Sasha was around to learn more about her family, plus she truly valued the time she could spend with both her mother and daughter.

After breakfast, Elaine followed her mother back to her home and collected the box. "Thank you," she said. "I'll let you know as soon as we find out anything about the book."

Virginia gave her a hug and a kiss on the cheek. "It's so good to see both of you." She hugged and kissed Sasha too.

Soon, Elaine and Sasha were speeding down I-295 toward Portland. There was good reason Maine was called The Pine State. Trees lined both sides of the freeway, both the evergreens and the budding branches of deciduous trees. The farther south they traveled, the brighter the day grew. Gradually, the sky transitioned from heavy clouds to thin gray skies and then to patches of blue. They passed Brunswick, where Bowdoin College was and where they'd stop later in the day on their way home.

Then they passed near Freeport, home of the flagship L.L. Bean store. At Yarmouth, they crossed over the Royal River as it made its way to Casco Bay.

By the time they reached Portland, the sky was completely cloudless. "Goodness," Elaine said. "I was beginning to think I'd never see a blue sky again. I need my sunglasses."

Sasha turned her face toward the window. "Isn't it beautiful?"

"Yes," Elaine said. "I long for sunshine in Lancaster again. The rain has gone on for so long."

"It will stop, sooner or later," Sasha responded. "In the meantime, I think it's kind of cozy."

"Cozy? You're soaking wet half the time, with all of your training," Elaine responded. Then again, maybe training in the rain with Brody was what she was really talking about.

Soon they crossed the strip of land between Back Cove and Casco Bay. The water was smooth as glass and sparkled in the sunlight. They arrived at the Maine Historical Society, on Congress Street, a few minutes later and found a parking place on the other side of Monument Square.

After paying the entry fee to the museum and confirming Patrick Stark was volunteering in the library, Elaine led the way with Sasha close behind. They'd been to the historical society before but not into the library. Book stacks filled both the main floor and the mezzanine level, creating a scholarly atmosphere.

Elaine approached the librarian at the front desk and said she was looking for Patrick Stark.

"He's processing a new collection," the woman said. "Please wait here."

After a few minutes, the librarian returned, followed by Mr. Stark, who wore archival gloves on his hands. He had a surprised expression on his face as he approached.

"Hello," he said to Elaine. "What are you doing here?"

The librarian slipped behind the desk and ducked her head.

"I have a few questions for you about my missing book," Elaine answered.

"Stolen book," Sasha added.

"What?" Mr. Stark crossed his arms.

Elaine quickly introduced Sasha to the man and then said, "We believe it was stolen. It never showed up. I wanted to ask you a few clarifying questions about information you gave me that day and also some specific questions about that night."

"*Moi?*"

"*Oui,*" Elaine answered.

"Do you think I took it?" Mr. Stark sounded offended.

Elaine smiled. "I don't know, but I know you were there that night. I was wondering if you could provide information that would help us determine who took the book."

Mr. Stark turned toward the librarian. "Do you mind if I talk with these two ladies in the boardroom?"

"That would be fine," she answered. "It's unlocked."

"This way," Mr. Stark said.

Elaine and Sasha followed him through the book stacks, under the mezzanine level, and into a room in the back of the library.

"Please sit," he said.

Elaine wondered at his formality. Was he getting ready to confess to taking the book? Perhaps he had it with him.

They sat in wood chairs around an old oak table.

Mr. Stark cleared his throat and then said, "I must confess—"

Elaine sat straighter.

Sasha shifted in her chair.

"—that I am shocked your book hasn't turned up. I was sure it had been simply misplaced that night by the bookstore owner. She had a lot to manage in a very stressful and chaotic situation."

"Yes," Elaine said. "She certainly did."

"I was there that night, for a short time. I tried to help carry books, but with my cane . . ." He held it up. "I wasn't much help, I'm afraid. I stood under the eaves of the library for a while and watched the others work, wishing I could do more."

"Did you see anything suspicious?" Elaine asked. "Did anyone get into Bristol's car? It was the red Toyota parked closest to the street."

He shook his head. "But I have to say other people knew about your book by then, and several people were talking about it."

"Such as?"

"The owner of the place where I stayed—Green Glade Cottages."

"Macy Atherton?"

"Yes, that's right," he said.

"When did you find out the book was missing?"

"The next morning, from Macy."

Elaine's brows shot up, expecting that she'd caught him—or else Macy—in a lie. "When you checked out?" Elaine asked. Macy said he'd left a note instead of personally checking out. Clearly, someone was not telling the truth, intentionally or otherwise.

"No, I bumped into her on the path to my car when she was delivering a stack of towels to one of the other cottages. She said she'd found out the night before that the book was missing."

Elaine hesitated for a moment, unsure of what to say next. Regardless of her uncertainty she said, "Macy indicated she didn't see you that morning. And that she found out at Murphy's General Store that the book was stolen."

A puzzled expression passed over his face. "Perhaps she mistook me for someone else then." He shrugged. "I have no idea why she'd say that."

"I don't either," Elaine said.

"What time did you leave that morning?" Sasha asked Mr. Stark.

"Seven, maybe seven fifteen."

Sasha's voice had a hint of accusation in it. "Why so early?"

"I slept horribly the night before." He lowered his voice. "I don't want to malign the Green Glade establishment, but the bed was the worst I've slept in for years. I woke up at four o'clock and couldn't get back to sleep. I didn't want another night of misery, so I decided to pack up and come home." He shifted in his seat. "I'm sure it was an anomaly. All of her reviews are favorable with no comments about uncomfortable beds." He shrugged. "Nevertheless I sent her an e-mail to alert her to the problem."

He leaned closer to Elaine. "Look, I'm really sorry that your book went missing, but I didn't have anything to do with it. And I don't have any information that can help you get it back. Frankly, I'm astounded by all of this. I can't imagine anyone purposefully stealing a rare book like that."

When Elaine didn't respond, he added, "Please believe me. I swear I didn't have anything to do with such a travesty. I hope more than anything that you're able to recover the book."

"I want to believe you, Mr. Stark, I really do, but you also told me that day in the book store that the historical society is working on a rare books exhibit, but I can't get that information corroborated from anyone I've spoken with here."

"Of course not," he said. "It's in the early planning stages and the curator for the exhibit is on vacation this week."

Elaine's eyebrows shot up.

Mr. Stark grimaced. "Look, I shouldn't have said anything about the exhibit. It was premature of me. But, in time, I'm sure the exhibit will come to fruition."

Elaine didn't entirely believe the man, but there wasn't any way to prove him wrong. "Thank you," she finally responded, "for your answers. If you come across any information about the book, say, if you see anything online or if anyone contacts you about it, would you please let me know?" She took a Tea for Two business card from her purse and extended it to him. "I'd really appreciate it."

"Well, I don't go online and I'm a nobody, so I doubt if anyone would contact me." He took the card. "But of course, if I hear anything, I'll let you know."

"Thank you," Elaine said.

He pushed his chair back. "Will you take some time and look around? Before you head back to Lancaster?"

Elaine glanced at Sasha.

"Yes," Sasha answered. "We'd like to."

Mr. Stark pushed himself up, leaning on his cane. "Our docents are practicing tours of Longfellow's house. That part of the museum doesn't open for another week, but they're looking for people to practice on. Would you like to join the tour?"

Elaine looked at Sasha, who nodded her head.

"That would be lovely," Elaine said. "Thank you so much."

Elaine remembered the time Ben, the children, and she visited Longfellow's childhood home. Jared had been ten and Sasha five when Ben had been stationed in Hawaii at the time. They came to Maine to visit Elaine's parents in Augusta and had driven into Portland for the day.

Her heart warmed at the memory. It seemed like yesterday—or maybe as much as a year ago. Not over twenty.

CHAPTER THIRTEEN

The Longfellow home had been restored since the last time the Cooks had toured it, and Elaine enjoyed seeing both the rooms and the changes. Everything was freshly painted in original colors, the wallpaper had been re-created, and the woodwork had been rebuilt as it would have been during the nineteenth century.

The Longfellows had occupied the home from the late 1700s to the early 1900s, quite a span for one family. As Elaine and Sasha stepped through the parlor, Elaine could imagine Henry's parents and siblings—there were eight children in all—gathered around the fireplace on a cold day, reading together.

Although her family didn't have an original home any-more, they certainly had their memories, and now Tea for Two acted as a new gathering place where everyone could meet and celebrate together.

There certainly was no place like home, that was for sure. She loved that Jan's grandkids—and hers when they visited from Ohio—felt about Tea for Two the way Jan and Elaine had felt about their grandparents' home.

Elaine gazed out the window to the garden. Her eyes landed on a lilac bush, which she knew would soon start to bud. She couldn't wait. Again, she imagined the Longfellow children, but this time playing in the garden on a spring day. She shivered a little, thinking about how quickly the years passed. Thank goodness for those who preserved history, books, and photographs. She turned her attention back to the tour guide, but her thoughts soon drifted to the box of photographs from her mother. Hopefully something in the box would shed light on the mysterious book and the estranged relationship between Nana and her sister.

"Mom," Sasha said, bringing Elaine back to the present, "look at that writing desk. It's so small—but beautiful."

Elaine nodded. It was made from a dark wood and had a flip top. All of the furnishings were from the Wadsworth or Longfellow families and some were hundreds of years old. Their home had been the first brick building in Portland and was much older than the Victorian house that was home to Tea for Two.

After the tour of the home, they toured the gardens, following the meandering path through what had been the Longfellow family's yard.

The garden had been added long after the historical society had taken over the care of the home, and had grown quite a bit since the last time Elaine had visited.

"Ready to go?" Sasha asked when the tour concluded.

"Not yet," Elaine answered. "I want to go back into the historical society and talk with the acquisition curator."

Sasha stopped. "Why?"

"Just in case the book shows up here."

Sasha started back toward the main building. "Oh, that's a good idea."

It took a few minutes for the volunteer at the front desk to track down the acquisitions curator. A man in his early thirties, wearing jeans and a blue oxford shirt, appeared fifteen minutes later and asked how he could help Elaine. She explained about the missing book and then made her request.

"We go through a lengthy verification process to prove ownership and provenance," he answered. "So hopefully a stolen item would never make it into our collection. Do you know how much the book is worth?"

"As much as $3,000, probably more."

"Then I'm sure it won't show up here," he said. "We don't have that kind of money at this time to purchase items and I doubt a thief would want to donate it."

"That makes sense," Elaine said. "Could I leave you my business card, just the same?"

The man nodded and took the card. He read it quickly. "Do you own this tearoom? In Lancaster?"

"Yes, with my cousin," Elaine answered.

"My wife and I were thinking of going up there last weekend, but the rainy forecast kept us away."

"You'll have to come sometime soon," Elaine answered. "The rain won't last forever." At least she hoped not.

"We will," the man said. "My wife and I just moved here from New Mexico. We're looking forward to exploring more."

"You'll love Lancaster," Elaine said. "Stop by the tearoom when you get up our way."

"We'll keep that in mind," the man said. "And I'll make sure and let you know if I hear anything about your book."

Elaine thanked him. The best advertising, she mused again, was word of mouth. So many people that she met through her sleuthing ended up coming in the tearoom. It was always a joy to see them again. Life was all about making connections.

She turned to go but then remembered one last thing she meant to ask about. "Excuse me," she said. "When will the exhibit on Maine books be on display?"

"Pardon?" the man asked.

"One of the volunteers, in the library, mentioned that a new exhibit is in the works called Maine Books. That a curator is working on it."

He shook his head. "That sounds like a good idea, but I haven't heard anything about it."

"Wouldn't you, as the acquisitions curator, be privy to that sort of information?"

He nodded. "There's no such exhibit in the works, unless it's just in the brainstorming phase. We have meetings to discuss that sort of thing. After someone proposes an exhibit, I do a survey of potential artifacts." He rubbed the side of his face. "Perhaps someone in the organization has the idea for such an exhibit, but there's no formal plan for it."

"I see," Elaine said, wondering if she could believe anything Mr. Stark said. She thanked the acquisitions curator for his help, and she and Sasha left the building.

ELAINE POINTED HER car south, grateful the sun was still shining.

"So where's our destination?" Sasha asked.

"It's a place you've been before," Elaine answered.

"Pre-memory?" It was a common joke of Sasha's. Elaine would make the mistake of asking Sasha if she remembered when they lived in such and such a place or visited a specific city. *Was I even born yet?* Sasha would often ask. Or she might say, *Wasn't I a toddler then, Mom?*

"Early memory." Elaine smiled. "I'm positive."

As she pulled into Crescent Beach State Park, Sasha said, "You're right. I do remember this place."

As the Atlantic came into view, she said, "I nearly froze to death even though it was a warm day. Weren't we stationed in Hawaii then? And in Maine on vacation?"

"That's right." Elaine was pleased Sasha remembered.

"I went running out into the water, right?"

"Yes." Elaine pulled into the empty parking lot.

"Dad ran in and saved me." Sasha smiled.

"He saved you from the cold—not from drowning." Elaine turned off the engine and the two climbed out of the car and walked toward the water's edge.

All those years ago, the children had been excited to see the Atlantic and had wanted to play in the ocean, and Sasha couldn't comprehend the water would be cold. She ran into it and then screamed. Laughing, Ben ran after her and scooped her up over his shoulder. Swimming in Maine was much different than swimming in Hawaii.

"Yes, I remember it all," Sasha said, patting Elaine's arm as they stood on the shore and gazed out across the still blue water. "I felt so protected by him, like always." She smiled a little, her eyes glistening. "I miss him."

Elaine sighed. "So do I."

Sasha swiped at her eyes and met her mother's gaze. "But I really like Nathan. I hope you know that."

"I do," Elaine answered. "Thank you." She took Sasha's hand and squeezed it. "So do I."

After a few more minutes of reminiscing, Elaine asked, "What do you want to do for lunch?"

"Brody told me about a place back in Portland, on the waterfront," Sasha said. "It's a café with a healthy menu."

"Sounds good."

Fifteen minutes later, Elaine parked near the café and then the two walked along the dock to reach it. A cool breeze blew off the bay, teasing the sails of the boats moored along the dock.

Elaine valued her time with Sasha and, after reminiscing about the past, she wanted to talk about the future. "Have you thought more about signing up for one of those dating sites?"

"Mother," she said, "are you just going to ignore the conversation we had this morning about Brody?"

Elaine shook her head. "No, this is entirely a different topic."

Sasha shook her head, just a little. "You're relentless." She leaned closer. "No, I'm not going to sign up for a dating app, not at the moment. And as to Brody...even though we just discussed this, please don't worry. It's not like anything can happen. We enjoy working out together. He's returning to North Carolina and I'm returning to Colorado, but for the record, he's one of the most honest and nicest people I've ever met. If we were both going to be in the same place, I'd definitely be interested in him."

Elaine's eyebrows shot up before she could stop them. She quickly tried to put on a poker face but it was too late.

Sasha sighed. "See?"

Elaine shook her head. "My reaction had nothing to do with Brody. It had to do with thinking you could know someone was honest after only knowing them a few days."

Sasha frowned. "I have pretty good intuition when it comes to honesty."

"All right," Elaine said. "And you're probably right. Just know there are people in this world who can fool others— even you."

Sasha definitely heard what Elaine had said, but her eyes drifted past her mom and out the window to the bay. "It's so clear today," she said. "You can see the islands."

There were around two hundred islands out in the bay, from quite large to barely a dot on a map. Of course only a handful were visible from the Portland area. The bay was huge. If Elaine remembered right, it was two hundred square miles.

Once their salads arrived—an avocado and tuna one for Sasha and shrimp Louie for Elaine—their conversation fell back to Sasha's childhood memories of trips to Maine. Finally she said, "It must have been hard for Grandma and Grandpa to have us so far away."

Elaine nodded. "I'm sure it was, but they never complained. They were just so happy when we visited."

"I know what it was like as a child having a dad in the military, but I've never asked you what it was like to have your husband make a career of it." Sasha speared a grape tomato. "Did you ever wish Dad hadn't?"

Elaine smiled slightly. "Sure, when he was in Saudi Arabia during Desert Storm and you and Jared were little. That was hard. His orders were for two years and the expectations were the war would last much longer than it did. It was difficult when he was in Iraq in 2005 too. But he was so fulfilled serving in the army. That made it worth it for me, plus he was doing such important work, taking care of his troops and protecting our country, protecting all of us. I was more worried about you kids than I was myself."

Elaine put her fork down. "How did the positives and negatives weigh out for you, as a child?"

"There were definitely good things. The travel. Living in different places. Learning to be flexible. On the other hand, making new friends was sometimes difficult. I see you in Lancaster, where you grew up, bumping into people from your school years all the time, and wonder what that would be like." She speared another tomato. "Honestly, I worried about Dad when he was deployed. Then I always thought, once he retired, I'd have more time with him. Losing him so soon was such a shock."

"I know," Elaine said, reaching for Sasha's free hand and squeezing it.

"So yeah, I guess the jury's still out when it comes to the life of a military family." She tilted her head a little. "And if your goal in asking was to get me to think about what it would be like to be in a relationship with a military man, don't worry. I've already thought it all through, long before I met Brody."

"And what was your verdict?"

Sasha wrinkled her nose. "I guess the verdict is still out on that too. I guess it would depend on the man, right? If he was worth following around the world. If I were sure he'd make a good husband and father. If I fell madly in love with him."

Elaine nodded. "That's certainly how it all played out for me when it came to your dad."

"So then why do you worry about this, Mom? Time will tell, right?"

Elaine couldn't help but worry, when her intuition, which was contrary to Sasha's, told her to be leery of Brody.

On the other hand, Sasha commenting earlier about feeling protected by her dad shed some light on her attraction to Brody. Ben had been a true soldier—physically capable, loyal, and dedicated to caring for others, especially his daughter. Perhaps Brody reminded her of her father.

THEY ARRIVED IN Brunswick just after 3 p.m. Elaine had always loved the tree-filled village with its Federal and Greek Revival mansions, charming homes, and brick buildings.

Harriet Beecher Stowe had written much of *Uncle Tom's Cabin* in Brunswick when her husband taught at Bowdoin

College. Elaine remembered hearing that it was a vision during a communion service at the college chapel that inspired Stowe to write the story.

Elaine found a place to park near the Hawthorne-Longfellow Library and then walked to the building where Dr. Day had his office.

"It's on the second floor," she said to Sasha. Up the stairs they went and found the right room. Elaine knocked softly and then with more force. Finally a voice called out, "Oh! Come on in!"

She opened the door to find a man, probably a few years younger than she was, behind a big desk. The room was lined with shelves that were overstuffed with old books, manuscripts, busts of authors, and old photos.

The man stood. "You must be Elaine Cook."

"Yes," she answered. "And this is my daughter, Sasha."

"Sean Day," he said, stepping out from his desk with his hand extended. "I'm so pleased to meet both of you."

"Likewise," Elaine responded as she shook the man's hand. Then she stepped back and Sasha stepped forward, greeting him also.

He motioned for them to sit in the two straight-back chairs in front of his desk. "I'm so sorry that the book has gone missing," Dr. Day said, settling back down in his chair. "I can't tell you what a thrill it was to see it. I'm certain the autograph is authentic—Henry W. Longfellow. It's so straightforward and easy to decipher. Not like some handwriting."

Elaine thought of the note in the back of the book.

"Do you have any leads on finding it?" the professor asked.

Elaine shook her head. "But we're continuing to gather information. I was hoping you could tell us about that afternoon when you viewed the book."

"Of course," he answered.

She pulled out her notebook. "Do you mind if I take notes?"

"Not at all," he answered and then leaned back a little in his chair. "I met Bristol several years ago at a symposium here at Bowdoin on Harriet Beecher Stowe. I've seen Bristol a few times since then, so I wasn't surprised when she called me about the book. If I was going to view the book anytime soon, I needed to do it that afternoon because I was leaving for a conference in New York the next day."

Elaine nodded. Everything he'd said so far matched what she'd heard from Bristol.

He leaned forward. "It wasn't raining when I left Brunswick, but it was pouring by the time I neared Lancaster. I almost turned around, but decided to keep going. When I arrived at the bookstore, there were several customers in the shop so Bristol showed me the book in her office. I was absolutely impressed by it. 1847. Autographed. It's a real gem. I told Bristol that if the owners ever wanted to sell it, I'd love to be given the first chance at buying it." He swept his hand wide. "As you can see, I collect books and author memorabilia. I don't have a family, so this is what I dedicate my free time and extra money to."

"I see," Elaine said.

He stood and walked over to the closest shelf. "I have a first printing of *The Scarlett Letter*—1850. And an 1853 edition of *Uncle Tom's Cabin*, along with several early editions of Mark

Twain's work. I also have quite a few early editions by Edgar Allan Poe." He shrugged as if that was only the tip of the iceberg. "If the author has a connection to Bowdoin, like Hawthorne, Longfellow, and Stowe, all the better, but I'm interested in any American literature, nineteenth century in particular."

"Is that what you teach?" Elaine asked.

Dr. Day nodded. "Along with twentieth century."

"That sounds fascinating."

He smiled. "It certainly is to me."

Elaine aimed to redirect the conversation back to the missing book. "Did any of the customers seem to notice you on the afternoon you viewed the book?" Elaine asked.

"Yes, one did. An older man who walked with a cane. He volunteers at the Maine Historical Society."

"Patrick Stark?"

"Yes, exactly."

Elaine thought it interesting he'd stayed at the bookstore until Dr. Day arrived.

"He seemed to know all about the book. He introduced himself and talked about his work at the Maine Historical Society. I've done a lot of research in that library, and I would have been happy to speak with him much longer except that I was worried about flooding." Dr. Day steepled his fingertips. "I needed to catch a flight out of Portland the next morning and didn't want to get stuck in Lancaster."

He paused for a moment and Elaine asked what happened next.

"A customer came in and said there was standing water outside, that the entire lawn was swampy with water. Bristol ran out to check—something must have been wrong with the drainage system because the water began rising quickly. She called her husband and a few others to come help move books. I considered staying, but like I said, I had a flight to catch the next day and didn't want to be stranded, so I left."

"Where was the book when you left?"

"In the office. Bristol relocked it."

"Was this before or after she ran outside to check the water level and then call people?"

"Before," Dr. Day answered. "I left the office with her when the customer raised the alarm. She locked it right after we stepped out, before we exited the building."

Sasha shot Elaine a look, probably because she felt her mom was being too pushy. Elaine ignored her. She needed to understand exactly what had happened as best she could. But as far as she could tell, his story matched Bristol's.

"What did you do after you left the building?"

"I headed straight to my car and left town immediately. Like I said, I didn't want to risk getting stuck in Lancaster and missing my flight." His expression became even more sympathetic than it had been. "I really am sorry about the book going missing. It's heartbreaking."

"Thank you," Elaine responded. "And thank you for answering my questions. I really appreciate it."

He nodded. "I'm happy to help any way I can. I know I'm not as devastated as you must be about it being stolen, but it really is a shame. I hope you'll be able to find it."

"Thank you," Elaine said. "If anyone contacts you about the book, would you let me know?"

"Absolutely," he answered.

As they stood to leave, Elaine noticed a copy of *Evangeline* on Dr. Day's shelf. The spine was worn and the title faded some.

"What year is that edition?" she asked, pointing to the book.

"It's not that old," he said. "And it's not signed. Like I said, I really would like to purchase your book—if you find it and you're ever interested in selling it."

"What's considered 'not that old'?" Elaine asked.

"Mine is 1866. Right after the Civil War. By then, he'd been retired from teaching for over a decade and kept writing. He'd become world renowned by then. In fact, in 1874 he was paid $3,000 for one poem."

"What would that be worth now?" Sasha asked.

"Over $60,000."

"That's incredible!" Sasha ran her hand through her hair. "Poets back then must have been the rock stars of their day."

Dr. Day grinned. "That or something like professional athletes today."

Elaine glanced around the room again, recognizing a bust of Longfellow. Times certainly had changed.

As they left, Elaine thanked Dr. Day again and asked if she could contact him if she had any other questions.

"Of course," he answered. "And please let me know when you recover the book."

She promised she would.

Ten minutes later, after Elaine pulled away from the college and turned onto the highway toward Augusta, Sasha Googled Dr. Sean Day. "He's listed on the faculty at Bowdoin College," she said. "No surprise there. And he pops up as the speaker at several symposiums and conferences. On nineteenth-century American authors, mostly."

No surprise there either, Elaine thought.

"I don't see any red flags. He doesn't sell books on Amazon. Or eBay. Or anywhere else I can find." She continued clicking on her phone.

Elaine really didn't think Dr. Day had taken the book.

"Oh my," Sasha said, squinting in the later afternoon light as she looked at her phone screen.

"What is it?"

"Patrick Stark is an entirely different matter," Sasha said. "Maybe it's a different person, but there's someone by that name selling books on Amazon, eBay, and a couple of other sites." She clicked a few more times. "A few are pretty old and he's asking up to $300 for a copy of *Uncle Tom's Cabin*." Sasha looked up from her phone and at her mother. "What do you think?"

"The fact that he sells books online isn't enough to prove that he took our copy of *Evangeline*."

"But this Mr. Stark has been pretty fishy, right? Saying the historical society plans to do an exhibit when they don't? Leaving Lancaster a day early, in the early morning?"

Elaine shrugged, keeping her eyes on the road. "It's all true. But none of that proves he took our book."

CHAPTER FOURTEEN

Even though the next day was Saturday, Bill Bridges arrived just after 8 a.m. to install the chandelier. Jan was halfway through the baking and was just pulling a tray of blueberry tarts from the oven when she heard his truck out front.

She wiped her hands on her apron, waited for a moment to see if Elaine was nearby, and then hurried to the front door to let Bill in.

He stood on the porch, shielded from the rain. It wasn't pouring, but it was a steady drizzle.

"Good morning!" Bill stepped into the entryway. "I'm finally here to hang that chandelier." He nodded toward the Bookworm. "Then I'm going to be hanging new Sheetrock for Bristol."

"I didn't realize everything was cleaned up over there," Jan said.

Bill nodded. "They've had fans running all week. I shifted some other jobs around to get the Sheetrock done so she can get the carpet installed and then haul all those books back in. I know that every day she's closed, she's losing business and money."

Jan couldn't help but be sympathetic. It didn't take long for a small business to fall into the red.

She headed through the west parlor toward the dining room. "Hopefully this won't take long." All he had to do was disconnect the existing light fixture, which was awfully plain, and install the chandelier.

As they entered the dining room, Jan turned on the overhead fixture, sending light bouncing through the crystals of the chandelier on the table.

Bill whistled. "Isn't that a beauty? Remind me where you found it."

"The Department of Public Works, of all places," Jan said. "We stopped by to check on our drainage system and a couple of the guys who work there had just hauled it out of the backroom. Patty Cane said we could have it."

Bill whistled again as he stepped up to the chandelier and touched one of the crystal pieces. "How in the world did it end up in the Public Works building?"

"No one there knew," Jan said.

Bill tapped the side of his face. "I'm having a déjà vu moment."

Jan raised her eyebrows. "You've seen this before?"

"Well, I don't know if it's the same one or not, but about a year ago I did some work at a mansion on the other side of the lake, at the end of a side road down by the shore. There's a wrought iron gate across the driveway. It's the one with the stone turret."

Jan shook her head. She couldn't place the house, but it had been a while since she'd been in that particular area. He turned toward the chandelier again. "I'm certain the one I saw was at least very similar to this one, if not exactly like it." He stepped closer and pointed at the chandelier. "This one was originally gas—not electric. And I'm guessing the one on the other side of the lake was too. The mansion would have been built before electricity was used, let alone wired to that side of the lake."

"Fascinating," Jan said. "We'll have to look into that. Perhaps it would offer a clue to where the chandelier originally came from—if it did come from that mansion, as you suspect."

Bill shrugged. "Maybe it didn't. Maybe these were common back then, sold by Sears or something." He chuckled and then turned toward the doorway. "I'll grab my ladder. And then I'll need to turn off the breaker to this room."

"Of course," Jan said.

Bill took a deep breath. "Smells good, as always. You must be baking." He looked around. "If I remember right, there's a different breaker for the dining room than for the kitchen."

Jan nodded. That's what she remembered too. "I have an apricot scone ready for you after you're done. And a cup of tea."

"Great," Bill said. He glanced back up at the smaller, existing light fixture. "That one's smaller but the structure is large enough for the bigger chandelier. I don't think this will take long." He stepped into the west parlor. "I'll let you know when I have this installed and am ready to claim my reward."

As Bill headed out the front door, Sasha and Elaine both came down the staircase. Sasha wore running tights and a rain jacket, and Elaine was dressed for the day.

Jan told them about the mansion across the lake where Bill had seen a similar chandelier, if not an identical one. She repeated the description of the mansion as Bill had said it.

"Are you kidding?" Sasha put her hands on her hips. "Brody and I have run by there several times. The front gate is padlocked and there are No Trespassing signs placed all around the perimeter."

"How odd," Jan said.

"It looks as if it might be a construction site."

Elaine gasped. "Do you think someone plans to tear it down?"

"I don't know," Sasha answered. "I'll see if anyone's around today that I can ask. Brody and I plan to run out that way. He'll be by in a few minutes."

Jan thought a brief look of concern passed over Elaine's face, but she couldn't be sure.

Through the glass in the front door, Jan could see Bill approaching with his ladder. She quickly opened the door for him.

He told Elaine and Sasha good morning and then continued on through the parlor. Before Jan closed the door, Brody pulled up out front.

"Here I go!" Sasha bolted out the door, calling over her shoulder, "Goodbye!"

Just as Jan was ready to close the door, Bill came back. "Gotta get a second ladder and then my tools," he said.

Jan held the door wide and said, "Just let yourself back in."

"Will do." He stepped out onto the porch and down to the walkway.

Sasha waved as she and Brody started running down Main Street. He gave a wave too and a wide grin.

"He certainly is handsome," Jan said.

Elaine made a little squeaky noise but didn't respond.

"What's up?" Jan asked. "Do you still feel as if he's a prime suspect?"

"Not really," Elaine answered. "But I do feel as if he's hiding something."

"From Sasha?"

"I don't know," Elaine answered, leading the way back into the kitchen.

The front door opened and closed. Bill was back. Jan took the tarts out of the oven, and Elaine started filling the tins of tea on the counter from the boxes in the cupboard.

A moment later, Bill came through the kitchen on his way to the back porch to the electrical box. He nodded and then began whistling as he stepped through the door.

A moment later all of the lights in the kitchen and the stove turned off.

"Oops." Jan stepped to the back porch door. "Did you get the wrong breaker?" she asked Bill.

"Did you lose electricity?"

"Yep," Jan answered.

"Sorry," he said after a moment. "I can't get the kitchen breaker to reset—it probably just needs some time. I'll get the chandelier changed out as fast as I can and then address the second problem too."

An hour later, with just thirty minutes until opening, Bill still wasn't done.

"I'll go check," Jan said.

"And I'll go start a fire in the fireplace," Elaine responded. "If the electricity doesn't come on, we can heat water the old-fashioned way."

"Good idea," Jan said. They had an old cast-iron kettle on display and a hook hanging in the fireplace. They might as well use it.

Jan stopped at the doorway to the dining room. Bill had pulled the dining room table over to the far end of the room and had a section of drywall resting on top of the second ladder, which was taller than the first, with the chandelier balanced on top.

He was working to connect the electrical cord from the chandelier to the wiring coming out of the ceiling.

"How's it going?" Jan asked.

"Not so well." Bill's voice was muffled with his face so close to the ceiling. "I'm having a hard time getting the wires connected."

It appeared the cord from the chandelier wasn't long enough to give him any slack. "Can I help?" Jan asked. "I can get our ladder and give you a hand holding the chandelier."

"Actually," Bill said, "that might be just what I need."

Jan hurried to the garage and grabbed the tallest ladder they had and then returned to the house.

"Place the ladder on the other side of mine," Bill said as he lifted the chandelier from the makeshift platform.

As Jan set up her ladder, Bill said, "I should have brought along an assistant to help."

"Hopefully I can do it," Jan said. Once she had the ladder up, she climbed until she was even with Bill. Because of the high ceiling, she was much higher than she felt comfortable with, but she was willing to give it a try.

He lifted the chandelier to the ceiling. "Can you help steady it while I finish splicing the wires?"

"I think so." Jan reached up and held the chandelier, while he held up the cord from the chandelier and began screwing on the nuts that would join the wires.

"I'll tuck these up after I'm done," he said. "And then put a collar around the base of the chandelier. I have a few in my truck you can choose from."

"Sounds good," Jan said. Even if the chandelier was lighter than Bill had anticipated, it was still heavy for her and steadying it took all of her strength.

Bill held the wires with one hand and then managed to unwind electrical tape from a spool with the other. By the time he taped the wires, Jan's arm was beginning to ache.

"Can you help me lift it all the way?" he asked.

"I'll try," Jan answered, wishing they'd recruited Brody to help before he went off running with Sasha.

Bill began lifting the chandelier and Jan stepped up another rung of the ladder.

She tried to ignore the footsteps in the west parlor, but she couldn't ignore Elaine asking, "How's it going?"

"Ask us in a few minutes," Bill managed to say.

Elaine hurried to the middle of the room. "I'll hold your ladders."

"Thanks," Jan muttered, concentrating as best she could, but feeling a little safer with Elaine below.

"I just need to get the cord over the hook in the ceiling," Bill said. "Then I can steady it."

A few moments later, he gave out a huge sigh. "Got it. You can let go."

He held on to the cord as he tucked the wires up into the ceiling and then pulled on it, sending the chandelier up to the ceiling.

"You can go ahead and get down," he said to Jan. "But could you do me a favor and go choose a collar out of the back of my truck, on the left side? And then after you bring it in, call Bristol and tell her I'll be there as soon as I can. I had no idea this would take so long."

Jan complied while Elaine continued to hold Bill's ladder. They only had ten minutes until opening now.

She hurried to the truck, chose an ornate collar that matched the chandelier, and then headed back into the house, checking the fire in the east parlor first. The flames were roaring and Elaine had placed the kettle on the hook over the fire. Hopefully if Bill couldn't get the electricity on soon, they could make at least a couple of pots of tea.

Once she climbed back up her ladder, she gave Bill the collar and then descended again. He asked if she'd get his electric drill from his toolbox. She obliged quickly and then scampered back up the ladder and handed it to him.

After that she hurried back into the kitchen and called Bristol. Now there were only five minutes left until opening.

The phone rang and rang and just when Jan expected the call to go to voice mail, Bristol answered. She was out of breath and sounded stressed.

Jan took a deep breath and tried to put her own stress aside. If she and Elaine couldn't serve a guest at exactly 10 a.m., the world would not come to an end.

"Are you all right?" Jan asked Bristol.

"I will be," she said. "I'm still trying to figure out things with the insurance company and how to pay for the repairs to the drainage system, and now Bill is late arriving to get started on the drywall."

"That's why I'm calling—at least as far as your last worry," Jan said. "Bill's been delayed. He's installing a chandelier here and it's taking longer than expected."

"Tell him not to worry. A half hour isn't going to make much difference at this point." Bristol sighed. "I keep worrying we might flood again anyway, with the drainage system being in disrepair and all."

"What does the insurance company say?"

"They'll pay for the damages but not the drainage system," Bristol answered. "All this rain has me worried it might overflow and I'll have to dry everything out again."

"Yes, it seems the drainage system is the top priority."

"Except that I don't have the money right now—especially when I'm not bringing in any income."

Jan thought of her earlier idea to do a fund-raiser for the Bookworm. She'd talk with Elaine about it again as soon as she got off the phone, but she wouldn't mention anything to Bristol until they came up with a plan. "Aside from the drainage system problem, once you get the Sheetrock work done, you can have the floors installed and then you can open back up," Jan said.

"I know." Bristol sounded as if she might cry. "It all feels so overwhelming right now—and like such a risk. The forecast says more rain is on its way."

It did seem a little crazy not to fix the drainage system first. "Well, Bill will be over soon. He might have some ideas about the drainage system. And I'll come by and check in on you as soon as I can."

"Thank you," Bristol said. "You and Elaine have been so kind, especially after I essentially lost your book."

"It's not your fault," Jan said. "Please don't dwell on that. You have other things to worry about."

"Thank you," Bristol said. "I'll let you go. I know it's opening time for you."

After she said goodbye, Jan looked at the time on her phone: 10:00. It was time to go flip the Open sign.

As she did, a car parked on the street—an older model that she thought she'd seen before but couldn't quite place.

A woman climbed out of the driver's seat, walked around the car, and started toward Tea for Two. It was Abigail Samson, Brody's mom.

Just as Abigail reached the door, the kettle in the fireplace began to whistle. And then, to Jan's relief, the lights flickered and came back on.

Jan showed Abigail to a table in the east parlor, not far from the fireplace, and handed her the menu.

As Jan grabbed a potholder and then unhooked the kettle and took it off the fire before placing it on the hearth, Abigail said, "It's so cozy in here."

"Isn't it?" Jan responded. "We don't always heat water in the fireplace though." She laughed and then told Abigail the entire story.

"Could I see the chandelier?" she asked, her eyes wide.

Jan smiled. "Follow me." She led the way through the west parlor and into the dining room, announcing to Elaine, "Look who's here!"

"Oh," Elaine said, seemingly surprised. But she greeted Abigail quickly and then introduced her to Bill, who was back on the ladder, securing the collar.

"Nice to meet you," Bill said. "Isn't this a beauty?"

Abigail agreed. "It looks amazing in here—as if it were designed for this room."

Enough sunlight was coming through the window to reflect off the crystal. The room would be dazzling in the afternoon light, especially during the late spring and summer.

"What brings you in today?" Elaine asked Abigail. Jan feared she detected a bit of apprehension in her cousin's voice.

"I was hoping maybe I could corner Brody and get him to talk with me," Abigail said. "He's been avoiding me for the last week."

Elaine's tone changed to concern. "Really?"

"Oh, I'm sure it's nothing. He's just been so quiet. I'd been looking forward to three weeks of conversation with him. Instead it's been crickets."

"Do you think it's because he's off with Sasha every day?" Elaine asked. She imagined he talked then, or else Sasha wouldn't still be spending time with him.

"Maybe," Abigail smiled. "Although I'm actually relieved he's found a friend while he's here. That's nice for him." She sighed. "I just thought that maybe he'd talk with me in a public place instead of evading my questions at home."

"So this is a coup," Elaine joked.

Abigail laughed. "You could say that."

Bill descended the ladder. "All done," he said. "I'll head over to Bristol's now."

Jan thanked Bill as she handed him two scones and a tea to go. Just then the front door opened.

"More guests," Elaine said. "We'd better get this show on the road." She put her arm around Abigail's shoulder. "Did Jan put you at a table by the fire?"

"She did," Abigail answered.

The two walked into the entryway, and then a second later, Elaine said, "Sasha. Brody. I didn't expect you back so soon."

"We've been gone an hour and half," Sasha said.

Brody turned toward his mom. "I saw your car out front. What are you doing here?"

"I thought I'd try out the tearoom. Want to join me?"

"Sure..." His voice faded.

Jan stepped into the west parlor where she could see everyone in the hall.

"Sasha, while they sit down, would you help me in the kitchen?" Elaine asked. "Bill just now turned the electricity on after hanging the chandelier and we're a little behind."

Sasha glanced at Brody, then said, "Sure." But she didn't sound too happy about it. Jan understood Elaine wanted to give Abigail time with her son, but keeping Brody and Sasha apart didn't appear to be an easy task.

Jan followed Elaine and Sasha into the kitchen. Elaine began whispering to Sasha, explaining that Abigail wanted time alone with Brody.

"All right," Sasha said, washing her hands. "I'll go up and get a shower and then come back down and help."

"Before you go," Jan said from the doorway, "did you find anything out at the mansion?"

Sasha shook her head. "We ran up the driveway to the gate, but couldn't see anyone on the other side. It's odd, because the yard is well taken care of, but no one was in sight."

"Maybe one of us can go take a closer look sometime," Elaine said.

As Sasha walked back into the hall, Jan turned around toward her. Brody stood in the doorway to the east parlor. "Will you join us?"

"I was going to go get a shower," Sasha answered.

"No fair." Brody grinned. "Come sit with us. If Mom can tolerate me, she can more than tolerate you."

"Yes." Abigail's voice sounded sincere. "Come join us, please."

Sasha glanced over her shoulder, as if she perhaps expected her mother to tell her what to do.

Elaine shrugged and then nodded toward the parlor. Abigail was either fine with it—or else resigned to it. She probably was just now realizing that it would be hard to have Brody to herself when Sasha was in the same building.

A few minutes later, as Jan concentrated on baking another batch of tarts, Elaine came into the kitchen with the order for Abigail, Brody, and Sasha.

"Well," Elaine said as she started a pot of Irish Breakfast brewing, "they're having a good time in there, joking and laughing. You'd never know Abigail wanted to have a serious conversation with her son."

"You should join them." Jan placed a savory scone—bacon, cheddar, and chive—on a plate for Brody.

"Oh, I don't want to interrupt." Elaine had a sad expression on her face.

"You need to get to know Brody better," Jan said. "What better time than now?"

"I guess you're right," Elaine said, pulling three teacups from the shelf.

"Guess?" Jan joked.

"Hope," Elaine retorted. "I should have said, 'I hope you're right.'" A smile crept across her face.

"That's my girl." Jan grinned back at her cousin. "Just take it a day at a time. Sasha and Brody are working out together, that's all. She's not moving to North Carolina or Korea or some other far-flung place."

"At least not anytime soon," Elaine muttered, placing the teapot on a tray. Jan knew North Carolina seemed so much farther away than Colorado at the moment. At least with Sasha in Colorado, Elaine could still hope she'd relocate in Maine someday.

Jan didn't respond to Elaine's comment. She understood why her cousin was negative toward Brody, but she wondered if Elaine might eventually see him in a different light and regret her initial response.

CHAPTER FIFTEEN

Sunday afternoon, after church followed by lunch at the Pine Tree Grill with Jan, Bob, and Nathan, Elaine retrieved the box of photos her mother had given her the Friday before from where she'd put them in her office.

She texted Sasha, who was up in the guest room, and asked if she wanted to join her and Jan to go through the box.

Sasha texted back: *Give me a minute.*

Jan stepped into the east parlor with a pot of tea on a tray and an assortment of the lemon tarts and cookies she'd made over the last two days. "I thought a little treat was in order."

"Great," Elaine said. "Sasha is going to join us."

"Perfect," Jan answered and then sighed.

"What is it?" Elaine asked.

"I should have asked Tara to come by. The more members of the next generation who can absorb our family history, the better. Don't you think?"

Elaine completely agreed. Besides, it would be fun for Sasha to have Tara involved. "Of course. Call and see if she can join us."

Jan smiled. "I might as well give it a try." She put the tray down on a table and pulled out her phone. Tara picked up right away, and a moment later, Jan was saying, "Great! See you soon!"

"She's on her way," Jan said as she ended the call. Which meant she'd arrive immediately; she only lived a few blocks away.

Tara stepped into the entryway just as Sasha came down the stairs, and the two hugged each other. Tara was a couple of years older than Sasha. When they were little that couple of years made more of a difference than it did now. Currently, they were in the same stage of life. Twenties. Single. And very independent.

Tara wore a stylish sweater, a string of glass beads, and jeans. Her light-brown hair was twisted up on her head and she wore big hoop earrings. In contrast, Sasha wore a pair of running tights and a sweatshirt. Her hair was a little bit darker than Tara's, but not much, and was looped on top of her head through her ponytail holder. Both young women were beautiful and looked as if they could easily be sisters.

As the two stepped into the parlor, Tara rubbed her hands together. "What kind of family treasures have you found?"

Elaine explained that her mother had given her the box of photos and memorabilia after she and Sasha visited on Friday.

"We're hoping to find some clues as far as who 'T' is," Jan explained. "From the note in the *Evangeline* book that I told you about."

"Sounds great!" Tara pulled up a chair to the table and Sasha did the same.

"You've had a front-row seat to the whole missing book thing," Tara said to Sasha. She grinned and then teased, "And I heard you've had someone sitting beside you the whole time."

"Not sitting." Sasha smiled back. "Running. And shooting. And working out."

"Oh, he sounds perfect for you!" Tara ran her fingers through her string of beads. The two girls couldn't be more different, so it had been great to see them grow closer over the last few years.

Elaine picked up the box. "Why don't we go up to the sitting room instead? It's more comfortable up there and we can spread out a little more."

"Sounds good," Jan said, placing the teapot and cups back on the tray. "Isn't this fun?" Jan asked Elaine as their daughters led the way upstairs.

"Yes, I'm so thankful for our family." She truly was.

Five minutes later—with the tea poured and the women spread out on the window seats—Elaine began pulling photos and papers out of the box and passing them around.

Some were labeled on the back but others weren't. There were photos of Virginia as a teenager with her brother, who was Jan's father. One was dated 1957, when the two would have been eighteen and seventeen.

"Ah," Tara said. "I don't know that I ever saw a photo of Grandpa as a teen."

He appeared to still be blond in the photo and was holding a fishing pole. The siblings stood beside water.

"Perhaps it's Lake Chickadee," Tara said.

"It could be," Elaine answered.

Besides photographs, there were newspaper clippings, graduation announcements, baby announcements, and even a few church bulletins. Plus a stack of greeting cards still in their sealed envelopes, all addressed to Gladys Good.

Elaine held one up as she pointed to the name and then the return address.

Jan raised her eyebrows but didn't say anything.

All of the cards were from Nana—but all had been returned, unopened. Elaine, thinking about her mother's story about the two sisters, put the cards in a separate stack.

"Nana found value in all sorts of things, didn't she?" Jan held up a newspaper clipping about George IV dying and his daughter becoming Elizabeth II.

Elaine reached for it. "Mom was a young teen when this happened. She's talked about it before."

"It must have impressed all of them," Sasha said.

Elaine kept digging. The lower layers of photos were older and more fragile. There was a photo of a soldier from World War II, most likely their great-uncle Tim, although the photograph wasn't labeled. Was he the "T" from the note in the back of the book, after all? What in the world could Nana have done that would have offended him?

Going back a few more years, there was a wedding photo of Nana and Grandfather Pritchard. Nana wore a light-colored skirt and jacket and Grandfather wore a tailored suit. It was the middle of the Depression and Elaine could imagine how tight their money must have been. She passed the photo on to Jan, who looked at it closely with both Tara and Sasha. Tara commented on the skirt and jacket, which launched a discussion about wedding attire throughout the years.

Elaine kept digging and found what she thought was probably her grandmother's graduation photograph. Nana smiled sweetly, showing off her dimples. Her dress was white and whimsical. Next was a photo of Nana with a boy and a younger girl. Elaine flipped the photo over. This one was labeled "Lena, Tim, and Teeny."

"Teeny," she read again.

"Who's Teeny?" Jan asked.

"I don't know—but she could be Nana's younger sister. Gladys was the name Mom told me." She held up the photograph. "If this is her, she was definitely petite. Do you think her nickname could have been Teeny?"

Jan nodded. "It's a possibility—that certainly could explain the 'T' at the end of the note."

Elaine's heart raced a little. Had they solved that part of the mystery? If so, would it shed any light on the history of the missing book?

THAT NIGHT BEFORE she went to bed, Elaine remembered the stack of returned cards and sat down in the wingback chair in the corner of her bedroom. Under the lamplight, she sorted the envelopes chronologically by the cancellation dates on the stamp. Gently she opened each one. The first was dated in June of 1937, the year Nana and Grandfather married, and was just a few lines. Nana asked her sister if they could meet and talk things through.

The next one was dated a year later. Nana asked Gladys again if she would meet her. This time she added another paragraph, saying:

It's time to put what happened behind us. You were young—now we're both older. There's no reason to be embarrassed about what you said. I don't care, and I hope you don't either. I want my sister back, more than anything. Please answer this letter, call me, or stop by and see me. Your loving sister,

Lena

The next letter was similar but the fourth one added more information. Their grandmother wrote:

Neither Nolan nor I hold your youthful infatuation against you. I know you believed at one time that I stole Nolan from you, but that's not what happened. I hope that you don't still hold that thought against me, against us.

In the next letter, Nana wrote:

I know you have the false idea that I "stole" Nolan from you. That's simply not true and all three of us know it.

But now, besides your false ideas, you've taken my copy of Evangeline. *If you fancy yourself "searching the world" for Nolan the way Evangeline did for Gabriel, please stop. Or if you decided that if you couldn't have my husband you'd take the book I valued most, then please know your actions are both childish and petty.*

Teeny, I'm dumbfounded by the way you're acting. Our parents didn't raise us to behave so poorly. You're married now, with a life of your own. Please bury the hatchet and give me a call.

Elaine put the last card into its envelope. Teeny *was* Gladys.

She'd had been infatuated with Elaine's grandfather and had believed Nana stole him from her. Then she stole the copy of *Evangeline* that had been in the family for decades and promised to Nana.

But the thing was, Gladys, or Teeny, must have intended to give the book back, because why else would she have placed the note in the back of the book?

Elaine stacked the envelopes together, retied them with the yarn, and then placed them back in the box. As she climbed into bed, her heart ached over the rift between her grandmother and great-aunt, even though it had happened many years ago and both were long passed. It had affected their extended family, even though Elaine hadn't been aware of it until now.

She'd drive out to Ronald Good's auto shop as soon as possible. She and Jan didn't have many relatives left anymore. They needed to claim all they could.

THE NEXT DAY, after the tearoom closed, Elaine asked Jan if she wanted to go with her to find Ronald Good.

"I'd love to, but I don't think I should. I need to get a few items mixed up for tomorrow." Jan washed her hands as she spoke. "I'm going to tackle macarons for our French-themed bridal tea. They're a little difficult so a head start will be good."

Elaine left the cleanup to Rose and headed north. A drizzle of rain fell, just enough to have the windshield wipers on low. As she drove, she began to think through the situation she'd soon face. Perhaps Ronald Good had held a grudge against Elaine and Jan's side of the family all of these years, as it seemed his grandmother had. Perhaps he knew exactly who they were and that was why he hadn't returned Jan's call. Or perhaps he had stolen the book and that was why he hadn't called her back. Elaine tightened her grip on the steering wheel. Perhaps she'd walk into his shop, and he wouldn't speak to her at all.

Her heart sank. Finding a long-lost relative was a milestone, something to celebrate. Suspecting he might have stolen a treasure from her and Jan would be a big letdown. She wasn't sure how to reconcile the two thoughts.

Whether he stole the book this time or not, it was clear it was the second time it had been stolen. Gladys had pulled it off the first time—but who was responsible for the second?

Elaine continued on for several miles, mulling the situation over and over in her mind. Finally, she felt compelled to pray and asked God to prepare Ronald Good for her visit and to give her the right words to say to him. She wanted to convey compassion, to dispel any lingering resentment he might have.

She drove into Waterville, crossed the bridge over the Kennebec River, and then to the outskirts of the town, following the GPS on her phone. She turned off the highway and not too much farther was the auto body shop. There was only one car in the parking lot: a new red Mustang.

Elaine parked, turned off the motor, and then said another prayer. As she walked to the door, she took several deep breaths and purposefully walked tall, squaring her shoulders.

She pushed open the door. Inside was a typical office space. A counter divided the entryway and a workspace that held two desks and file cabinets. A waiting area was just past the entry-way. But no one seemed to be around.

Then a woman, around thirty, stepped through a side door. She wore dress slacks and a sweater. Her blonde hair was cut in a stylish bob. "May I help you?"

"Hi, I'm looking for Ronald Good," Elaine said. "I'm Elaine Cook. My cousin Jan Blake left a message with you, I believe?"

"Oh, of course." The woman stepped forward and extended her hand. "I'm Cami Walters," she said as she shook Elaine's hand. "I did take the message, and passed it on to Ronald, of course." She tilted her head to the side as she released Elaine's hand. "Don't tell me he didn't call you back?"

"He didn't," Elaine said.

Cami shook her head in a friendly way. "Sorry about that. I'll ask him about it when—"

The door opened and an older woman stepped into the shop. She wore a velour running suit, and her gray hair was styled in a chin-length bob.

"Hello, Agnes," Cami said. She turned to Elaine. "Excuse me just a minute."

Elaine nodded and stepped back to the wall.

Cami slipped behind the counter and began shuffling through some paperwork. As she collected the payment, Agnes asked how the Goods were doing.

"I'm not sure," Cami answered.

The woman leaned closer and lowered her voice. "I heard Mrs. Good is in the hospital, down in Boston."

"Well, she hasn't been admitted. But she's having quite a few tests done."

Elaine's stomach fell. She'd feared the worst—that Ronald Good was ignoring her on purpose—when it sounded as if he was dealing with some sort of emergency.

"Any idea when they'll be back?" Agnes asked.

Cami shook her head. "Hopefully soon, though."

A few minutes later Cami had finished the transaction and handed the woman a key. "Your car is parked on the side of the building. Thank you so much for your business."

"Of course," Agnes replied. "This is the best body shop around. I've been bringing my cars here for the last thirty years. I just hope everything is fine and that the Goods will be back soon."

Cami agreed.

As the woman left, Cami told Elaine that she would remind Mr. Good about the message.

"Oh goodness," Elaine said. "I couldn't help but overhear your conversation. I don't want to add any more to his plate right now."

"I'll just remind him," Cami said. "If he has time, I would think he'd call."

"Thank you," Elaine said. "And could you add some new information to my message for him, just in case it makes a difference? I just found out on Friday, from my mother, that Ronald is a cousin. His grandmother and my grandmother were sisters."

Cami's eyes lit up. "Isn't that something? And to think you just found out."

"Yes," Elaine said. "So naturally I'm anxious to meet him. But, of course, not until he's back and has the time."

"Of course," Cami agreed. "I'll let him know that too." She smiled.

Elaine returned the smile. Perhaps Ronald's wife was quite ill. Elaine couldn't fault the man for not calling her back, not at all.

"Aren't you from Lancaster?" Cami asked.

Elaine nodded.

"I'm so sorry you had to drive up here for nothing."

"No, it's fine," Elaine said. "You've been very helpful."

Cami walked with Elaine to the door. "Oh, it's raining again," she said. "Figures."

Elaine smiled. "We're bound to have sunshine sooner or later."

"Later, apparently," Cami joked. "Definitely later." The woman seemed kind and competent.

Elaine guessed the Mustang in the parking lot belonged to her, which indicated she was probably a lot of fun too.

"Thank you so much," Elaine said. "I really appreciate your help."

"Have patience," Cami said. "Ronald's a nice man. He'll return your call as soon as he can. You can count on it."

For the first time since finding out about this long-lost cousin, Elaine felt optimistic. Ronald Good's employee saying nice things about him was a good sign . . . at least she hoped it was.

THE NEXT DAY, as Elaine, Jan, and Rose readied to open the tearoom, Sasha came in from her run with her arms full of loose flowers: daffodils, hyacinth, and tulips.

"Where did you get all of those?" Elaine asked as she plugged in the electric kettle.

"I admit, from the flower shop. They were having a sale, and I couldn't resist." She put the flowers in the sink. "Remember when we used to make May baskets when I was little?"

Elaine nodded. She remembered it well. No matter where they lived, they put together a basket of flowers for their neighbors. In Hawaii it had been plumerias, orchids, and gardenias. "Oh goodness," Elaine said, jarred out of her reverie. "May baskets! That means April's finally over." What a relief. Maybe the rain would stop soon. "It's finally May!"

"Yes," Sasha said. "I thought it'd be nice to put together floral arrangements for the tables today," Sasha said. "In memory of our May Day baskets."

"That's lovely," Jan said and then grinned.

Not too long after they opened, Rose's father, Clifton, stopped in along with Rae Burns. Elaine guessed Clifton was taking a midmorning break from his orthodontic practice. Perhaps he had a patient cancel.

He was a distinguished-looking man with his white mustache and beard—and entirely bald head. He pulled the look off with style. Both Clifton and Rae greeted Elaine, and she gave them a wave before darting into the east parlor and taking the order of two older women, who chose the mini maple croissants, coffee cake, and a pot of Irish Breakfast tea. After Rose showed her dad and his new girlfriend the crystal chandelier in the dining room, she seated them in the west parlor. A few minutes later she took their order.

As they waited, Elaine stepped over to their table and said hello. The two had been dating for a month or so and Elaine was thrilled that Rose was positive about the relationship. Elaine knew that it wasn't easy for a daughter to see her surviving parent date someone else, but, like Sasha, Rose was able to look to the future and what was best in the long run.

As Elaine gazed down at Rae and Clifton, she was struck with how beautiful Sasha's flowers looked on the table. Arranged together, the flowers didn't appear weatherworn at all. Beauty was so important. The beauty of nature. Of relationships. Of a thriving business.

The front door chimed. Elaine hurried to the entryway to seat the next customers. To her surprise, both Macy and Bristol stood in the entryway.

"Oh, how lovely," Elaine said, directing them to the east parlor and a table near the fire. Yes, May had arrived but the rain and the chill continued.

"Would you tell Jan we're here? She had an idea about a fund-raiser," Macy said. "For the Bookworm."

"Yes, she mentioned that to me," Elaine said. But she had no idea that Jan had approached anyone else about it. And certainly not Macy, but what a good idea to include her. Elaine smiled. "I'll go get her."

When she stepped into the kitchen and told Jan who was waiting for her, she said, "Oh, I meant to tell you I contacted Bristol and asked if she wanted to brainstorm."

"What about Macy?"

"Macy's here?"

Elaine nodded.

"Oh." Jan raised her eyebrows. "Bristol must have asked her to join us." She untied her apron. "I won't be long."

"Take your time," Elaine said. "Rose and I can handle things."

A few minutes later Elaine plated Bristol and Macy's orders—a pot of oolong and two lemon tarts. After she brought out their tea and goodies, Jan followed Elaine back into the kitchen.

"What would you think if we hosted an English High Tea to raise money for Bristol to fix her drainage system?"

"Do you think we could raise enough?" Elaine guessed the repairs could be several thousand dollars.

"We'd sell overpriced admission tickets," Jan said, followed by a grin.

"Of course." Elaine smiled back. And she knew supporters of the bookstore would be happy to pay the extra money.

Jan nodded toward the parlor. "Could you join us for a few minutes?"

Elaine nodded and followed Jan back to the table. As they approached it, Macy said to Bristol, "I'd like to ask people to donate books to auction off too. That would definitely increase the revenue." Macy glanced up and asked, "What do the two of you think?"

Honestly, Elaine thought the whole thing sounded like a lot of work, but nevertheless she liked the idea of it. And she was willing to put in the work for Bristol's sake.

She asked, "Who all would be involved?"

"I'll organize it all," Macy said. "If the two of you can come up with the goodies and tea."

"Definitely," Jan said. Macy could be grating, but below her sometimes dour exterior, she was nothing if not generous.

"We'll need to get a date figured out right away," Bristol said.

"I'll go get the calendar," Elaine answered. "Be back in a minute." But just as she stepped into the entryway on her way to her office, the front door opened again.

It was Trooper Benson. He tipped his hat and said, "Elaine."

"Hi, Dan," she said, her heart accelerating. Had he found the book?

"I just wanted to stop by and let you know I haven't had much time to spend on the case, what with all my other cases, but I'm making time now. I was wondering if you could update me. Have you come across any new, pertinent information?"

Elaine hesitated. She'd done a fair amount of digging but hadn't come up with anything concrete. Still, it would help him to know what she'd done. She told him about her trip to Portland and Bowdoin College. And also about her attempt to meet Ronald Good.

"But no one offered any new information?" the trooper asked.

Elaine shook her head. "Sadly, no."

"Well, let me know if anything comes up," he said. "In the meantime I'll start by heading over to the Bookworm."

"No need," Elaine said. "Bristol is over here."

"Oh." The trooper pointed first to the left and then to the right with a questioning look on his face.

"Left," Elaine said. "How about a cup of tea?"

"Have any coffee?" he asked.

"Sure," Elaine answered. "And a couple mini maple croissants?"

"No doughnuts?" he joked and then laughed. "Of course I'd like Jan's specialty. Thank you."

Elaine hurried back into the kitchen and began a pot of coffee. Then she plated the croissants.

As Elaine loaded the dishes in the sink into the dishwasher, Sasha came in with a book in her hand. "My copy of *Evangeline* arrived," she said. "I thought I'd go read until Brody..." She glanced around the kitchen. "Unless you need help in here."

"No, I'm fine," Elaine answered. "Where are you and Brody off to today?"

"The shooting range."

"He didn't run with you this morning?"

She shook her head. "He was helping his mom." Her phone buzzed and she pulled it out of her back pocket. "He's early." She looked up at Elaine. "I'll see you this afternoon."

Elaine told Sasha goodbye, washed her hands, poured Trooper Benson a cup of coffee, and then remembered to retrieve the calendar from her office. By the time she returned to the east parlor, Jan, the trooper, Macy, and Bristol were all having a lively conversation. Everyone except for Macy was laughing, but even she had a smile on her face.

Elaine placed Dan's coffee and croissants in front of him and then slipped the calendar out of her apron pocket. "Excuse me for a moment, Dan. Do you mind if we talk dates for a fund-raiser?"

"Don't mind me," the trooper said. "I'll just enjoy my treats." He took a big bite.

"We have a bridal tea this Saturday," Elaine said, which would be too soon anyway.

"And then next weekend is Mother's Day."

"What if we do something that Thursday before, for a late afternoon tea, after you've closed?" Macy asked. "We might attract more people if we call it a pre-Mother's Day tea."

"That's just over a week away," Elaine said. "It's not much time to plan."

"I'll get it done," Macy said. "I'll design a flier and distribute them today and take out an ad in this week's paper. I'll also ask Pastor Mike put it in the Lancaster Community Church bulletin, plus make some phone calls and get others to talk it up around town. Everyone loves the Bookworm—I think you'll be pleased with the turnout—if you're all in agreement about the event."

Jan nodded her head, and so did Bristol.

"It's a plan then." Elaine took out a pen from her pocket and wrote the event on the calendar. It felt good to be doing something to help Bristol. Elaine just hoped they could earn enough to make a difference for the future of the Bookworm.

CHAPTER SIXTEEN

The next day, not long after Elaine had flipped the tearoom Closed sign, her cell phone rang. She dug it out of her apron pocket to find Dr. Sean Day's name on her screen. She quickly answered it.

After greeting her, Dr. Day said, "I just had a phone call about an old copy of *Evangeline*."

Before Elaine could find her voice, he continued, "I've set up an appointment tomorrow, in a coffee shop on College Street, just off the campus. I thought a public place would be better. That way you could be in the shop and see if you recognize the contact person."

"Good idea," Elaine said. "I'll call the trooper here and see what his opinion is—hopefully he'll come along too." Brunswick was in Cumberland County and Elaine wasn't sure what the protocol would be, even though Dan Benson was a state trooper. Perhaps he would travel that far or perhaps he'd ask an officer in that area to be on the premises of the coffee shop.

"I'll definitely be there," she said. "What time?"

"Three in the afternoon." Dr. Day told her the name and address of the coffee shop. "I'll see you then," he said.

As Elaine slipped her cell back into her pocket, she realized she wanted someone to go with her. Jan. Sasha. Nathan. Any one of them would do. She didn't want to go by herself. She'd see who could accompany her, after she put in a call to Trooper Benson.

As it turned out, Dan didn't have time to drive to Brunswick the next day. He said he'd call the Cumberland County sheriff's office and get back to her.

He called back in a few minutes.

"They're short staffed," he said. "They'll try to send someone over but couldn't make any promises."

Elaine was beginning to think that none of the law officers in the area believed the theft of a book, even a rare one, was that big of a deal.

"If you go, don't confront the person, even if a deputy is there. He or she could be armed," Dan said. "Write down a description and any other pertinent information though."

"Will do," Elaine said.

Jan decided she shouldn't go; if she did they'd be understaffed. Sasha had already made plans with Brody to go to the shooting range. She said she'd reschedule if her mother needed her to, but Elaine said she'd see if Nathan was available.

Elaine gave him a call. He answered his phone with, "Hello, sweetheart." His voice always warmed Elaine. She explained her predicament.

"Let me look at my calendar," he said, followed by the rustling of papers. "Let's see, May 3...In the morning I'm headed to Farmington—I have an estate auction out that way on Saturday...But, yes, tomorrow afternoon is free. I'd love to go with you."

"Thank you," Elaine said.

"I'll pick you up at noon. We can get a late lunch before the"—he chuckled—"sting."

Elaine laughed and explained what Trooper Benson said.

"Got it," Nathan said. "I'll leave all of my Inspector Gadget tools at home. Maybe we can video the guy though. Pretend we're taking selfies and get him in the background."

"Sounds like a plan," Elaine responded, relieved that Nathan could go with her.

THE NEXT DAY, Elaine and Nathan stopped for lunch in Augusta and then continued on their way to Brunswick, arriving a half hour early. The clouds hung heavy but it wasn't raining.

Nathan described an auction he'd done a few years ago in one of the beautiful old colonial-style houses on South Street. "The home had been in the family for over two hundred years. The furnishings they'd collected over the years were amazing."

Elaine's heart lurched a little. If only the Pritchard family had such a heritage, but people moved and died and sold houses. The exception was a home that stayed in a family for so many years, like the Longfellow family. It wasn't the norm.

Nathan found a parking place not too far from the coffee shop. Once he turned off the engine of his Cadillac, he asked, "Should we wait a few more minutes or go in?"

"We might as well go in," Elaine said. "I might be less likely to give away that I know Dr. Day if we're already seated."

"Sounds good," Nathan said, taking the keys from the ignition. He reached Elaine's door to open it while she was still gathering her purse and umbrella.

"Thank you," she said, taking his arm. He glanced down at her, his blue eyes twinkling. "And thank you for coming with me. I really appreciate it," she added.

"My pleasure," he answered. "Any excuse to spend time with you." He grinned and she patted his hand.

The coffee shop had an industrial motif with stainless steel tables and chairs and open duct work in the ceiling. Elaine ordered an espresso while Nathan ordered a cup of black coffee.

Elaine checked the time on her phone—2:55—as they started walking toward a table at the back of the shop, where they could see whoever came into the shop but hopefully not be obviously visible themselves. No matter where Dr. Day sat, they'd be able to see him.

Dr. Day arrived at 3:02. He seemed a little frazzled. He nodded, slightly, and then ordered a cup of coffee. He sat at a table near the front of the shop.

Then they all waited and waited. And waited some more. Every time someone came into the shop—a couple of students, two women in their thirties, a mom with her little boy—Elaine perked up but then each time it obviously wasn't who they were waiting for.

At 3:40 a man wearing a pair of khakis and a golf jacket came in. He waved at Dr. Day and stepped over to his table. He didn't pull out a book or anything and didn't sit down. He wasn't the right person either.

"What do you think?" Nathan whispered.

"That Dr. Day got stood up."

"But why?"

Elaine shook her head as Dr. Day told the friendly man goodbye. A moment later the professor stood and walked to their table. Elaine quickly introduced him to Nathan and after the two men shook hands, the professor said, "Sorry. Maybe the man who called me had second thoughts."

"Do you have his phone number?"

Dr. Day shook his head. "He called me on my office phone and wouldn't give me his number. Our old, antiquated phone system doesn't have caller ID."

"I see," Elaine said. She hoped whoever contacted Dr. Day hadn't seen her through the window. And she hadn't told anyone besides Jan and Sasha, except for Nathan, she was coming.

"I'm sorry you wasted your time," Dr. Day said.

"It wasn't a waste," Nathan said, smiling at Elaine.

She smiled back and then asked Dr. Day if he had any idea who else the thief might contact about the book. "Do you have colleagues who might be interested in the book?"

He rubbed his chin. "Perhaps. I can't see any of them stealing the book though."

"Of course not," Elaine answered. "But they might buy it, inadvertently."

"True." He frowned.

Elaine took out her notebook as Dr. Day rattled off the names of a handful of professors from colleges on the East Coast or in the Midwest.

"Do you know of any other collectors who might be interested in it—who aren't in the academic world?" she asked.

"No. I don't go to many of those rare book types of conventions. I mostly attend academic conferences."

"Of course," Elaine said. "Thank you so much for your help. Will you let me know if the man contacts you again?"

Dr. Day nodded as he glanced at his watch. "I need to run. I have a faculty meeting at four."

Elaine and Nathan followed Dr. Day out the door. "Do you think whoever called Dr. Day could see me through the window?" Elaine asked Nathan, trying to position herself outside the shop to see the table where they'd been seated. She couldn't manage to find an angle that worked.

"Of course not," Nathan said. "Track down the e-mails or phone numbers for the names Dr. Day gave you. Perhaps the thief decided someone out of the area was a better idea."

"But it wouldn't be worth it for them to travel somewhere. The book isn't worth that much."

"He could ship it."

That was true. Feeling discouraged, Elaine walked with Nathan to his car. She was no closer to solving the mystery than the night the book was stolen.

THAT EVENING, ELAINE searched the Web and came up with e-mail addresses for the professors Dr. Day had mentioned. She sent each a message, alerting them about the stolen book and asking each to call her if they had any information. The next morning she called the colleges they taught at and asked to be connected to their phones. None of them actually answered, but she left voice mails, figuring two messages were better than one.

As she dashed into Murphy's General Store for a few last-minute ingredients for the bridal shower on Saturday, she saw a flier about the fund-raiser for the Bookworm in the window. Macy wasn't kidding when she said she'd handle everything. A couple of women Elaine didn't recognize were reading the flier and commenting on it.

The flier read:

Pre-Mother's Day Tea, Bring Your Mother or Leave Her at Home if You Don't Want to Bring Her

Elaine chuckled at the line and kept reading.

But Buy a Ticket or Tickets and Support the Bookworm Drainage System Repairs so our favorite bookstore never floods again

And Bring a Book to Be Auctioned! And Bring Your Checkbook to Buy a Book!

The additional information included that Macy was selling the limited tickets, forty to be exact, and to buy them soon, before they sold out.

The border around the flier was made up of teapots and cups and the information was in a box that looked like an old book. It was definitely an eye-catching flier.

Elaine knew how much the bookstore meant to Macy, but she was still impressed with how dedicated she was to helping Bristol.

The next morning, before opening, Jan baked up a storm—petits fours, macarons, and tarts—for the bridal party tea and Elaine mixed up egg salad and sliced cucumbers for the tea sandwiches. The French bleu tea had arrived and all seemed to be in order for the day.

Rose handled the customers while Elaine prepared the dining room for the tea, thoughtfully setting the table for ten. As the afternoon sun started to shine through the west window, the chandelier dazzled in the light. Elaine breathed a prayer of thanks for the gift of the beautiful fixture. It would add so much to the bridal shower and every event they held in the dining room, whether for customers or family.

Elaine imagined holiday dinners with Jared and his family here, along with Sasha. And perhaps Nathan and his sons and their families too. Along with Jan and her children and grandchildren and Bob too, of course. She smiled at the large group they'd grown into and the sense of community they'd all developed. God had truly blessed her.

After Ben died, Elaine had felt so isolated. It was with Jan's support that Elaine had stepped back into life. What a relief to realize that love never stopped growing and that one's circle could always expand, drawing in more and more people.

After the table was completely set, Elaine stood back and took it all in. The china, the cloth napkins, the lilacs in the center all added elegance to the setting, but it was the chandelier that truly completed the ambiance. Light reflecting from the bulbs sent shimmers bouncing around the room.

As soon as the tearoom closed at 4 p.m., Rose, Jan, and Elaine quickly changed into their Victorian costumes. Elaine chose her crimson damask gown with the lacy apron to protect it. Once they were all back downstairs, Elaine helped Jan finish plating the food for the tea and then as the starting time neared, rushed to the front door to welcome their guests. The bride and her mother, Mavis, who was quite young, were the first to arrive. Both had their long dark hair twisted low on their heads in French rolls. They carried gift bags for the bridal party and both were dressed in loose white gowns with pink sashes around the waist.

"I like your gowns," Elaine said.

"Thank you," Anna said. "I like yours too."

"Ours are Marie Antoinette style, *chemise à la reine*," Mavis added.

"Well, they're beautiful!" Elaine exclaimed.

Mavis smiled. "Anna is majoring in French literature."

"Yes, you mentioned that before. It shows," Elaine said, motioning toward their gowns. "This entire tea is going to be absolutely lovely." She remembered that the wedding would be in a chapel on the way to Augusta. Someone—she wasn't sure if it was Anna or Mavis—knew how to plan events.

When Elaine led them into the dining room, Mavis *oohed* and *aahed* over the new chandelier. The clouds had parted and the lowering sun shone through the window now. The entire room glowed in the late-afternoon light. Soon the bridesmaids arrived too, all dressed in the same flowing white dresses.

Because the tearoom had closed, both Rose and Elaine waited on the group while Jan kept everything running in the kitchen.

Rose gave a talk about the three different types of French tea they were serving—the *vanille*, the *noir* with a hint of chocolate, and the new *bleu*. Then Elaine spoke about the history of tea in the afternoon in England and the differences that evolved as the practice gained popularity in France.

"The French may have been drinking tea before the British, but only the elite and the bourgeois drank it in France. It never trickled down to the masses as it did in Britain. Therefore the French have never been known for their tea drinking the way the British are," Elaine explained. "However, the French greatly influenced the foods that were paired with tea. Pastries and delicacies, the more decadent the better, were soon introduced. Unfortunately, tea, along with the French royal family, went out of style during the French Revolution and coffee became the beverage of choice."

Elaine paused for a moment and then took up the story once more. "Late in the last century, tea began to come back into vogue. Not the traditional British tea though. The new French blends were lighter and infused with flavors. Words like 'climate' and 'aroma' all became terms thrown around in the French tea conversation and tea began to appeal more to consumers in France."

Next Jan spoke about the French macarons. "They're a meringue-based confection with ganache or butter cream filling. They were first produced in Venice in the eighth century. Catherine de Medici brought them with her to France when she married Henry II. Through the years, the macaron has evolved—jams, liquors, and spices were added. It wasn't until around 2010 that macarons became popular in the United States. Please enjoy these..." She gestured toward the table where three platters of macarons rested—red velvet, strawberries and cream, and chocolate hazelnut. "Along with the petits fours, tarts, and tea sandwiches."

Mavis began to applaud and then all of the attendants followed. As the women ate, Mavis and the attendants shared stories about the bride, and Elaine and Rose replenished the pots of tea and food as needed. After they'd finished eating and Elaine and Rose cleared the dishes away but refilled all of their teacups, the bride passed out the gift bags. The attendants pulled out books of French poetry, perfume, and drop pearl earrings for them to wear on the wedding day.

Elaine stood at the doorway, a pot of vanille in her hands, marveling at the elegance the chandelier added to the room. Just as she started to return to the kitchen a popping noise stopped her. She turned back. The bride screamed and her mother, Mavis, stood quickly. Sparks began to fly from the ceiling and crystals began to rain down on the table.

"Evacuate, quickly!" Elaine shouted.

CHAPTER SEVENTEEN

"Tell Jan to turn all of the breakers off. Immediately. And you call 9-1-1," Elaine commanded Rose as the younger woman hurried back into the dining room, eyes wide.

The bride's mother, Mavis, stood with her mouth agape, staring at the dangling chandelier. "What happened?"

"I'm not sure," Elaine answered. "There's a simple explanation, I'm sure. Everyone must exit immediately though, just in case there's an electrical problem." Loudly, she said, "I'm so sorry about this, but please hurry, everyone."

The bride and attendants began grabbing their purses and heading toward the west parlor, but her mother continued to stare at the chandelier.

"Let's keep moving," Elaine said. "I need everyone out."

"Oh." Mavis met Elaine's gaze and then grabbed her purse. Elaine ushered her into the east parlor. "Continue on out the front door," she said.

As Elaine followed the last guest into the entryway, both Jan and Rose appeared.

"What happened?" Jan asked.

"I don't know except that the chandelier exploded."

Jan's hand went to her mouth. Sirens wailed in the background.

"Come on," Elaine said. "We need to let the fire department check out what's going on before we go back in."

Thankfully it wasn't raining, although the sky hinted that it might start again soon. The fire truck parked on the street and Elaine ran toward the firefighters, all of whom she knew, to explain the situation while Jan and Rose calmed the bridal shower attendees.

The volunteer firefighters entered the house first and once they determined there was no danger of fire, they allowed Jan, Elaine, and Rose to collect the gifts and coats of the shower guests.

The chandelier was dangling on the cord, swinging precariously. Thirty or more crystals had landed on the table and some had bounced onto the floor. Elaine was thankful that none of them had seemed to break.

"I'll handle this," Jan said. "You go talk with our guests."

Elaine and Rose took out the coats and purses that had been left behind and apologized profusely to each guest. The bride's mother told her not to worry about it.

"We had a lovely time," Mavis said. "Thank goodness no one was hurt and that your beautiful place didn't burn down. Hopefully you'll be able to repair that lovely chandelier. I was so mesmerized by it."

Elaine felt overcome with gratitude that nobody was injured. Mavis was right. It could have been much, much worse.

When she returned to the dining room, the firefighters had the chandelier disconnected from the ceiling and Jan had spread a quilt over the table.

"Put it right here," Jan said.

"Yes, ma'am," Rachel Leon responded.

Des Murphy, the de facto leader of Lancaster's firefighters, then told them that there wasn't any damage to the ceiling and that nothing had burned. "But you'll need to get an electrician to see to it right away," he said. "Obviously something malfunctioned."

Elaine promised they would and then began to gather up the teardrops of crystals while Jan walked the firefighters out. She'd need to figure out how to rehang them on the chandelier.

By the time she found Jan in the kitchen, her cousin had already called Bill Bridges.

"He's hanging Sheetrock over at the Bookworm," Jan said. "He'll be right over."

Elaine couldn't imagine that Bill had made a mistake in connecting the chandelier. Hopefully he could figure out what went wrong. Perhaps the chandelier was defective. Maybe that was why it had been mothballed in the Public Works building. Maybe this wasn't the first time it had exploded.

BILL RUSHED INTO Tea for Two, saying, "I saw the fire truck but never would have thought it might be the chandelier. I assumed a guest had an emergency."

Elaine followed him to the dining room, telling him what happened as she hurried to keep up with him. "It was enough of an explosion that it knocked the chandelier out of the ceiling and sent crystals flying. Thankfully it held until the firefighters could disconnect it."

Bill had reached the dining room. First he examined the chandelier, which was sprawled out on the dining room table again. He examined the electrical wires and then the bulbs inside the chandelier. "These seem to be what exploded," he said. "But we need to have an electrician come out and take a look at the whole thing and determine if it was the bulbs or the wiring. I don't think I made any mistakes installing it, but I need someone to verify that—and if that's not the problem, figure out what is. I took out the exploded bulbs and replaced them with clear ones that I had."

"Thank you," Elaine said but then she must have frowned because Bill asked, "What is it?"

"We have a fund-raiser for the Bookworm this coming Thursday. We'd hoped to use this room."

"I'll put a call in to Roland Nance." He was the electrician in town. "Hopefully he can be out here in a day or two."

"Thank you." Elaine wouldn't hold her breath. She knew how busy Roland usually was.

"I'm sorry," Bill said.

"It's not your fault," Elaine answered. "I appreciate you coming right over."

He nodded and then placed his hand on the table. "It's amazing the cord held."

Elaine agreed. "And that the crystals that fell didn't break."

Bill apologized again.

"There's no reason to believe it was the installation," Elaine said. "You've always done good work for us—thank you for contacting the electrician. This will all get straightened out."

Bill nodded. "It will, in time."

Elaine hoped it was sooner rather than later.

SUNDAY AFTER CHURCH Elaine and Jan hosted an impromptu potluck at Tea for Two, inviting Bristol and Mark, Rose, Brent, and Emma, Abigail and Brody, and of course Nathan and Bob. Tara and Jack had other plans and couldn't make it.

They sat in the east parlor instead of the dining room, but everyone ventured in to look at the chandelier.

Nathan examined the bulbs. "Did you change these?"

"Just the ones that exploded," Elaine answered. "Actually, Bill did, but he left the others."

He leaned closer to one of the original bulbs, pointing to the filament. "I'm really curious how old these are."

"They couldn't possibly be original, could they?"

"That would make them over a hundred years old. Electricity came to this area around 1900. I've never seen any kind of light fixture with original bulbs."

"They're clear glass," Elaine said. "Like in the old days."

Nathan nodded. "I assumed they were replicas but maybe not. If they are the original bulbs, then this chandelier didn't get much use—although the old bulbs were made to last much, much longer than our modern ones."

A few minutes later, just as they all gathered to say grace, a knock sounded at the front door.

Elaine answered it and found Macy on the porch, peering inside. "I didn't realize you were having a gathering," Macy said. "I thought Sunday was your day off. I had a question about the upcoming tea—if you think we could accommodate a few extras. I've had a great response."

"Of course," Elaine said. "And, please, come on in. We're having a potluck. We'd love to have you join us."

"Oh no," Macy said. "I wasn't invited."

"You are now," Elaine responded with a smile. "We'd be honored to have you."

"All right." Macy stepped into the foyer, nodding at the others who'd gathered around.

After Nathan said a blessing, they all filled their plates from the food spread around the kitchen counters. Once they sat down in the east parlor—they'd placed the tables together in one long row—Bob asked Brody when he would return to duty.

"Soon," he answered.

Again, Elaine noted he was being vague.

"And where will you go?"

"Back to North Carolina, sir."

Bob laughed. "You don't have to 'sir' me."

"Yes, sir," Brody said and then grinned.

As they talked more about what was next for Brody as far as the army goes, Abigail leaned toward Sasha and Elaine and said, "Honestly, Brody has never been very up front with me about his army career or anything about his personal life. But lately I feel as if he's perhaps keeping some sort of information from me."

"What do you mean?" Sasha asked.

"Oh, I feel like he's purposefully not telling me what's next for him."

"What do you...?" Sasha's voice trailed off.

Abigail shrugged. "I'm not sure." She lowered her voice. "He's just reminding me of his dad."

Sasha's eyes grew large.

Abigail put her hand on Sasha's arm. "Not about women—don't get me wrong. He did have a girlfriend in Virginia, but they broke up. He's not like his father that way. But Brody's never been very transparent." She sighed.

Elaine felt uncomfortable with Abigail sharing so much, especially when Brody was farther down the table, but before she could say anything more, Abigail continued. "I've asked him three times where he's being transferred, and he's changed the topic each time."

"He hasn't told you?" Sasha's voice was a little high.

Brody shot her a look.

Sasha lowered her voice. "What do you mean? He's going back to North Carolina, right?"

"Yes." Abigail shrugged. "But he hasn't been specific beyond that."

"Maybe he can't be," Elaine said, surprised to find herself defending Brody. She knew that happened sometimes in the service, although she wasn't convinced that was the case with Brody. More likely he had another reason.

"He probably doesn't want to be up front with me because he doesn't want me to know his business."

"I'm sure he'll tell you in due time or when he can," Elaine said.

Nathan asked Abigail about her house renovations and Elaine pretended to listen to that conversation, but she was really mulling over the problem of Brody. It certainly didn't sound as if he'd had a good example of how to treat women or to live honestly. Then again, she couldn't assume that just because his father had been "unreliable," as Abigail had described him, Brody would be too.

Lost in her thoughts, she slowly became aware that Jan, Macy, Sasha, Rose, and Brent were talking about the chandelier. Jan mentioned the house across the lake. Elaine turned toward their conversation.

"The mansion with the turret?" Macy leaned forward.

"Yes," Jan said. "Do you know anything about it?"

"If I remember right, my grandmother knew the son in the family."

"Really?" Jan's voice was full of hope.

"The father was a millionaire from Boston who relocated here, for some reason." Macy put her fork down. "My grandmother went to high school with the son. He was the star quarterback. Sadly, he lost the family fortune during the Depression."

"Oh dear," Jan said.

"Yes," Macy said. "As far as I know, he left Lancaster by the early thirties." She gave the others an arch look. "I think my grandmother must have had a crush on him in high school. That was why she followed his story."

"What happened to him after he left? And to the house?" Jan asked.

"I don't know what happened to him—I assumed he went to Boston, that there were still relatives there. And I think the house was bought and sold several times through the years."

Elaine said, "Sasha said it looks as if they're getting ready to do some work on the property."

Macy pursed her lips. "I hope they're not planning to tear it down."

"Yes." Elaine couldn't imagine why someone would do that unless the mansion was in horrible disrepair. It sounded as if the history of the place alone would make it worth saving. "Do you happen to remember the name of the original owner?"

"As a matter of fact, I do," Macy said. "I always thought the name sounded like the hero of a romance novel. Dennis Gray was the original owner—and his son was Dennis Gray Jr. Or perhaps Dennis Gray II." She grinned.

"How interesting." Elaine smiled in return. "I think I'll go over there tomorrow and see what I can find out. Bill Bridges said he saw a chandelier similar to ours, if not identical." She paused. "But why in the world would a chandelier from a mansion end up in the Public Works building?"

Macy shrugged her shoulders. "Maybe there was something wrong with the chandelier. Could be it was defective and removed from the mansion. That same defect might have made it explode here."

Elaine nodded in agreement. Macy might be right, but that didn't explain why the chandelier would have been taken to the Department of Public Works, of all places.

THE NEXT MORNING, just before eight, as Elaine vacuumed the west parlor, her cell phone buzzed in the pocket of her sweater. She pulled it out and glanced at the number. It wasn't one she recognized. She turned off the vacuum and answered the phone, expecting a business call.

"Hello, this is Elaine. How may I help you?"

"Ernie Baker here," the man said. "I'm returning your call about that book found at our old house."

Elaine nearly dropped her phone. Finally! "Mr. Baker! How good to hear from you." She stepped toward the fireplace.

"Sorry I didn't return your call earlier. I just now listened to your voice mail. We were on a Caribbean cruise and left our cell phones at home—you know, we wanted to truly get away."

"That's understandable." Elaine thought it sounded like a fabulous idea. "Abigail Samson told me she called you about the book she found in her house," Elaine said. "I wanted to double-check with you and see if you talked with anyone else that day about the book."

"As a matter of fact, I did," he said. "We'd been in that house for thirty years. Never would have thought there was a rare book trapped in the wall." He chuckled. "Isn't that something?"

"Yes, it certainly is."

Mr. Baker chuckled again. "When Abigail told me about the book, I'll admit it did puzzle me for a while."

It seemed the man was a talker.

"At first, when she read the name in the front, it wasn't familiar to me. But then I remembered Lena was your grandmother, and I told her the Pritchard cousins had that new tea place in town. Two for Tea, right?"

"Tea for Two," Elaine corrected with a small chuckle. Two years in business and they were still "new." A decade from now they probably still would be.

"So I told her to take it to you and your cousin. But after we hung up, I kept thinking about that book and how it got in the wall of the house. I thought maybe someone had bought it at an estate sale or something years ago—although I doubted it was anyone in my family who did that. I started thinking about who owned the house before us. The last owner inherited the house from his father, who inherited it from his mother. So three generations lived in this house. The book could have belonged to any of them, although I doubted to the youngest. But naturally, I thought to call him, since his father had died so long ago. His grandmother too."

Elaine murmured, "Of course."

"I called him at the auto body shop he owns, up past Waterville."

Elaine murmured, "Uh-huh."

"Do you happen to know him?"

Elaine quickly explained that she didn't, but she'd just found out he was a cousin of hers.

"Well, that all makes sense then," Mr. Baker said. "There has to be some sort of story behind the book and Ronald being a long-lost cousin." Mr. Baker paused for the first time during the entire conversation.

"I agree," Elaine said. "But we haven't quite figured that out. Your information may help."

"Oh, good."

Elaine leaned against the brick of the fireplace. "So what did he say?"

"What did who say?"

"Ronald Good."

Mr. Baker burst out laughing. "I got ahead of myself. I told him about the book, but he said it wasn't his, at least not that he knew of. And, regardless, it belonged to Abigail Samson because she bought the house so she could do whatever she wanted. Including give it to the Pritchard cousins."

"Oh." Elaine realized she was gripping her cell phone a little too tightly and tried to relax. Perhaps Ronald Good had known about her and Jan all along.

"Anyway," Mr. Baker said. "That's all I know." He chuckled again.

"Thank you for calling me back," Elaine said. "I really appreciate it. You've been very helpful."

"Great!" He paused a moment and then said, "It's eighty-two degrees here in Arizona. How's the weather there?"

Elaine turned toward the window. "Rainy," she answered. "With a chance of downpours. And approximately forty-two degrees."

Mr. Baker groaned, in a good-natured way. "I hope it warms up before we head back."

"We heard you've purchased a condo in Portland."

"Yes," he said. "We have a place overlooking Casco Bay, but we'll come back to Lancaster to visit. Maybe we'll stop by your tearoom sometime." Elaine could imagine him grinning even though she had no idea what he looked like. "We only have a few days of golfing left before the weather is too hot, and we need to hit the road. Right now, I have a tee time! Gotta go."

With that he was gone. Elaine slipped her phone back into her pocket and pushed the switch on the vacuum. As she ran it back and forth over the floor, she thought of Ronald Good. If he didn't come back from Boston soon, she was tempted to go down there and find him. She couldn't help but think he was avoiding her.

THE NEXT DAY, after closing time, Elaine called Cami to check in. Cami was apologetic that Mr. Good still hadn't called. "He's usually much more on top of things than this," Cami said. "I'll tell him again."

"Oh dear," Elaine said, feeling bad that she'd called again. "No need to give him another message. Just ask him to call me when they return home."

She thanked Cami and hung up. She hoped they would connect with Ronald Good but perhaps it wasn't meant to be. However, she'd at least like to rule him out as a suspect. What he'd said to Mr. Baker had all sounded good, but perhaps he had the foresight to cover his tracks.

Elaine turned toward Jan, who was loading the dishwasher. "I should have been asking everyone what time events took place that afternoon. When did Abigail call Mr. Baker? When did Mr. Baker call Ronald Good? I know Abigail dropped it off in the late afternoon. Would Ronald have had time to arrive here and see me take it over to the Bookworm? And notice I didn't return with it? And then hang around and steal it?"

"I'll call Abigail and ask if she remembers what time she called Mr. Baker," Jan said as she squeezed soap into the dispenser in the door. "And you call Mr. Baker back—ask him what time Abigail called him and then what time he called Ronald."

"Good idea," Elaine responded. "But I'll text Mr. Baker. He said the number I have is his cell phone. He may still be golfing, and I don't want to interrupt him with a call."

Elaine typed out her questions to Mr. Baker, half listening as Jan reached Abigail. After greeting her and explaining her questions, Jan said, "So you waited a bit?" She paused and then said, "Great. Thank you."

Elaine finished her text and sent it just as Jan slipped her phone into the pocket of her apron and said, "Abigail said she didn't run the book over right away. She finished up her work and put her tools away first."

"So how long did she wait?"

"She said an hour or so," Jan answered. "It might have been longer."

"So if Mr. Baker called Ronald immediately afterwards," Elaine said, "then Ronald would have had enough time to drive over here, hoping to intercept the book."

Jan thought for a moment. "Ronald would have had to have wanted the book really badly to wait around for an opportunity to steal it. But maybe, once he saw you take it over there, he planned to steal it after the bookstore closed."

"But why in the world would he want to steal it at all?" Elaine asked.

"Maybe he's the one who hid it."

Elaine crossed her arms. "But why wouldn't he have retrieved it before he sold the house?"

"Maybe he forgot," Jan answered. "Or didn't care—until he found out the book was being taken to us."

Elaine grimaced. "That would mean the grudge in the family ran pretty deep."

Jan shrugged. "I hope not, but it's a possibility."

That was it—there really wasn't a way to figure out what was going on until they could meet and talk with Ronald Good. And perhaps, even if they could meet with him, he wouldn't tell them what they needed to know. Perhaps they'd never know what happened.

Elaine hoped they'd be able to find the book, but at this point, who knew? Well, somebody did. But that didn't mean that she and Jan ever would.

"I'm going to take a little break and call my mom," Elaine said. "Then I'll come back down and clean up."

"Take your time," Jan said. "Are you going to ask her more about the rift in the family?"

Elaine nodded. "I'm hoping she'll be able to give me some sort of information that will help." She hit her mom's number on speed dial as she started up the stairs.

Her mother answered the phone with, "Hello, dear."

"Hi, Mom." They exchanged pleasantries and then Elaine updated her on the book and the situation with Ronald Good as she stepped into the upstairs sitting room. "Do you think he would have carried a grudge?"

"I have no idea," Virginia said.

"Did his father?" Elaine asked as she settled onto the window seat.

"I really didn't know his father," Virginia said. "Except from a distance."

"What do you mean?"

Virginia's sigh was audible, even over the phone. "We actually went to school together."

"What?"

"It's true. He was two grades ahead of me. We went to grade school together, but I had no idea who he was then. Mother and Aunt Gladys saw each other at a school play that both my cousin and I were in my sophomore year. Mother tried to speak with her sister, but Gladys wouldn't have anything to do with her. It took me a few days to get the story out of Mother, but she finally told me that she and her sister had been estranged all of these years. When I tried to speak with Ronald, he refused to talk and avoided me until he graduated."

"So it seems he shared his mother's opinion."

"At that time," Virginia said. "I found out about his death years later. I regretted I never had the chance to get to know him, but honestly if his behavior in high school was any indication of his character, I probably didn't miss much."

"What about his son? Wouldn't he have gone to the same school that I did?"

"I think he's several years older than you. The two of you were never in the same school at the same time."

Elaine had reached the sitting room. She sat down on the window seat and curled her legs underneath herself. "It's all so sad," she said.

Virginia agreed. "We'll never know exactly what happened."

"Maybe Ronald Good will have some clues."

"Perhaps," Virginia said, but she didn't sound very hopeful. "It's not uncommon for a family to have some sort of rift. It's one of the reasons I long for heaven. We'll have no more strife in our relationships."

"It's so sad they couldn't work things out on earth though."

"I know," Virginia said. "But it's a cautionary tale to all of us. I know of mothers and daughters who are estranged. Women who used to be best friends. Brothers and sisters. Cousins. Once Mother told me the story about her sister, I vowed to do all I could to stay in a good relationship with all of those I love."

"That's good advice," Elaine said. "I'm certainly thankful for our relationship, Mom."

"So am I, dear." Virginia's voice was warm and kind. "You and your brother have been my greatest joys. I did anything I could to make sure my relationships with my parents, brother, and husband were good. And now my focus is on you, your brother, my grandchildren, and now my great-grandchildren. Family is so important."

"You're absolutely right, Mom," Elaine said. "And you've certainly set a good example for all of us."

After they disconnected, Elaine sat on the window seat, looking out over the front yard to the street, and up the hill to the church steeple. A drizzle of rain fell from the steely gray sky. But then the sun edged out through the clouds and a sliver of afternoon light cast a shimmer over the rooftops of the town.

She would never stop needing her mother. When she spoke with her she felt ageless—she could be a teenager or a young mom or a new widow. Her mom, no matter her age, had always shared her wisdom through everyday conversations with Elaine.

Did Elaine offer her own children the same? Jared had Corrie, so he didn't call much to chat or ask for advice. It wasn't that he didn't call—he did. It was just that his intention was to catch Elaine up on the latest things the grandchildren were involved in or what his family as a whole had been up to. She absolutely welcomed those calls, and she never felt as if she was in danger of jeopardizing her relationship with Jared.

She didn't feel as if she was in danger of jeopardizing her relationship with Sasha either—not really. But she knew she needed to be careful not to offer Sasha too much advice, not to voice her opinion too often. So why did she keep pushing her concerns about Brody? She'd come to his defense the day before, but she'd also felt more concerned considering that his own mother felt he was being secretive.

She settled against the window seat, feeling thankful for her family, the beauty around her, and her home. All brought her joy and drew her closer to the Lord. She breathed a prayer of gratitude just as a text came in from Mr. Baker. He said that he'd called Ronald Good as soon as he got off the phone with Abigail.

Elaine sent back a thank-you text, stood, and then headed down the stairs just as Sasha came through the front door dressed in her running tights and a waterproof jacket, splattered with rain. As the door swung shut, Elaine saw Brody's pickup pulling away.

Before Elaine could speak, Sasha said, "You know that mansion across the lake? The one with the security gate that's been padlocked? "

Elaine nodded.

Sasha untied and then kicked off her wet running shoes. "The gate was open today. We ran up far enough to see a van."

"Really?"

"Maybe there's someone there we could talk to. Want to drive over there? I'll go with you."

"Yes," Elaine answered. "I'll tell Jan."

"And I'll change into sweats," Sasha said. "I'll meet you back here in a flash."

Elaine waited a moment, watching Sasha run up the stairs. Her daughter would return to Colorado in less than a week. Elaine's heart skipped a beat. She longed for Sasha to move closer. What a blessing it would be someday, when Elaine was old like her mother, to have her daughter close by.

Elaine couldn't help but wish that Sasha would find someone to date, marry, and settle down with in Maine. She wondered for a half second if Brody felt positive about Maine, if perhaps she'd feel more positive about him. She shook her head. As long as he seemed secretive, she wouldn't. No matter what.

CHAPTER EIGHTEEN

As they drove, Sasha mentioned she'd been trying to read *Evangeline*. "It's a little difficult," she said. "That whole epic poem format feels really dated."

Elaine smiled. "I had to read it in high school. It's a great slice of history."

"Yeah, horrible history. Running off the Acadians. Dispersing them all over. Separating families and lovers. The story of Evangeline and Gabriel is so sad—especially that they weren't reunited until he was dying. It's such an unjust story."

Elaine nodded in agreement.

They were silent for a moment as they drove past the boat launch and swim area and on around the lake. Then Sasha started talking about her training and how nice it was to run and shoot with Brody. "He's good for me," she said. "He's really pushed me to run faster and shoot with more confidence."

Just because he was helping Sasha improve athletically didn't mean that he was the right man for her, but Elaine bit her tongue from saying so. They turned the corner and started along the far side of the lake.

"It's up ahead," Sasha said. "On the left."

Elaine slowed. "The gate's open," she said as she put on her turn signal. "Shall we?"

"Why not?" Sasha responded. "The gate was closed when we ran by but not padlocked, so we headed up the driveway, far enough to see a work van. If it's open now, that means they're not done for the day."

Elaine turned and inched up the paved drive. There was no sign of any vehicles now. "Maybe whoever was here forgot to close the gate behind them."

"I doubt it," Sasha said. "It's been locked up pretty tight."

Trees lined the driveway. The green buds of deciduous trees fanned out, creating a tunnel of green specks that waved back and forth in the breeze above the car. The dark green of the pines towering over them created a bit of a gothic feel.

In front of the trees was a stone wall that appeared to be a century or more old but was in surprisingly good shape. Wildflowers grew along the base, along with emerald-green grass. It felt as if they'd stepped back into history. It was peaceful and yet ominous too.

The pavement gave way to a cobblestone circular parking area, but there were no other vehicles around. After parking under the branches of an old oak tree, Elaine turned off the motor and she and Sasha stared at the mansion for a moment.

A wrought iron gate in the middle of a hedge of roses led from the circular arrangement of bricks to the walkway to the mansion. It was constructed of stone and several large leaded glass windows graced the front, along with more windows on the lake side of the house. The most prominent feature of the mansion was the three-story turret. At the base of the turret was a double wooden door entrance and at the top was a small leaded-glass window.

"We could go take a peek," Sasha said. "We might be able to see the chandelier that Bill mentioned."

Elaine looked in the rearview mirror, toward the driveway, thinking of the No Trespassing signs. "I wish the workmen were still here."

"It won't hurt just to look," Sasha said. "We're not going inside or anything."

"All right." Elaine took the keys out of the ignition.

Sasha opened the gate and Elaine stepped through first. The path was cobblestone too. The entire setting was enchanting, as if from a fairy tale, but Elaine's heart still raced. She followed Sasha to the first window.

The light was growing dim and at first Elaine was afraid they wouldn't be able to see through the leaded glass. She squinted. The room was huge and completely empty. A cavernous fireplace, made of stone and big enough to step inside, lined the far wall. However, no chandelier hung from the ceiling. No light fixture at all was visible.

Elaine ran her hand through her hair. "Bill said the chandelier was in the dining room, which this room isn't. I'm guessing the kitchen would be in the back of the mansion. And the dining room would be close to it. Let's see if we can go around back."

Sasha led the way. The cobblestone walkway continued around the side of the house. For being abandoned, the garden was in good shape. More rose bushes lined the path and they'd been recently pruned. Beyond that was a berry patch—which would soon sprout raspberries, blueberries, and strawberries. They rounded the side of the building to the backyard. A wall of ivy spread along the edge of the property.

The grass was already thick and definitely cared for. Elaine could imagine games of croquet across the lawn. She turned toward the lake. A short fence, just a couple of feet tall, separated the yard from the beach. The view was magnificent. Elaine could make out a dock but there were no boats moored to it. Beyond, Lake Chickadee was choppy and several sailboats raced across it, propelled by the strong breeze. The wind also blew the tops of the trees this way and that.

"Any chance that van you saw belonged to a yard service?" Elaine asked, marveling again at how well cared for the yard was.

"I don't think so," Sasha said.

"Because this grass has been recently cut—and nothing about this yard looks like it belongs to an abandoned mansion." They'd reached another cobblestone area, a sort of patio off the back of the building. A french door led to the inside of the mansion. Elaine and Sasha stepped up to the windows. It was a smaller room, perhaps a study or library or small sitting room. Again, there was no light fixture hanging from the ceiling.

"Maybe it's the next room," Sasha said. They continued along the patio to the next set of windows. "Bingo." Sasha pressed her nose against the glass. "Double bingo."

Elaine stepped up to the window. Sure enough, a chandelier hung down from the ceiling of another large room—a chandelier that looked identical to the one back at Tea for Two.

Elaine couldn't hide the enthusiasm in her voice. "Bill was right—and the chandelier is still here."

Sasha took out her phone and took a couple of photos, distracting Elaine until a rustling behind her caught her attention. As she started to look over her shoulder a deep voice called out, "Step away from the window and put your hands on your head."

ELAINE EXPECTED TO have a gun pointed at them as she and Sasha turned around slowly, their hands on their heads. But there was no gun. Just an old man pointing a garden hoe.

"What business do you have here?" he boomed. His voice was much bigger than he was. In fact, he was quite small, dressed in coveralls and a yellow rain coat and hat. He looked as if he could have stepped out of the 1940s.

Elaine quickly introduced herself and Sasha and then nodded toward the dining room. "We have a chandelier that matches the one in the mansion. We'd been told so anyway—and came out to confirm it."

Sasha took a step forward, but the old man waved the hoe around and she froze, but managed to say that she'd been running earlier and had seen that the front gate was open and there was a van in the driveway.

"But it's a gated property. Surely you didn't think you were welcome here."

"Well, yes, but we hoped someone would be here who could give us some information we're looking for."

"The worker left," the man said.

"But he didn't lock the gate," Sasha said. "Perhaps he's coming back."

The old man grunted. "I don't know about that."

"Well, may we talk with you?" Elaine asked. "About the mansion—about the chandelier."

"I don't know anything about that either."

"Well, what about the mansion? We've been told it belonged to a Dennis Gray way back when."

"I've heard that too," the man said. "But I never met this Dennis Gray."

Elaine guessed the man was born about the time Dennis Gray left Chickadee Lake. "Was there a workman here today?" she asked the man.

He nodded.

"What was he doing?" Elaine asked.

The man shrugged. "I couldn't tell exactly. He wasn't here long. Maybe just looking around inside the house, to see what needs to be done. The roof has been leaking with all of this rain."

"So who owns the house now?" Sasha asked.

"I don't know—not for sure."

Elaine crossed her arms. "Well, did someone hire you to take care of the gardens? And the yard. Or do you do it for free?"

He shook his head. "I'm paid. My father took care of the property until he grew ill." He nodded behind him. "I grew up in the caretaker's cottage. I helped my father tend the gardens and then took over when he died. I receive a check each month from a bank in Portland."

Elaine realized he hadn't introduced himself to them. "What is your name?"

"Anthony Nichols." He reluctantly shook their hands.

Elaine didn't recognize the name, but she guessed the man might be about her mother's age, which was really old to be doing all of the yard work he did. But she guessed the work probably kept him young and fit. He appeared to be in great shape.

"I'm sorry we alarmed you." Elaine pulled out a few of her business cards from her purse. "If the owner comes out to look at the property or if the workmen return, would you please give them my number and ask them to give me a call? I really would like to talk with someone about the chandelier."

The man took the cards, although he seemed reluctant to do so.

"Thank you," Elaine said. "I really appreciate your help on this."

Mr. Nichols nodded but Elaine got the feeling he wasn't going to be much help, given he didn't even know who wrote his checks. She and Sasha told the man goodbye and then started around the house again, stepping quickly. As they reached the front, a van came up the driveway.

"Uh-oh," Sasha said.

"Maybe we'll get a better idea of what's going on though." Elaine put on her friendliest smile and stepped through the gate. The van had Schmidt & Sons written on the driver's door. She waved as a man in jeans and a sweatshirt climbed out of the front seat. He appeared to be in his early thirties and wore a Red Sox cap.

"We were just talking with Mr. Nichols," Elaine said.

"Who's that?" the man asked.

"The caretaker."

The man shrugged. "I don't know who you're talking about."

Elaine quickly explained that a man by the name of Anthony Nichols saw to the gardens.

"I wasn't hired to come out to look at the gardens," the man said. "Just the mansion."

"Good," Elaine responded, "because we're looking for information about the chandelier that's inside."

"Well," the man said, "I don't know nothing about that either."

"All right." Elaine smiled, hoping the man would cooperate. "Can you tell us who owns the house?"

The man shook his head but then started digging in the pocket of his sweatshirt. "I have a card here that my boss gave me." He held it up. "This is who contacted us."

"Could I take a picture of the card?" Elaine stepped toward him.

"Suit yourself."

Elaine asked the man what his name was as she pulled out her phone.

"Bud," he answered. "Bud Johnson. I'm from Augusta."

Elaine introduced herself and Sasha and then shook the man's hand. Then he held the card so Elaine could snap a photo with her phone.

Elaine did, reading the card as she did. *Denny Gray.* She gasped. Dennis Gray had been the original owner, according to Macy, and then his son had the same name. "Does it still belong to the original family?" She thought Macy said it had been sold several times over the years.

The man shrugged. "I have no idea. All I know is someone wants some work done."

Elaine sighed in relief. "I hoped that the plan was to renovate it."

He shivered. "If I owned it, I'd raze it."

Elaine couldn't help the alarm in her voice. "Why would you do that?"

"Because the location is great, but the place is haunted."

"Do you really believe that could be possible?"

"Yep." His eyes grew wide. "I've worked in a lot old houses before. There've been creaks or a groan, that sort of thing, but it's just the old structure shifting or wood swelling. But this place is different." The man paused and shivered again.

"What do you mean?" Elaine asked.

"It's hard to explain. I heard some stories before I came down here, but I didn't believe them. And the first hour or so everything was fine. But then weird noises started in the dining room. I couldn't find anything. Next, they started in the living room. Again I couldn't find anything. Then a shadow passed through the hall where there are no windows. I'm telling you, it's creepy."

"Anthony Nichols didn't say anything about it being haunted."

The man shook his head. "Like I said, I don't have any idea who you're talking about. I haven't seen anyone on this property."

"He lives in a caretaker's cottage, past the rhododendrons and trees."

"Did you actually see the cottage?"

Elaine shook her head and glanced at Sasha. She grimaced a little and then said, "We didn't have any reason not to believe Mr. Nichols."

"Well, I didn't see a cottage or a man. In fact, I got so spooked being out here by myself that I drove into town for a break, just to get away from it."

"But you're going back in now?"

He exhaled, sharply. "Just to get my tools," he muttered. "I'm telling the boss to send someone else. Yeah, this house definitely creeps me out."

CHAPTER NINETEEN

D o you think it's really haunted?" Sasha asked as Elaine turned from the driveway back onto the road.

"I don't believe in that sort of thing," Elaine answered. "There's always a scientific explanation. If no one had ever told him the place was haunted, I doubt he would have come to that conclusion about the noises he heard and the shadow he saw. It's simply the power of suggestion."

When Sasha didn't answer, Elaine asked, "What do you think?"

"That there all sorts of things in life that can't be explained through science."

Elaine waited for Sasha to make herself clear. When she didn't, Elaine finally asked, "Such as?"

"Oh, you know, relationships. That sort of thing."

"Does this have to do with Brody?"

Sasha sighed.

"What's going on, sweetheart?"

"I thought I'd just run with him. Do some shooting. That's all. I'm going back to Colorado. He's going back to…North Carolina. Or wherever." She paused again.

"But?"

"We talked about this. It can't work. And I wouldn't say that I am even fully interested—it's been such a short time. But, like I said, I really enjoy spending time with him and I'm not looking forward to telling him goodbye."

"What are you saying?"

"Nothing. Except that I'm definitely attracted to him. He's kind and ambitious. He takes his faith seriously. He's responsible." She turned toward Elaine and grinned. "Not to mention handsome and athletic."

Elaine gripped the steering wheel a little tighter.

"I know you don't approve of him," Sasha said. "But for the life of me, I can't figure out why. He's everything I've ever wanted in a husband."

"He's a fine young man," Elaine said. "I especially enjoyed getting to know him a little more yesterday."

"Then what is it, Mom? Is it that you hope I'll move to Maine and you're afraid instead I may be living all over the world?"

"Being married to a soldier is difficult."

"You were married to a soldier."

"Yes." Ben had been deployed to war zones and had certainly been in dangerous situations. Everyone in the army was a soldier, whether they were directly part of the action or not. Brody, however, was a Green Beret—not only would Sasha be by herself, but her husband would be off fighting in the most dangerous places imaginable. He would be in combat or he would be training for combat. Plus, he would be gone much of the time unless peace was miraculously made around the entire world.

"Mom."

Elaine sighed. "It's a hard life."

"I know," Sasha said. "Remember, I lived it too."

"You did." Elaine knew Ben's service was hard on her children. There were a lot of benefits—living all over the world, growing to love other cultures, and learning at an early age to trust God with their father. But having him gone for long stretches of time and missing school and sporting events and family time was hard on all of them.

"So I know at least a little about what I'd be getting into." Sasha turned her head and gazed toward the lake as they rounded the corner toward the boat launch.

Elaine didn't reply to her daughter. Being married to a soldier was a whole lot different than having one as a parent. But Elaine wasn't sure how to tell Sasha that. Elaine certainly didn't regret being married to Ben or any of their adventures. It was the life God had planned for her, for them.

But to be honest, the thought of marrying Nathan and staying in Lancaster filled her with relief. Moving around the world, always wondering when the next deployment would be, and fighting panic when Ben was in a war zone had taken a toll on her she didn't fully realize until he retired.

She didn't want that for Sasha.

As they approached Tea for Two, Elaine spotted Brody's truck first. "Did you have plans?" she asked Sasha.

Sasha stopped staring at the lake and turned her head. "Not that I know of."

Brody stood on the porch, waving. Sasha waved back.

Elaine pulled into the driveway and Brody bounded toward them. As soon as the car stopped, Sasha jumped out. Elaine opened her door slowly.

After greeting her, Brody asked Sasha if she'd like to ride into Augusta with him. "I have a long list from Mom," he said. "Nails. Sheetrock. Plaster. Fun things like that."

He had a tarp over the back of his truck, which was a good thing because it seemed probable it was going to start raining again.

"I'd love to," Sasha said. "Mom and I went out to that mansion, and I haven't gotten cleaned up since our run."

"You're fine." He grinned. "I promise we won't be stopping at a five-star restaurant or anything."

Sasha said she'd just be a minute and dashed up the stairs, while Elaine invited Brody to kitchen. "We'll see what Jan has left over from today."

Brody patted his stomach. "I'm watching what I eat."

Elaine laughed. "Good luck watching what you eat here."

They found Jan putting a tray of key lime cheese bars away in the fridge. Brody politely took one. "Tell me more about your Special Forces—your Green Beret unit," Elaine said.

"Well, as with most, we're all close. We'd do anything for each other." He turned toward Jan. "This is delicious."

"Take another," Jan said.

He hesitated for a moment but then went ahead and took a second one.

"Eat up. It won't be long until you're back on army food," Elaine said. "MREs? Mess hall food? Army base fare?"

Brody shrugged. "None of it is as good as this, let me tell you." He turned toward the back porch where Earl Grey meowed loudly.

"Someone needs to be fed," Jan said.

"I'll do it." Elaine headed toward the door. She might as well. She wasn't getting any information out of Brody anyway. Maybe Jan would have better luck.

When she returned, the two were talking about her recipe for the key lime bars. A few minutes later Sasha came down. It appeared as if she'd managed to get a quick shower, and she was dressed in jeans and a sweater, with her raincoat over her arm. "I see the mother hens have been plying you with food."

Brody held up the bar in his hand. "It's a good thing you came down when you did."

Sasha shot Elaine a suspicious look and then waved. "See you two later," she said.

Elaine didn't have a chance to wave back. Her daughter was halfway up the walkway, matching Brody's stride, her head turned toward him.

THE NEXT AFTERNOON, as Elaine sat down in her cozy office, rain began to pelt the window. A moment later it turned to hail. She didn't bother to look out the window at the pots of plants on the deck. Would the dreadful weather ever end?

She opened her e-mail, trying to distract herself, and worked backwards. She had an inquiry from a bride-to-be about using Tea for Two for a small wedding on a Sunday in August. Then a reply from a professor in Chicago to her e-mail. He said that no one had contacted him about the book, but he'd let her know if someone did. She deleted several junk e-mails and then read an e-mail from a professor in Missouri. His reply was essentially the same.

She closed her e-mail and then opened up her browser, typing in "Denny Gray, Augusta, Maine." Absolutely nothing came up. Then she typed in "Dennis Gray." A few accounts about the original owner of the house came up and then a couple about his son. The stories lined up with what Macy had said.

Was this contemporary Denny Gray a real person? A business? A ruse?

Feeling restless, she decided to go check on Bristol and see how she was faring with putting the bookstore back together. Perhaps Jan would want to go with her.

Fifteen minutes later both of them entered the Bookworm with plates of leftover pastries. It was almost six but workmen buzzed around the store. Two men measured the floor while three other men hung the last section of Sheetrock. Bill worked behind them with a taping machine.

Elaine finally spotted Bristol in her office and followed Jan across the subfloor.

Through the open door, Bristol caught sight of them. Her face broke out into a smile.

"We brought treats," Jan said. "For you to take home or to share with the workers."

"Ah, thanks," she said. "There are some paper plates on the table over by the windows. I'll have them grab some as they leave."

As the women headed toward the table, Elaine asked how things were working out with the insurance company.

"We're getting closer," Bristol said.

Elaine asked exactly what that meant.

Bristol sighed. "I'm still worried about the drainage system and the cost of repairing it."

"We'll keep praying," Jan said. "In the meantime, Macy is stopping by tomorrow morning to go over last-minute details for the fund-raiser."

"Thank you," Bristol replied. "Honestly, whether the event makes much money or not, it's going to be a great distraction. I'm really looking forward to it."

"Then it'll be a win-win," Elaine said, "a success no matter how much money is raised." She was grateful to Macy for pushing the event and sincerely hoped it earned enough to make a difference for Bristol.

"When do you expect to reopen?" Jan asked.

"In a week. I'm meeting with the insurance agent again tomorrow," Bristol said. "I'm not going to have the flooring installed until I know that what the insurance company is paying will cover it."

"That's understandable," Elaine said.

Bristol tilted her head, causing her ponytail to swing. "I'm so thankful for everything you two are doing to help. You've been so gracious about the book. And such good neighbors to me, as always. I'm just so sorry your book went missing on my watch."

"None of that," Elaine said, wagging her finger. "We're not giving up hope. I really believe we'll still find the book."

CHAPTER TWENTY

Before leaving the Bookworm, Jan asked Bill about Roland Nance, the electrician.

"I left a message." Bill held his taping machine in his hand. "But he hasn't called me back yet. I'll let you know as soon as he does. I know you need that chandelier back in place by tomorrow. If the electrician doesn't get back to me tonight, I'll string it back up by noon, but you won't be able to turn it back on."

"All right," Jan said. "That sounds like a backup plan." Not a good one, but it was better that having the chandelier spread over the dining room table.

Jan thanked him and then followed Elaine out the door. As they walked back to Tea for Two, Jan asked who her cousin's top suspect was for their book thief.

"I hate to say it, but I'd say it's Ronald Good."

It pained Jan to think a cousin, even one they'd never met, would steal the book. "Really?"

Elaine shrugged. "Well, it certainly feels like he's been evading me. That by itself seems suspicious to me."

"Unless his wife is very ill. Then it would be understandable that he hasn't returned your calls."

Elaine shrugged. "He calls Cami every day. How hard would it be to make a two-minute phone call to me? Until we have a chance to speak with him, I'm not going to rule anything out."

As they reached the front porch of Tea for Two, a thought came to Jan. "I have a friend—Nancy—who lives north of Waterville now. We were neighbors back in Augusta. Anyway, her husband is in the auto body business. I'll give her a call right now and see what they know about Ronald Good."

"Good idea," Elaine said, leading the way into the house. "I haven't ruled out Patrick Stark entirely. Or even Brody. Both certainly knew about the book and what it was worth. Plus they both had motivations to take it."

Jan nodded. "Let's hope my friend can give us some insight." As it turned out, her friend didn't answer, but Jan left a voice mail.

The cousins had a simple supper of soup and a half sandwich each. Soon after that Bob stopped by, and he and Jan went for a walk before it grew dark. Jan was grateful it wasn't raining, but the evening was gray and overcast. Still the light that wafted through the cloud cover cast a golden hue over the lake. A sailboat headed toward the boat launch and flock of geese flew overhead, making their way north.

"What a beautiful evening," Jan said. It was cool but not cold. Perhaps warm days were just around the corner after all. Jan brought Bob up to speed on both the book and the chandelier, including Elaine and Sasha's trip out to the old mansion.

"So no resolution to either case." He smiled a little, his chocolate-brown eyes full of concern. "I'm sorry."

"Thanks," Jan said. "Once we can meet with Ronald Good, we should have some answers about the book. And there has to be some explanation to the chandelier exploding."

As they continued walking, Bob brought up the second chandelier. "That would be great if you could get that one too, if the owner doesn't want it or would be willing to sell."

"That's a great idea," Jan responded. "We could put it in one of the parlors. Or perhaps the entryway."

"Ask Bill about it. Maybe he knows the owner of the company hired to renovate it."

"I'll do that," Jan said, then chuckled. "The only drawback would be if we end up with two exploding chandeliers."

THURSDAY MORNING JAN rose long before dawn, showered, fed Earl Grey, and settled into her routine in the kitchen. She needed to bake enough goodies for the day and also for the fund-raiser for the Bookworm that afternoon. Rose would make the sandwiches and set up the dining room—once the chandelier was out of the way—and then set the other tables between when the tearoom closed at four and the fund-raiser tea began at five.

Hopefully Macy had sold enough tickets to make the event worth it. Jan sighed and chastised herself. No matter what money they brought in, Bristol would feel supported and that was what truly mattered.

She'd started on the chocolate chip scones when her cell began to buzz. It was 5:30 a.m. and the first rays of light were coming through the window—it really was much too early for anyone to call unless it was important. She quickly answered it.

"What in the world?" her friend Nancy blurted out. "You're related to Ronald Good?"

"Well, hello to you too." Jan laughed, stepping away from the mixer. "How did you know I'd be up so early?"

"You're always up early." Nancy chuckled. "Sorry. Your voice mail surprised me, and I decided to call first chance I got." She paused a moment and then added, "Which happened to be 5:30 a.m."

"So do you know Ronald Good?"

"I know of him. The auto body business is a small world, plus we have mutual friends, so I've heard of him and his wife through the years."

"Good things?" Jan asked.

"Completely," Nancy said. "They're upstanding people. Hard workers. Good businesspeople who are fair to their employees. They give back to the community in all sorts of ways—Little League, the fire department, Meals on Wheels. That sort of thing."

"Do you know anything about his wife's health?"

"Only because I called our mutual friend last night. I mean, I knew his wife had some health issues recently, but not exactly what's wrong with her. My friend said they've been down in Boston for testing. But they're back now."

"They're back?"

"Yep. In fact I noticed his car outside the shop when I drove into town this morning." Nancy worked at the hospital, in the cafeteria.

"That's great," Jan said. "Thank you so much for your help."

"You're welcome," Nancy said. "I hope you can meet him soon. From everything I've heard he's a great guy."

As Jan hung up, she wondered about what Nancy said. Jan knew that there was always the possibility that a "great guy" wasn't always what he seemed. People could look good—and still do bad things. Perhaps there was something about the book that made Ronald Good snap and then react out of his normal character. Every person had their buttons, that one thing that pushed them to act in a surprising way.

Jan breathed a prayer for direction concerning the case.

When Elaine came into the kitchen, Jan told her about the phone call.

"I wish we could go up today," Elaine said.

"You could," Jan answered. "I bet Sasha would ride along."

Elaine shook her head. "I'd rather we go together. Besides, there's too much to do here. Macy is coming at nine to go over the details. And hopefully we'll be busy today."

Jan nodded. She knew their revenues were down compared to last year due to all the rain. Tourists weren't venturing out as much this spring as they had the year before.

"We could try visiting Ronald's shop again tomorrow," Jan suggested.

"But we'll have no idea if Ronald will be there or not."

"You could call…"

"But if he knows we're coming out, he might disappear."

"That's true," Jan said. "I could ask Nancy to let me know if his car is there tomorrow."

"Great idea," Elaine said. "We'll come up with a plan then. Right now, let's not think about it and concentrate on raising money for Bristol's new drainage system."

Macy arrived right on time. Elaine brought her back to the kitchen and the three went over the menu again and the order of events. Macy had everything under control and said she would emcee the tea. She planned to hold the auction in the west parlor so those in both the dining room and east parlor could crowd around the doorways and see what was going on. "What's the status on the chandelier?" Macy asked.

"Bill Bridges plans to put it back in place," Jan answered.

Macy flinched. "You're going to use it tonight?"

"Not unless Roland can come check it out before this afternoon, and I sincerely doubt that will happen." The two left the kitchen and Jan got back to work as she shook her head. Surely Macy knew they wouldn't endanger their guests.

The morning progressed with Rose coming in to prep, help Elaine with the serving, and work on what needed to be done for the tea in her slow minutes, which turned out to be few and far between. The tearoom was soon humming with conversation, laughter, and the clinking of silver against china.

Jan had prepared enough macarons to have them as the special of the day and they were flying out of the kitchen like hotcakes. She had to guard the ones for the tea to keep Rose and Elaine from selling those after they quickly ran out of the extras.

After her run and shower, Sasha helped too.

"How's Brody doing?" Jan teased as Sasha mixed up the cucumber and cream cheese filling for tea sandwiches.

"He didn't run with me this morning," Sasha said.

Jan hoped they hadn't had a spat. "Oh? Why not?"

Elaine stepped into the kitchen as Sasha said, "He had an appointment with the VA, up at Bangor."

"Whatever for?" Elaine asked as she placed an order.

Sasha shrugged. "He didn't say."

"A medical appointment? Has he been injured?"

"Mom." Sasha turned toward Elaine. "Like I just told you, he didn't say and I didn't press him."

"Sorry," Elaine said as she stepped toward the teapot cupboard.

Jan could just imagine how this fit into Elaine's concern that Brody was keeping a secret, but none of them said anything more about it as Sasha quickly changed the subject.

"There were two work vans out at the mansion today," she said. "And the gate was unlocked again."

Elaine began speculating about how much it would cost to renovate the mansion as she brewed a pot of coconut oolong tea. Soon Elaine left the kitchen and Rose arrived with an order for one savory and one apricot scone, along with a pot of English breakfast tea.

Bill arrived at noon to install the chandelier. Jan walked with him to the dining room as he said that he did hear back from Roland but it wouldn't be until next week that the electrician could take a look at it. Bill apologized again, and Jan told him not to give it a second thought. "It's not your fault," she said, quickly moving on to telling him he was right about the identical chandelier out at the mansion on the other side of the lake.

"One of my buddies told me that place is going to be renovated," Bill said.

"Yes. Elaine got a card from the party that's bought the house but she can't find any information on it. The name on the van of the company that's been hired to renovate it is Schmidt & Sons. Have you heard of them?"

"Out of Augusta?"

"Yes," Jan said.

"I'll look into them and see what I find out," Bill said. "In the meantime, I'll get the chandelier back in place—although I won't hook it back up to the electricity."

"Sounds like a good plan," Jan said. There was no way they would risk anyone's safety—or the reputation of their tearoom—no matter how beautiful the light from the chandelier had been.

Rose started setting up for the tea before closing time. They'd decided to do a buffet instead of serving each guest individually, so Rose placed the tables in the entryway where the buffet would be.

Just as the tearoom closed and after Jan, Elaine, and Rose had changed into their Victorian costumes, Macy showed up with boxes of books that would be auctioned off.

"Someone should look through them for the missing copy of *Evangeline*," Jan joked as she helped Macy carry them in from her car.

"Honestly, do you really believe I didn't already think of that?"

"I was just joking," Jan said. "I know you would have alerted us if the book had shown up."

Macy rolled her eyes as she placed the box she was carrying on the floor next to the wall of the west parlor. "It's amazing," she said, "what people are willing to donate for a worthy cause. Some of these books have been in families for years but the younger generation doesn't seem to want them."

"Oh, that's too bad." Jan was grateful that both Tara and Sasha were interested in family heirlooms and history. She knew Brian wouldn't value a book that had been in the family for years. But Avery would. Different people treasured different things, that was all there was to it.

"We're going to have a full house," Macy said.

Jan had planned for that but was relieved to have it confirmed. Perhaps they'd make enough to help Bristol out after all.

While Macy unpacked the books, Jan helped Rose set out plates, napkins, and cutlery. Then she began to place the trays of scones and cookies on the tables, saving the sandwiches and cream puffs for last.

A couple of minutes before five, the tea party participants began to arrive. Macy stood at the front door and took tickets one by one, greeting each woman and asking her to take a seat until the event began.

Bristol was one of the last to arrive. By then Macy already had the guests going through the buffet line.

"I'm so sorry," Bristol said. "I was meeting with the insurance agent."

"How are things going?"

"All right. There will be enough to cover the carpet so I'll go ahead and have that installed."

"That's great news," Jan said.

"It looks like a wonderful turnout," Bristol said.

"It really is," Jan answered. "We have a full house."

Jan directed Bristol to the west parlor and then showed her to the head table, where Macy was sitting with her plate of food and cup of tea.

"I'm so grateful for everything all of you have done," Bristol said. "Right after the flood, I wondered if I'd have to throw in the towel when it came to the Bookworm, but through the support of all of you I've been able to go on." She turned toward Jan. "What an amazing event—thank you."

Both Jan and Elaine nodded toward their friend.

Then Bristol turned toward Macy. "You, my dear, are the one who made this entire event possible. The money raised will go toward a new drainage system and hopefully keep a flood from ever happening again at the Bookworm."

Macy pursed her lips and then muttered, "I didn't do much."

"Yes, you did. Look at everyone who is here." She swept her hands toward the women returning to their tables, their plates full of little sandwiches and cream puffs and fruit and scones, and their cups full of tea. "And look at all those books you've collected. Macy, I know the Bookworm means a lot to you, but you've really blessed me by doing this."

Macy nodded her head and then, raising her teacup, said, "Well, I've always been a big fan of C.S. Lewis's quote: 'You can never get a cup of tea large enough or a book long enough to suit me.'" She took a drink and then put her cup down. "I figured combining tea and books was sure to be a big winner."

"Well, you were right," Jan said.

"And I can't imagine my life without the Bookworm." She put her cup down and stuck out her tongue. "So there."

Everyone laughed. That was the Macy they all knew and loved.

The event went off without a hitch. All the women enjoyed the food and tea. Macy ran the book auction, and the guests bid on the books, including several classics from over a century ago, such as *Swiss Family Robinson*, *The Secret Garden*, *Little Women*, and *Jane Eyre*. None of the editions were rare, but all of them were old. One by one, after the women purchased a book, most of them gave it to Bristol, telling her to sell it at the bookstore for additional revenue. Jan teared up again as she watched. People could be so generous and supportive. She brushed the back of her hand across her eyes.

And yet in this very community someone had stolen a book that had once belonged to her and Elaine's grandmother. People could be good and giving but they could also be the opposite, that was for sure.

CHAPTER TWENTY-ONE

The next morning before opening for the day, Elaine called Cami at Ronald Good's auto body shop one more time.

"Oh, hi, Elaine!" The woman sounded happy to hear from her. "Ronald is back in town—he plans to come in today although he's not here yet." She sighed. "I'll tell him you called again."

"Thank you," Elaine said. "I imagine he has a lot of catching up to do after being away."

"Some, but it shouldn't take him too long. I'm guessing he'll give you a call soon. I'll remind him first thing when he comes in."

Elaine thanked Cami and ended the call. She wouldn't call again. Ronald Good seemed to be avoiding her. The best thing to do would be to go out and surprise him. Rose was coming in to work in the tearoom all day, so perhaps Elaine and Jan could get away and drive up to Waterville during the midafternoon. Maybe Sasha would go with them.

Just as Elaine flipped the Open sign over, Macy opened the door and she and Bristol stepped into the entryway.

"Good morning," Elaine chimed. "How is our amazing event coordinator? And how is the recipient of said effort?"

"The money from the event, combined with the savings I have from the business, means I'll be able to get the drainage system updated right away. The business is going to survive!" Bristol said, beaming.

"Amen," Elaine said. "Do you have a reopening planned?"

"Hopefully Tuesday," Bristol said, rubbing her hands together. "The carpet is going to be installed today. If all goes well, we'll move the books on Monday."

"Wonderful!" Elaine said. "What an answer to prayer."

"Speaking of," Bristol said. "I'm still praying your book will show up."

"I hope so," Elaine said, hugging her friend. "Time will tell—we'll leave it to the Lord."

Bristol hugged Elaine back, saying, "Taking home all of those old classics last night was bittersweet. None of them are nearly as old as your book, but every one of them is a treasure. Some women value jewels. I, however, value books. I just really hope yours still turns up."

"Don't give it another thought," Elaine said. "What will be will be." She glanced from Bristol to Macy. "How about a cup of tea and an apricot scone with clotted cream?"

"Well," Macy said, "I probably should get back to work."

"Oh, come on," Bristol said, linking her arm through Macy's. "Let's celebrate! We can raise our teacups to you and Jan and Elaine! The three of you have been such good friends to me. Let's celebrate together."

Macy's eyes may have grown a little misty, but Elaine couldn't tell for sure. "Well, I guess I could have one cup," Macy said. "If you insist."

Just after noon, Roland Nance stepped into the tearoom. He wore a work belt with tools low on his hips. "Bill Bridges sent me to take a look at the exploding chandelier."

"Thank you so much for coming." Elaine led him to the dining room, explaining that Bill had rehung it but hadn't rewired it.

"I'll take a look and see what I can find," Roland said. He retrieved a ladder from his truck, and then Elaine left him to work alone. Fifteen minutes later, the electrician appeared in the entryway as she took a customer's credit card. He paced around until she was done.

She feared bad news by the way he was acting, but he said, "I couldn't find a thing wrong with the wiring in the chandelier or the ceiling. Bill did a fine job with the installation."

"What about the lightbulbs?" Elaine asked. "It seems they might be quite old."

He took off his cap and rubbed his head. "I don't know anything about old lightbulbs, to be honest. But I went ahead and rewired the chandelier."

"Oh." Elaine was surprised to hear that.

"I think it should be fine."

Should be? "What if it's not?"

Roland took a card from his pocket. "Give me a call, and I'll give it a second look."

Elaine took the card. "All right," she said. "What do I owe you?"

He waved his hand. "Actually, I owed Bill a favor. He felt so bad about the whole exploding chandelier incident that he called it in, on this occasion." The man winked. "So nothing today."

He retrieved his ladder and then left as quickly as he arrived.

Elaine hurried into the dining room and switched on the light. The chandelier lit up beautifully, just as it had before. But she quickly turned the switch off, unsure if she could trust it.

By midafternoon, Sasha agreed to go up to Waterville with Elaine and Jan. Jan had finished making the salted caramel chocolate pecan bars again—for the next morning. They'd been a hit before, especially with Bob, and Jan had decided to make them again.

Rose was fine finishing serving and cleaning up, so the three made plans to leave at three. But just as they put on their coats, Brody pulled up to the curb outside of Tea for Two.

Elaine figured her daughter would choose to go with him, but as he came up the walk, Sasha turned to her mother and said, "What if we ask Brody to come along?"

Elaine wanted to say "Absolutely not," but she bit her tongue. He was still on the suspect list. How awkward would it be to have him along? Then again, when the topic of the book came up, Elaine could monitor his reaction.

Elaine shot Jan a look. Her cousin nodded.

Jan turned toward Sasha. "Go ahead and ask him."

Sasha opened the door and stepped outside. Elaine and Jan held back, giving the couple a minute until Sasha called out, "Brody said he'd drive."

Elaine looked at Jan with raised eyebrows.

"Everything will work out," Jan said. "Chances are Ronald won't be in his auto body shop anyway. But we can know we tried."

Elaine hoped that wasn't the case. If Ronald Good wasn't there, she would ask Cami his home address—Elaine had already tried to find it online but couldn't. Hopefully Cami would be willing to give the address, but on second thought, as a good employee, she probably wouldn't.

Elaine sighed. If nothing else, maybe she could get a better read on Brody at least during the drive up to Waterville and back.

Elaine and Jan sat in the backseat of Brody's king cab pickup. It was comfortable and absolutely immaculate. Seventies music played on the radio, and Elaine couldn't help but wonder if he was playing it for her and Jan, specifically. Brody and Sasha teased each other about their last run.

"You were totally the tortoise," Sasha joked. "And I was the hare."

As they turned onto the highway, the rain started again. By the time they reached the outskirts of town it was pouring.

"I'm not going to miss this rain," Sasha said.

"I won't either," Brody replied, turning toward Sasha. But judging from the look he gave Sasha, he was going to miss her.

Elaine leaned back against the seat, her heart heavy for a moment. Colorado and North Carolina were a long way apart. She exhaled. *Thank goodness.*

She still hoped that Sasha would move to Maine sometime and find someone to settle down with. *In Maine.* Not in North Carolina or who knew where else.

"How was your appointment at the VA?" Sasha asked, her voice low.

Brody glanced into the rearview mirror, making eye contact with Elaine in the backseat, and then quickly at Sasha before his eyes fell back on the road. "Actually not very good," he said, his voice louder. It seemed he wanted all of them to hear.

Sasha turned toward him. "What's going on?"

"I had a medical exam. I've had quite a few in the last few months."

Sasha's voice was barely audible. "Oh."

"Yeah, I didn't want to say anything before." He exhaled. "I finally told my mom last night, and it's time to be honest about what's going on."

Elaine's heart fell, hoping it wasn't too serious.

"I was injured in Afghanistan five months ago. An IED exploded and I ended up with a traumatic brain injury. It was actually mild but I haven't cleared, over and over. Yesterday was my last chance."

"Wow," Sasha said. "I'm so sorry."

"Thank you." He glanced at her again, a pained expression on his face.

"What now?" she asked.

Elaine leaned forward, her weeks of suspicion changing to compassion.

"I'll be honorably discharged. The unit arrives back at Fort Bragg next week. I'll go down and see everyone to say goodbye and pack up my apartment."

Elaine could only imagine the pain Brody felt. "Will they have a ceremony for you? Perhaps an award?"

He cleared his throat.

"It's not bragging, Brody," she said. "We care."

"Yes, ma'am, I'll receive a Bronze Star for valor."

"Do you mind telling us what happened over in Afghanistan?" she asked. Sometimes it was good for a soldier to talk about it—she wanted to give him the opportunity, and she really did want to know.

He didn't answer for a long moment but finally he said, "We were in Kunar Province, in eastern Afghanistan, clearing a road. We had a dog handler with us and the dog indicated an IED was buried on the side of the road. Just as the handler flagged the spot, we came under fire."

Brody was terse in his descriptions, clearly not wanting to bring any attention to himself, but what Elaine gathered was that Brody had covered for everyone else as they retreated to safety and the IED exploded just as he started to follow. He was thrown to the ground, but thankfully survived. He was evacuated to Germany and then to the States.

"And you never told your mom about your injury?" Elaine asked.

He shook his head, glancing at her in the rearview mirror. "She had enough to worry about. It was considered a 'mild' traumatic brain injury. I thought I'd be sent back to Afghanistan right away, but with me not clearing the test I can't go back or even continue. The docs say I'm fine for civilian life—but I can't risk another explosion, which means I can't do my job." His voice was full of sadness.

Sasha's eyes were misty. "What will you do?"

He shrugged. "I'm not sure in the long run, but after I'm done in North Carolina I'll come back here and stay with Mom until I figure it out. I have some money in savings that I'm going to use to help her finish the renovation, so that's all settled."

Elaine leaned back against the seat, feeling mortified at how badly she'd misjudged Brody. He was a hero—not a thief. "Thank you for sharing all of that," Elaine said to him. "I'm truly sorry."

He nodded and glanced at her in the rearview mirror again for just a second. "I'm doing my best to trust God on this. His ways are not our ways. I know He's got my back."

Both Elaine and Jan murmured "Amen" at the exact same time. Then Jan reached over and patted Elaine's shoulder.

As grateful as she was for her cousin's reassurance, Elaine knew she deserved an "I told you so" from Sasha or at least a glance saying that, but none came. Instead, all of Sasha's attention was directed at Brody.

They all rode in silence for a few minutes. The emerald green of the countryside shone through even in the rain. Tall evergreens zipped by as Brody picked up speed. He and Sasha spoke quietly and this time Elaine couldn't make out their words. Jan had her head back against the seat, her eyes closed.

Elaine kept her eyes on the landscape. In no time they were passing through Waterville, a charming town with old brick buildings, wide streets, and massive trees. They crossed over the Kennebec River and then by the shopping center on the north end of town. Brody drove past the entrance to Waterville Park and a few minutes after that signaled to turn left. Elaine craned her neck to see the sign. *Good's Auto Body Shop*. They'd arrived.

Jan opened her eyes. "Are we here already?"

Elaine nodded as Brody parked next to Cami's red Mustang. "Do you want me to come in?" Brody asked. "Or wait here?"

"You might as well come in," Elaine said as she opened the back door of the cab. They might need his strong, quiet, calm, nonassuming presence—in other words, a hero. They all jumped down and Elaine led the way. As they entered, the sound of a saw from the garage pierced the air.

A thin man with salt-and-pepper hair stood on the other side of the counter next to Cami, who sat at her desk with a spreadsheet in front of her.

The saw stopped and a soft banging sound took its place.

Obviously not having noticed the people who just entered his shop, the man said, "Tell me about these numbers."

Elaine wondered if the man was having financial problems. That would certainly have given him extra motivation to steal the book.

Cami did notice them and her gaze quickly fell on Elaine. She stood, sending her chair rolling backwards. "Elaine," she said, "why didn't you tell me you were coming?"

"It was a little last minute," she answered and quickly introduced Jan, Sasha, and Brody.

Ronald Good introduced himself as he stepped around the counter and shook everyone's hand. "I'll let you speak with Cami," he said, giving his employee a puzzled look.

"Actually we're here to see you," Elaine said to Ronald. He seemed like such a nice man.

He looked confused.

Elaine did her best to keep her voice calm. "I've left several messages over the last couple of weeks. I understand you were in Boston for a while but thought we'd stop by in person because you didn't return my calls."

"Messages?" He glanced toward a tidy desk on the far side of the room and then shifted his gaze to Cami. "I didn't get any messages from you."

"I left them on your desk," she said. "And told you about them when you called."

Ronald appeared to be bewildered, but Elaine feared his obtuse expression was a front. Perhaps his politeness was too. "No, you must be mistaken. I don't recall you telling me about any calls besides business ones. And there weren't any such messages in the ones left on my desk."

Cami appeared as if she wanted to playfully roll her eyes at her boss, but she didn't. Apparently Ronald had done this before. Instead she politely stepped to her desk and picked up her phone. It appeared she was sending a text.

Elaine decided to carry on with what she needed to say. "Jan and I believe that you're a relative, a cousin of ours."

"Cousin?"

"Lena Pritchard was our grandmother. She had a younger sister by the name of Gladys—"

"—who was my grandmother." He smiled a little. "How odd we've never met."

"It seems there was some rift in the family, between the sisters."

"Yes, my father mentioned that a few times. But no one told me I had any cousins." His smile grew a little wider. "I'm pleased to meet both of you."

Elaine smiled back at him. Ronald Good wasn't what she'd expected, not at all.

"It's coming back to me now," he said. "Is this about that book? Mr. Baker called—he bought my family home years ago, and said that the book was going to the Pritchard cousins— but that all happened right before we went to Boston, and I'm afraid it slipped my mind."

"Yes, it does have to do with the book," Elaine said. "Were you aware of it before that phone call, by chance?"

"My father mentioned the book a few times years ago, when I was still in high school. He seemed to think it was quite valuable."

Cami stepped forward. "Is that the antique in the story you told me? The one your father said would pay for college, the one you never found?"

Ronald blushed. "Yes, that's the one. But the point of the story I told you was that I found another means to make a living without going to college, and everything worked out after all."

"Got it," Cami said. "Listen, I need to get to the bank before it closes." She grabbed her oversized purse, slipped her phone into it, and slung it onto the counter. As she did the bag fell to the side next to a basket of papers. She righted the purse and then grabbed a moneybag with the name Waterville First Bank on the side from the back of the till. With both items in her possession, she told Ron she'd see him on Monday.

She gave Elaine a warm goodbye and told Jan, Sasha, and Brody it was nice to meet them. After giving everyone one last smile, she stepped out the door.

"I really didn't get a message from you," Ronald said. "I'd remember if I did. Cami has a lot of good qualities as an employee but every once in a while—" He stopped himself and by the expression on his face appeared as if he regretted saying that much. He faced Elaine. "What exactly did you want to talk with me about?"

"The book that Mr. Baker called you about was stolen that same evening." She explained about it being at the Bookworm and then about the flood. "We're guessing someone took it out of Bristol's car."

"Oh no, that's awful," Ronald said.

"I was wondering if you could tell us about Mr. Baker's phone call—what time he called, what your response was, what you did next."

Ronald ran his hand through his hair. "It sounds as if you suspect I took it."

Elaine shook her head. She had—and might still, but she wouldn't reveal that to the man. She smiled. "Oh, I'm just gathering information. Trying to piece it all together, you know?"

He sighed. "Mr. Baker called around four or so. It was a Friday afternoon, like today. He told me the woman who had bought the house from him called about a book she'd found. He said he'd told her to take it to the Pritchard cousins at the tearoom in Lancaster. It was the first time I'd heard of you—the Pritchard cousins or that you owned a tearoom in Lancaster, or that there was even a tearoom in the town. We haven't stopped in Lancaster for years. We really just drive through it on our way to somewhere else."

Elaine nodded, encouraging him to keep talking.

"Anyway, I figured it was the book my father had mentioned a few times, that he thought was worth quite a bit. But it didn't belong to me, not anymore anyway, and I thought whatever this woman wanted to do with it was fine." He paused. "As far as what I did the rest of the afternoon? I was on the phone trying to schedule appointments for my wife in Boston. Finally, by closing time, I'd gotten everything sorted out. She had appointments on Monday morning to see a group of specialists. We went home that evening and I did laundry and cleaned the house." He chuckled. "My usual Friday night chores. Except I also started getting us packed. We decided to drive to Boston on Saturday so my wife would have a chance to rest on Sunday before her appointments on Monday."

"I see," Elaine said.

"Oh, I thought of one other thing. The Pattersons, good friends of ours, came over with dinner. So I didn't have to add that to the list of things I needed to do."

"My friend Nancy knows the Pattersons," Jan said.

"Nancy Harris?"

Jan nodded. "I knew her in Augusta, before she moved to Waterville."

"We've met Nancy but don't know her well."

Elaine leaned against the counter, puzzled. "Did you happen to tell anyone else about the book?"

"Just my wife." He turned toward the door to another room. "Peggy, could you come out her for a minute?"

A woman's voice called out, "I'll be right there."

"She came in for a couple of hours today to help us get caught up on everything," Ronald explained.

A woman pushing a walker appeared. She was thin, with her hair pulled back into a bun at the nape of her neck, and wore a long sweater over leggings.

Ronald quickly stepped to her side. "These are the cousins Mr. Baker mentioned. Elaine and Jan." He glanced toward the door where Sasha and Brody still stood.

Elaine quickly introduced them to the woman.

"And this is my wife, Peggy," he said. "She came down with Guillain-Barre syndrome a year ago and is still recovering. That's why we were in Boston."

"I see," Elaine said, feeling like a heel. Peggy obviously wasn't the thief. She could barely get around on the linoleum let alone an uneven parking lot, in the dark, in the pouring rain. And Ronald seemed to be as good as he appeared to be.

"I'm so pleased to meet all of you," Peggy said, reaching across the counter.

Elaine leaned forward and shook the woman's hand, putting her other hand on the countertop. As she did she brushed up under the basket of papers. There was something hard under it.

Peggy shook Jan's hand next and as she did, Elaine nudged the hard object a little harder. It was a phone. She pulled it out and glanced down as she did. A text popped up over a screen saver of Cami in front of her Mustang. *I'll be at the arranged location within minutes. I have the cash. Hurry.* The text quickly disappeared but not before Elaine registered it was from a P. Stark. Elaine handed the phone to Ronald. "This must have fallen out of Cami's purse."

"Thank you," he said. "I'm sure she'll be back for it in no time."

Elaine made eye contact with Jan, nodded toward the door, and then said to Ronald and Peggy, "It's been so nice to meet both of you." She stepped backwards as she spoke. "I'll be in touch soon, I promise."

As Peggy and Ronald told all of them goodbye, Elaine whispered to Sasha. "Hurry!"

They exited and ran through the rain to the truck, Elaine wondering if Cami had overheard Ronald's conversation with Mr. Baker. She hadn't even thought to ask about that.

By the time Elaine and Jan climbed into the backseat, Brody had the truck engine running. As he pulled out onto the highway and accelerated, Elaine told all of them about the text that she saw. Elaine doubted the meeting point was the bank, but Cami would have to go there at some point.

She figured they were probably ten minutes behind Cami. If the spot where she planned to meet Patrick Stark was close, they might have already completed their transaction. They might as well head to the bank and try to cut her off there.

If they didn't find Cami, Elaine would call back to the shop, explain what was going on to Ronald, ask him for Cami's home address, and hope to find her there.

As they passed Monument Park, Elaine spotted a blur of red through the trees.

She craned her neck. "Turn around!"

"Mom?" Sasha turned toward the backseat.

"I think she's in the park. There's a red car."

They were past the park entrance now. "What if it's not her?" Sasha asked.

Elaine hesitated for a split second, then said, "It's a chance we need to take."

CHAPTER TWENTY-TWO

Brody slowed the truck, glanced in his rearview mirror, and then turned the truck around in the middle of the highway. A minute later he turned into the park.

"See that red Mustang?" Elaine pointed to the right. "It looks like Cami's." It was parked next to a black Jeep.

As they approached, Elaine could see that a man and a woman were sitting in the Jeep. She squinted through the rain. The woman was Cami.

And the man was Patrick Stark, just as the text indicated. Maybe he wasn't a thief—but it appeared he wasn't above trading in stolen property.

As Brody backed in beside the Jeep, Cami jumped out of the vehicle and rushed toward hers.

"Go block the exit," Elaine instructed.

Jan grabbed her cell phone from her bag. "I'm calling 9-1-1. And then Trooper Benson."

"Good idea," Elaine said.

Elaine looked toward the entrance where a car was entering. She opened her door. "I'll go ask the driver of that car to stay put for a few minutes—"

"I'll do it, Mom." Sasha opened her door, jumped down, and took off sprinting toward the entrance as Cami started her car. Both Elaine and Jan quickly jumped out of the truck and stepped away from it.

As Cami started to back up, Brody quickly pulled out of the parking space and drove toward the exit, forcing Cami to wait, or run into Brody's truck. He gained the advantage and maneuvered his truck across the one lane in front of the exit.

Mr. Stark had backed his Jeep out of the parking place and started to follow Brody, but he was now attempting to turn around, probably because he realized he wouldn't be able to exit that way. Cami headed toward the entrance even though it was blocked, and the Mustang now faced the stopped car. As Sasha talked with the driver, Cami started honking the horn, over and over and over.

"Hopefully we're at an impasse," Elaine said. "And Cami doesn't ram that car."

Without saying anything, Brody turned off the engine and jumped out of his truck, slamming the door behind him. Then he sprinted toward the entrance, most likely to protect Sasha.

Jan hung up with 9-1-1 and called Dan Benson. "*Aww,*" she said as she watched Brody too. "He's going to— Oh, hello, Dan." She quickly explained the situation and where they were.

As she hung up, she said, "He's north of Lancaster and will be here as soon as he can."

Mr. Stark opened his door and the cousins started toward him. His eyes were wide.

"Do you have the book?" Elaine asked.

"What book?" Mr. Stark asked.

Elaine pursed her lips and didn't say anything more. There was no reason to argue with the man. The police would arrive soon enough.

Everyone held their positions for the next five minutes. Cami honked a few more times, like a petulant child. Then she opened her car door, but Brody stepped toward it and she slammed it shut again. Finally she lowered her head to the steering wheel and maintained that position until a police car pulled into the entrance, parking behind the driver who'd kindly cooperated with them.

A young policewoman approached Sasha and Brody. After a minute of conversation, the policewoman stepped toward Cami's car and motioned everyone else to join them.

"Let's go," Elaine said to Mr. Stark. Jan stepped to his other side. He hesitated but then began to shuffle along beside them.

Cami lowered her window but didn't get out of the car.

The policewoman appeared to know her. "What's going on?" she asked.

When Cami didn't answer, the officer called her by name and then said, "The sooner you're straight with me, the sooner we can get this matter settled."

Cami still didn't get out of the car.

The officer glanced toward Sasha and then back to Cami. "Did you steal a book? Like these people said you did?"

Elaine couldn't hear if Cami answered the question.

"I'll go get a search warrant for your car if needed, or you can cooperate."

A brown package came sailing out of the window. Elaine gasped. It landed on the wet pavement. Brody quickly scooped it up.

The police officer opened the door of the Mustang, saying as she did, "Cami, how about if you come down to the station and answer some questions? But you'll need to ride with me." She glanced toward Elaine and Jan. "I'm Officer Vicks. I need the two of you to come down too—but I'll trust you to drive yourself."

"You have no reason to suspect me of anything," Mr. Stark said. "I didn't have the book in my possession. I'm an innocent bystander."

Officer Vicks glanced at Mr. Stark. "Really?" The officer harrumphed and then said, "Well, regardless of the way you see it, you're at the scene of a crime and I'm taking you in for questioning. You can share the backseat of my cruiser with Cami. Prepare to shed some light on the situation—or I'll get a warrant for your home computer, smartphone, or whatever it is you do your business on. And a search warrant to see if you have some sort of cash on you." She turned toward Brody. "Would you pull Cami's car into a parking space please, lock it, and then return the key to her?"

Brody complied quickly and then gave the key to Cami. She tossed it into her large bag.

Then Mr. Stark, with a defiant look on his face, climbed into the cruiser. But he didn't appear to be quite as confident about the situation as he had been a few minutes before.

Cami's face had turned bright red under her blonde hair. She followed, without saying a word. Just as Elaine and Jan turned back toward Brody's truck, Trooper Benson pulled up behind the Waterville police car. Officer Vicks spoke with him for a moment and then he backed out onto the highway, followed by the cruiser.

Once Brody, Sasha, Elaine, and Jan were all back in the pickup, they followed too, all the way to the police station. Officer Vicks and Trooper Benson worked together to take all of the testimonies.

Elaine told them exactly what happened, from her arrival that day at Tea for Two when Rose told her about the book, to taking it over to the Bookworm, to the discovery that it was missing. She also mentioned Dr. Day and gave his contact information so her story could be corroborated. Dan told Officer Vicks that he'd already spoken with Bristol and her story matched Elaine's.

When Elaine had finished telling her story, Officer Vicks asked her to stay at the station for a while longer. It wasn't long until she came out from the room where they had given their statements and said, "We have a confession from Cami."

The officer sighed. "We went to high school together. She's not a bad egg—she just got into some credit card debt and apparently thought this would be a fast way to pay some of it off."

Officer Vicks went on to summarize exactly what had happened. Cami had overheard Ronald's conversation with Mr. Baker, he told them. She hurried over to Tea for Two to see what she could find out about the book in person, but just as she arrived, Elaine was taking the book over to the Bookworm.

She followed Elaine into the store, hiding between the bookshelves where she could hear the conversation but not be seen. She overheard Patrick Stark's interest in the book and that he volunteered with the Maine Historical Society, and Bristol's phone conversation with Dr. Day from Bowdoin College. Once Bristol hung up, Cami slipped out of the bookstore. She spent a couple of hours at the Pine Tree Grill, planning to try to break into the bookstore and steal the book after dark.

Vicks went on with the account and told them that when Mr. Stark came in and said the bookstore was flooding and all of the books were being moved out, Cami decided to try to snatch it in the chaos of the moment. She hurried to the library parking lot and hid along the building. When she saw Bristol come out with a canvas bag of books and put them in the backseat of her car, Cami thought the rare book might among them. She put on her gloves and opened the back door of Bristol's car. The top book in the bag was wrapped in brown paper and none of the others were, so she snatched it and hurried back to the restaurant.

Officer Vicks paused for a moment and then wrapped up his account. "She had an unsavory friend call Dr. Day and then she actually arrived in Brunswick at the coffee shop when you were there. But Cami spotted you and didn't go in."

Elaine grimaced. She thought she'd been so careful not to be seen, but obviously Cami had been extra careful in staking the place out before showing herself.

"After that, she contacted Patrick Stark, who agreed to pay her $5,000 for the book. He does have the money on him—in cash. He confessed too, once he knew that Cami did."

Elaine shook her head. Not in disbelief—it all made sense—but at the audacity of the theft and subsequent attempts to sell the stolen property. "Did they really think they could get away with it?"

Officer Vicks shrugged. "At first they thought it was the perfect crime—they truly believed everyone would just think that the book was lost during the move. Then, even though Elaine tried to contact Ronald Good, Cami still figured the law wouldn't care enough about a possibly stolen book to pursue getting it back." She smiled a little. "They certainly knew the monetary value of the book, but they underestimated the intrinsic value and that the two of you would keep trying to recover it."

Elaine sighed. "It once belonged to our grandmother, whom we both deeply loved. We couldn't let it go."

"Of course not," the officer replied.

"What now?"

"Cami will be charged with theft, but she may qualify for a diversion program."

Elaine cleared her throat.

"What is it?" the officer asked.

Elaine pulled out a business card she'd picked up at Ronald Good's shop. "Would you call Peggy and Ronald Good? Cami works for them. We ran out of there quickly this afternoon, once I saw a text from Patrick Stark on Cami's phone." Elaine smiled. "She's probably wondering where that phone is."

"She did mention that it was missing," Officer Vicks said. "And she wondered how you knew she was meeting Mr. Stark."

Elaine smiled again. "The text on her phone will shed light on the entire situation."

The officer raised her eyebrows. "I'll give the Goods a call right now."

Elaine thanked her. She'd contact the Goods too—but she preferred an officer fill the couple in on the crime their employee had confessed to.

Dan Benson came out of the interrogation room and shook Jan's hand and then Elaine's. "Thank you for all of your work on solving the case," he said. "You'll get the book back—eventually. Once the case is complete. In the meantime, it'll be kept as evidence."

"We understand," Elaine said. "Just keep it safe, please."

"We will," Dan said. "I'll log it into the evidence room personally."

"Thank you," Jan said.

"You two are free to go now," Dan said. "But call me if you have any questions."

"Definitely." Elaine chuckled. "You make sure and do the same."

He smiled. "Of course. And believe me, I'm taking notes on this case. You two did great work."

"Well, we had a lucky break," Elaine said. Patrick Stark's text had certainly been fortuitous.

Jan stepped out into the parking lot and headed toward the pickup, where Brody and Sasha waited for them. Elaine followed. The rain had stopped and the late-afternoon sun poked out from the clouds.

On the way home to Lancaster, Jan and Sasha chatted away about what had just happened. Elaine didn't join in the conversation. Instead she kept her eyes on the passing landscape.

She didn't remember it ever before being the vivid green that it was now. The budding trees were practically shimmering in the sunlight and yellow bloomed in the emerald-green grass on the hillside. She wasn't sure she'd ever seen anything quite so beautiful.

Hopefully the weather had finally turned.

Sasha interrupted her thoughts. "Brody and I'll drop the two of you off and then go on into Augusta for dinner."

"All right." Elaine reached forward and patted Brody's shoulder. "Tell your mom what happened—we told her we'd let her know when we found the book. And thank you so much for driving us. It worked out really well. And it was good to have you there." Brody was so calm and steady. He reminded her of Ben in that way.

JAN AND ELAINE fixed soup and salad for dinner and talked about Mother's Day. Sasha and Tara had both asked about coordinating lunch on Sunday, and inviting Brian and his family and Amy and hers. Sasha had said she'd already asked Virginia, and that she'd also asked Nathan and Bob to attend and man the barbecue.

Elaine and Jan both agreed it sounded like a lovely idea.

"What if we invite Ronald and Peggy Good too?" Jan suggested. "That way they can meet your mom and the whole family, at least those who live close by."

Elaine agreed that sounded like a great idea.

"I'll give them a call," Jan said. "I got the idea they don't have any children, although we didn't ask. I guess we'll soon find out if they have Mother's Day plans or not."

After they'd finished cleaning up, Elaine called Nathan and gave him a detailed account of the afternoon.

"Wow," he said when she finished. "So glad you caught the thief."

Elaine agreed. "At first I thought perhaps Brody had taken it. And then Ronald Good seemed to be the leading suspect. Both had viable motivations—but both turned out to be good men who did everything they could to help catch the real thief."

"You didn't accuse either one of them," Nathan said, reassuringly. "Even though you genuinely had reason to suspect them."

"That's true," Elaine said. Then she told him about Brody's health issues. "I was wrong about that too. He was being secretive about his injury—not about his next assignment."

"Poor guy," Nathan said. "But I have to say, I'm happy to hear he's coming back to Maine. At least for the time being. He'll be a great asset to our community."

Elaine agreed. And perhaps he'd be just what was needed to draw Sasha back to Maine, sooner rather than later.

After Elaine changed the subject to Mother's Day, Nathan said he'd already told Sasha it sounded like a great idea. Of course, his boys would be with their mom and wives and children, so Nathan said he'd like nothing more than to honor Elaine and spend the day with her and Sasha and all of the others. And man the barbecue with Bob.

After she hung up, Elaine found Jan in the sitting room, reading a book. Jan said she'd talked with Ronald Good and he and Peggy said they'd be delighted to join everyone on Sunday afternoon.

THE NEXT MORNING dawned bright and sunny. Every time Elaine looked outside, she squinted, and she spent a good half hour dusting. The sunlight exposed far more than the long, long string of gray days had.

Sasha left on a run before Elaine could speak with her. Brody's pickup wasn't parked outside so Elaine guessed Sasha ran alone, which gave Elaine a quick stab of pain. In a day she'd gone from hoping Sasha wasn't interested in Brody to hoping she was.

By the time Sasha returned, the tearoom was open—and busy. The sunshine had brought out a crowd of tourists. Elaine was grateful that Rose was working and they were able to keep up with the orders and serving the customers.

Sasha came in, a melancholy expression on her face. Elaine didn't have a chance to speak to her, and she went straight upstairs.

A half hour later she came down and helped Jan catch up on orders in the kitchen. By the time the tearoom closed, Sasha had gone back upstairs. When Elaine checked on her, after finishing the closing-up chores, Sasha was napping. Elaine didn't wake her. She'd meddled enough in her daughter's life—she needed to wait until Sasha was ready to talk instead of prying any more.

CHAPTER TWENTY-THREE

The next morning, on the way to church, Elaine asked Sasha if she needed a ride to the airport the next day. She'd be flying out of Portland.

Sasha shook her head. "Brody is driving back to North Carolina. He said he'd pick me up by 6 a.m. and drop me off at the airport with plenty of time to catch my flight."

"All right," Elaine said, happy that they would at least have that time together.

Pastor Mike gave a heartfelt sermon about motherhood. At one point in the sermon, Sasha took Elaine's hand in hers and gave it a squeeze. Elaine blinked back a tear. She so desperately wanted Sasha to move back to Maine permanently, but that was between Sasha and God. Elaine would have to continue to struggle with trusting Him on that issue.

As they left the church, Elaine spied Brody and his mother but she was interrupted before she could reach them.

When they arrived home, Sasha insisted Jan and Elaine relax out on the deck in the sunshine. "Tara will be here soon. We'll get everything ready."

At 12:30, Nathan and Bob arrived and started the grill. Soon after, Brian and his family pulled into the driveway and unloaded a box of food. Avery approached with a book in her hand. It was the copy of *Evangeline* that Virginia had given her. "I just finished it," she said to Elaine.

"Goodness," Sasha answered. "Did you really?"

The girl nodded. "I read the whole thing—Dad said the audio was too expensive."

"I read it too," Sasha said. "But it wasn't easy."

Avery agreed.

Sasha continued. "And it was all so sad. Evangeline and Gabriel being separated by the British and then her traveling for years trying to find him, only to have just a moment with him before he died."

"I know." Avery spoke gravely. "If only they'd had cell phones back then."

Elaine gasped but then realized the girl was joking. She began to laugh. Avery and Sasha joined in too.

It dawned on Elaine that in another ten years Avery would be a young woman and Sasha would be well into her midthirties. And perhaps there would be another little girl in the family. She shivered, just as her mother pulled into the driveway. She rushed out to meet her, followed by both Sasha and Avery.

The Goods were the last to arrive. Everyone else had gathered on the deck, except for Jan, Virginia, and Elaine, who waited at the front door for their guests. When Ronald parked the car, the three walked out to meet them. Virginia swiped at a few tears as she told Ronald hello.

Half an hour later, they all grabbed comfortable sweatshirts and jackets and sat around the tables on the porch, eating barbecued chicken, kale slaw, fruit salad, potato salad, and homemade rolls that Amy brought. Ronald and Peggy seemed comfortable with everyone, even though Peggy appeared tired. Ronald shared some of his story. Ronald's mother had died from cancer when he was a sophomore in high school. About that time his father started talking about a book that "could help" Ronald pay for college. It seemed that his father had hidden the book somewhere, but couldn't remember where. That was when Ronald realized his father was having health issues. "I'm guessing it was early onset Alzheimer's," Ronald said. "But that was the 1970s and we didn't know about that sort of thing. It appeared he was going crazy. He ended up dying of a stroke when I was twenty."

Empathy rushed through Elaine. The poor man had lost so much at such a young age.

"By then, I'd been working in an auto body shop for a couple of years. I'd already met Peggy and we knew we wanted to be together, so I sold the house, we got married, and then we bought the auto shop in Waterville and have been in business ever since." He smiled as he pushed his empty dinner plate away from the edge of the table. "Things worked out. God has blessed me with a loving wife and a good business. We never had children, but He's filled our lives with other things." He reached for Peggy's hand and squeezed it. "This last year, battling illness, well, it's only reinforced how blessed we are."

Touched by her cousin's wise words, Elaine said, "I appreciate your perspective so much. But I'm guessing you never were one to hold a grudge."

Ronald glanced out over the lake and then back at Elaine. "Honestly, both my grandmother and my father were pretty bitter people. My mother wasn't, though. Perhaps it's just the personality God gave me—maybe it's that simple—but I remember when I was in the fifth grade, one day in Sunday school, telling God I'd choose to be grateful instead of bitter. I think it stuck."

Elaine smiled, thankful to have found such a caring relative.

After strawberry shortcake for dessert, Ronald and Peggy told everyone thank you and that they should get going. Jan glanced at Elaine, who nodded. She knew exactly what her cousin's plan was.

Jan cleared her throat and said, "Once we receive the copy of *Evangeline*, we'll return it to you, Ronald."

"That's thoughtful of you," he said. "But I won't take it. I want you to keep it." He spread his arms wide. "I've gained an extended family. That's far more important to me than a book."

Peggy nodded in agreement. "This has been delightful," she said. "And we look forward to hosting all of you sometime in our home."

Virginia gave both Ronald and Peggy a hug and then the rest of the families said their goodbyes to the couple.

After they left, Brian asked what Elaine and Jan planned to do with the book once it was returned to them.

Elaine said, "We're not sure."

Jan cleared her throat.

"What is it?" Elaine asked. "Allergies?"

"Ha ha," Jan replied.

"Just joking." Elaine smiled. "What are you thinking?"

"Well, I've been thinking about Bristol and her needs and how good it felt to help raise the money for her drainage system."

Elaine agreed.

"And then I got to thinking about Abigail and how generous Brody said she was to others with no thought to herself."

"Yes, I remember that," Elaine said, turning to Brian. "Abigail is the woman who found the book."

He nodded. "I remember that part of the story."

Jan continued. "Then I thought of Brody saying he'd pay for his mother's house with money he's saved. But here he is an injured veteran. I know the value of the book won't cover all of Abigail's work, but I'd like for whatever it's worth to go to her."

Elaine wasn't sure how to reply. The book belonged to their grandmother and had a long family history. If Ronald had accepted it, the book would still be in the family.

Jan's gaze met Elaine's. "Bad idea?" Jan ran her hand through her short dark hair.

"No," Elaine replied. "I actually think it's a wonderful idea. And I think it's what Nana would have wanted us to do." At that moment, Jan reminded Elaine of their Nana and her care for others.

Elaine turned toward to her daughter, but before she could ask for her opinion, Sasha said, "Mother. Don't do that." Her face grew red as she spoke.

Elaine turned toward her daughter. "Why not?"

Sasha's face was beet red now. "I'll tell you later," she muttered as she stood and began collecting the dessert plates. Then she said, "You two should display the book in the tearoom, behind glass of course. And under lock and key. But it's yours to treasure. Enjoy it." Sasha turned toward her cousins. "Let's all clean up while Mom, Jan, and Grandma relax." She glanced toward Bob and Nathan. "You two can join our mothers."

"I'm going to go rest," Virginia said. "You young things"— she grinned at Elaine and Jan—"should go take a walk with your sweethearts."

"Rest in my room," Elaine said to her mother. "I'll come check on you when we get back."

The two couples obeyed Virginia. Chickadee Lake shimmered in the sunlight, and a crane flew just above the water.

The warmth of the sun beat against Elaine's arms and she turned her face heavenward. "What a perfect day," she said to Nathan as they fell a step behind Jan and Bob, who were deep in conversation.

"Yes, perfect," Nathan answered. "A perfect day—because I'm with you." He wrapped his arm around Elaine and pulled her close as she slipped her arm around his waist.

"I saw a book at Bristol's before the flood—one on back road trips in Maine," she said. "I'm going to buy it during the grand reopening this week. For the two of us."

"Sounds like a great idea," Nathan said, giving Elaine a squeeze. "Sunday afternoon drives, here we come."

ELAINE WOKE UP at five the next morning to songbirds outside her bedroom window, ready to greet the coming sunrise.

She climbed out of bed, deciding to go ahead and shower and dress. Sasha would be leaving soon, and Elaine wanted to be fully awake to tell her goodbye.

As she dressed, she made a mental list of what she needed to do before the tearoom opened, putting contacting Dr. Day and giving him an update on the book at the top of her list. But first she needed to speak with Sasha about why she thought giving the book back to Abigail wasn't a good idea.

Soon, she was heading downstairs to put water on for tea. As she reached the entryway, she saw Sasha's suitcase, backpack, and coat ready to go. When she stepped into the kitchen, Sasha stood at the window looking over the lake, a glass of water in her hand.

"Can I help you with anything?" Elaine asked. "To get ready to go?"

Sasha shook her head, turning toward her mother. "I packed last night."

"How about if I fix you some breakfast?"

Sasha started to shake her head, but then stopped. Maybe she realized it would mean something to her mother to feed her before she left. "Sure. Something light. Maybe a bowl of oatmeal?"

"You've got it," Elaine said, grabbing a pan from the cupboard.

They chatted for a few minutes as the water boiled.

Elaine kept the conversation light, but then Sasha said, "You're probably wondering why I didn't think you should give the book back to Abigail."

Elaine nodded but didn't say anything.

"Brody really does have the money to help his mom with the money she's short."

"I know he said that," Elaine said. "But doesn't he need to buy a new truck?"

Sasha shook her head. "He's decided he doesn't since his current one is only a few years old. When we first met him, he was out of sorts about his injury and wondering if he was forced to leave the army what he would do for work and all of that. But the truth is, he's saved like crazy. He could buy a new truck and help his mom and still have some money in savings."

"All right," Elaine said. "If you're sure."

"I am," Sasha said, "and so is Brody. He said he needed to trust God with his future—what he'll do for a job, where he'll live, all of that—rather than his bank account."

"This guy," Elaine said, "just keeps sounding better and better."

Sasha nodded, her eyes teary.

Elaine wrapped her arm around her daughter. "What is it?"

"I'm really going to miss him, Mom."

Elaine's eyes watered too. "Have the two of you talked about the future?"

Sasha nodded. "Some. He feels the same way, but we need to spend more time together. He'll try to come out to Colorado—he has a good buddy not too far from me. And I'll come back here as soon as I can."

Elaine's heart warmed. "I'll be praying for the two of you."

Sasha smiled a little. "I know you will. There's no way you can know how much I count on that."

Elaine kissed her daughter's forehead. She probably did know, but there was no reason to tell Sasha that. She'd counted on her own mother's prayers her entire life.

Elaine gave Sasha another hug and then dished up the oatmeal for her. Five minutes later there was a light tap on the door.

Sasha smiled. "He's right on time." She put her bowl in the sink and headed to the door, with Elaine following her.

Just as Sasha opened the front door and let Brody in, Jan appeared on the staircase. "Off so soon?" she called down.

"Yes," Sasha answered.

"Hold on." Jan hustled down the stairs. "I need to give you a hug."

As Jan hugged her, Sasha whispered, "I'll be back soon. I promise."

"You'd better be." Jan hugged her even harder and then let her go.

Sasha hugged Elaine one last time. "Thank you for everything and for our talk this morning. I appreciate it."

Sasha released her, and Elaine quickly swiped at her eyes. Then she turned to Brody and gave him a hug. He returned it and said, "Thank *you* for everything."

"Don't be a stranger when you get back," Elaine said.

Brody glanced at Sasha, grinned, and then said, "I won't be. I promise."

"I expect a detailed report about your awards ceremony. Pictures. The whole thing."

"You've got it." He grinned again and gave Jan a hug too.

Then he picked up Sasha's suitcase and the two headed out the door.

Sasha waved as she walked beside Brody. Elaine and Jan both followed them onto the porch and watched as Brody put Sasha's suitcase in the backseat of his cab. Then they both climbed into the front, and Sasha waved again as the truck pulled away into the bright morning.

"So," Jan said. "Will Sasha soon be coming back to see us *and* Brody?"

"Yes," Elaine answered. "Let's have a cup of tea and I'll tell you the whole story."

Jan rubbed her hands together as they stepped back inside. "We're blessed, aren't we?"

"Absolutely," Elaine answered. "Every morning, rain or shine, clouds or blue sky. We're blessed with family, a beautiful home, jobs we love, and an amazing community."

"Not to mention two terrific guys," Jan answered.

Elaine put her arm around her cousin as they entered the kitchen and then glanced out at the flowers on the deck. They didn't appear battered at all now. Instead they appeared sturdy and bright. Spring had definitely arrived, and with it, a renewed sense of hope.

"I've been thinking about that chandelier," Jan said as she poured their tea.

Elaine groaned. "Never a moment's peace, is there?"

Jan laughed. "Not in this house. That's our next project, right? To figure out what made it explode?"

Elaine's blue eyes twinkled. "Do you think we can if the electrician couldn't?"

"As a matter of fact, I do." Jan raised her teacup, as if proposing a toast, and Elaine clinked hers against her cousin's.

"Because if we put our heads together," Elaine said, "we can figure out anything, right?"

Jan laughed. "I certainly hope so."

As the two sipped their tea, Elaine breathed a prayer of gratitude for her cousin and best friend and all they shared together. Sasha was right. There was no place like home, especially when it was in Maine.

ABOUT THE AUTHOR

L eslie Gould is the #1 best-selling and award-winning author of twenty-six novels, including nine with Guideposts. She teaches college writing and enjoys studying church history, traveling all over the U.S. (and the world, when she can!), and researching pretty much everything. She and her husband, Peter, have been married for thirty-four years, live in the beautiful Pacific Northwest, and are the parents of four adult children.

From the Tea for Two Kitchen

Jan's Caramel Chocolate Pecan Bars

CHOCOLATE CRUST:

- 1½ cups all purpose flour
- ¾ cup unsweetened cocoa powder
- 1 cup powdered sugar
- 1 teaspoon salt
- 1 cup cold butter, cut into small chunks

PECAN TOPPING:

- 1½ cups pecans
- 10 ounces chocolate chips
- ½ cup or 8 T. butter
- 1 cup brown sugar
- ⅓ cup heavy cream
- 1 teaspoon vanilla
- ½ teaspoon salt

Preheat the oven to 350 degrees. Spray a 9 × 9-inch baking dish with cooking spray. Using a food processor, combine the flour, cocoa powder, powdered sugar and salt. Pulse until combined. (If you don't have a food processor, use a whisk to combine the dry ingredients thoroughly.)

Add in the cold butter pieces and pulse again just until the dough comes together in crumbles, similar to a streusel or shortbread. (You can use a pastry blender if a food processor is not available.) Press the dough firmly into the bottom of the prepared pan. Sprinkle the pecans over the crust, followed by the chocolate chips.

In a medium saucepan, melt together the butter, brown sugar, cream, vanilla, and salt over medium heat. Whisk until smooth and the sugar is dissolved, then pour the mixture over the chocolate crust.

Bake for 25 minutes. Let cool completely before cutting into squares.

Read on for an exciting sneak peek
into the next volume of Tearoom Mysteries!

Brimming with Questions
by Elizabeth Adams

Jan Blake sat back on her heels and looked around. She and her boyfriend, Bob Claybrook, had made some progress, but there was still several days' worth of work before they would have this place cleaned out. The storage unit hadn't been opened in nearly four years, and she'd forgotten how much stuff was in here.

"Ready to call it a day?" Bob asked.

"I guess we probably should. I'm about ready to go home," she said. "I sort of thought we'd made more progress than this."

She looked around at the piles of papers that surrounded her. Boxes were stacked as high as the ceiling toward the back of the storage unit, and pieces of antique furniture were scattered on top of plastic bins at the front and wherever there was room. Canvases and framed artwork were piled haphazardly on every surface. She knew there were boxes of old books and reams of papers and heaps and heaps of clothing, most of which would need to be tossed. Jan recognized the various pieces of the dining room set she'd grown up with toward the back. It was a good set, cherry, and carved in the French provincial style, but Jan didn't know what she'd do with it. Maybe she'd get Elaine's boyfriend Nathan to sell it at one of his antiques auctions.

"It's going to take time." Bob's light sweater was covered in dust and he'd been sneezing all morning, but he was smiling at her now. He was such a good sport, and she was so thankful he'd agreed to help her today. "These are your mother's things. Of course you're going to want to go through them carefully."

Jan nodded and looked down at the half-empty box in front of her. Maybe she'd packed it when her mother passed away, but it was more likely one of her kids had done it. She'd been so overwhelmed by planning the funeral in the midst of her grief while grieving that her grown kids had done much of the work of cleaning out her mother's apartment. They'd tossed everything in boxes and put it in this storage unit, until the estate could be settled. That had taken a couple of years—far longer than Jan thought possible for such a simple estate. Jan, as the only child, was the sole beneficiary, aside from some donations to charity, but somehow it had still taken years to work its way through probate. Then, once everything was settled, Jan had been in the midst of opening and running the tearoom, and, well, it had sort of fallen by the wayside. Sorting through her mother's things had seemed like such a difficult task on so many levels. Like such a big job. Looking around again now, she could see that she'd been right.

"Let me just finish going through this box, and then we'll call it a day."

Bob nodded, stood, and started to gather up the garbage bags they'd filled so far. He'd brought along a portable paper shredder and had been shredding old bank statements for the past hour.

Jan looked down at the box she was sorting. So far she'd found her mother's Bible—a precious find that she'd treasure—as well as some yearbooks and a couple photo albums. She had flipped through the photo albums and set them in a pile of things to bring home, and the yearbooks in a pile to deal with later. She reached back into the box now and pulled out a manila folder. She flipped it open and found a stack of old newspaper clippings. She almost set it aside, but then one of the headlines caught her eye. *Missing Infant.*

What in the world? Jan looked a little closer and saw that the article was about a baby, kidnapped from her mother's arms.

Portland. Dora and Larry Kellogg are still desperately hoping for clues in the kidnapping of their newborn daughter, Jane. Jane was just hours old when she was taken from her mother's arms in Portland General Hospital on Tuesday by a woman dressed as a nurse. The woman, who was not employed by the hospital and whose identity is unknown, then carried the baby out of the hospital, and neither the "nurse" nor the baby have been seen since. Local police as well as the FBI have been searching for any clue as to the child's whereabouts. Anyone with any information is encouraged to call the Portland police station.

Oh my. Jan couldn't imagine. What an awful thing to have happen. Had those poor parents ever gotten their daughter back? She shook her head, and turned to the next article in the stack. It was from the day before, the day the news had broken. *Baby Stolen from Hospital; Massive Manhunt Underway,* the headline read. There were not many more details in this story. Just that the woman who was dressed as a nurse had promised to take the baby to the nursery, but no one had any clue who she was. It was awful.

Then Jan noticed something strange. The first article to run, the one that had broken the story, had been published April 5, 1961. So the baby would have been born on April 4. That was her birthday.

"What did you find?" Bob asked. Jan looked up and saw that he had the garbage bags all gathered in the hallway. She'd forgotten he was even there.

"It's nothing important." She flipped through the other papers in the folder and saw that they were all newspaper clippings about the story. The press had covered the story for months—years even. There were stories clipped on the first, fifth, and tenth anniversary of the kidnapping. Why had her mother saved all this? "Just some old newspaper stories about a kidnapped baby."

"That's strange." Bob brushed the dust from his sweater.

It was strange, Jan thought. Maybe her mother had just been intrigued by the case. The baby had been born the same day as Jan, and in the same hospital. Maybe that was why Mom had been fascinated enough to track it for decades.

But the baby's name...was it really too much to believe babies named Jan and Jane were both born in the same hospital on the same day? They were both common enough names. But...Jan shook her head. Something about this felt strange.

"I think I'll take this with me," Jan said, slipping the folder into the bag of things she was going to take back to the house.

She would read through all the articles more carefully later. Probably there was nothing to it.

They drove in Bob's car back through the charming streets of Lancaster, Maine. Bob had a smile on his face, and the little town really was enough to make anyone cheerful on this beautiful June day. The sky was a lovely cerulean blue, and the trees still had that fresh green tint that meant summer was just beginning. And the little lakefront town, full of historic homes and charming small businesses, was in full bloom. Azaleas and rhododendrons were bursting with blossoms, and peonies, irises, viburnum and roses graced the yards and walks of just about every home in town.

But Jan was distracted, thinking about the folder of clippings she'd found in her mother's things. It was probably nothing. But still, she was curious.

When they got back to Tea for Two—the tearoom set in the grand Victorian home Jan shared with her cousin Elaine—Bob helped her unload the things she'd brought home but didn't stay so Jan and Elaine could start getting the tearoom ready to open for the day.

"What's all this?" Elaine asked, pointing to the pile of papers Jan had left stacked on the counter.

"Oh. Sorry. I'll move that all out of the way." Jan was taking teapots down out of the cabinets next to the sink.

"This is crazy." Elaine had lifted the cover of the folder and was looking at the top newspaper clipping, the one that ran in the *Portland Press Herald* the day after Jane was kidnapped.

"I know," Jan said. She set the teapots on the counter and reached for the kettle.

"Wait. I remember hearing about this," Elaine said. She was flipping through the clippings now, looking at each of the headlines. "This is about the baby who was kidnapped from the hospital by a woman dressed as a nurse. This was a big case. I remember hearing about it on one of those shows about unsolved crimes."

"Really?" Jan had had no idea the story was well known. Why hadn't she ever heard of it?

"Yeah. Apparently they changed a lot of things about how hospitals operate after this."

"I should hope so." Jan let cool water run into the kettle.

"But why did your mom have this stack of clippings about it in her things?" Elaine closed the folder and looked at Jan.

"I don't know." Jan said. She turned off the faucet. "There's probably no good reason. Just something she was interested in."

"But you brought it here instead of throwing it away."

"Yeah." Jan set the kettle on the stove. "I guess I wanted to look at it all carefully. Read through the articles a little more."

Elaine was giving her that look, the one that said she knew there was something Jan wasn't saying. "Why?"

Jan turned and busied herself pulling out the tins of loose tea they used most often.

"I don't know," Jan finally said. "But there's something fascinating about it."

"There is indeed," Elaine said. "A fifty-year-old mystery that was never solved? That would intrigue anyone, especially one about something like kidnapping."

Jan arranged the tins along the counter. Earl Grey was their most popular variety, so she set that in the front, with English Breakfast behind it. Elaine was waiting for her to say something, she knew, but Jan wasn't sure exactly what to say.

"I noticed that the baby was born the same day I was," Jan finally said. "At Portland General Hospital, where I was born."

"That's quite a coincidence," Elaine said. She still had her hand on the folder.

"And I noticed that the baby was named Jane. Which, you have to admit, is pretty close to Jan."

"It is," Elaine said, nodding. "Is that why you're so interested in these old clippings? Because it could have been you?"

It was an innocent enough question. Coming from anyone else, Jan would have taken it at face value. But she knew Elaine better than that. Or, more specifically, Elaine knew her better than that. But how could she even formulate the crazy thoughts that were going through her head into words?

"I don't know," Jan finally said.

Elaine didn't say anything. She just watched Jan, waiting for her to go on. Jan set the mint tea behind the rooibos.

"I guess I've always wondered," Jan finally said.

"Wondered what?"

"Oh, I don't know. If there was some mix-up at the hospital I guess. I mean, I know lots of kids always wonder that at some point about their families, but I don't know. I was never anything like my parents."

Elaine was nodding, listening. Jan went on.

"You know what my dad was like. So reserved and standoffish. And he was so into music. He was always playing his guitar, or singing in the church choir, or listening to his favorite songs on the record player. It was his passion. And I just…it's not that I never cared about music. I like music, of course. Who doesn't? But I just didn't ever love it like he did. I was never passionate about it, and I guess I sometimes felt like he was disappointed about that."

"Fair enough," Elaine said. "And?"

"I don't know. I guess there's also my mom, who of course I love, but who really found her release in painting."

"She was very good."

Jan shrugged. "She loved it. And I've got several dozen canvasses in that storage unit to prove it. But as much as I like art, I never really got it like she did. So both of my parents are these artistic types, and meanwhile I was always much more interested in science and empirical evidence. They always seemed baffled by how I could be related to them. And, yeah, I'll admit that sometimes I wondered the same thing myself."

"Are you suggesting that you think your parents might not be your real parents?" Elaine asked carefully.

"I don't know what I'm suggesting. I'm just thinking aloud." Jan had already set the tea tins in a row, and now she straightened them, lining each one up carefully. "But ever since I found those articles, I've realized a few other things."

"Like what?"

Jan felt a tiny bit ridiculous even speaking these thoughts out loud. But it was just Elaine. She knew Elaine would listen without making judgments. She took a deep breath.

"I've never seen a picture of my mother pregnant, for one thing."

"Okay. Have you seen other pictures from around that time?"

"Yes. There are pictures from my parents' early marriage, and a lot from when I was young, but none of my mom pregnant with me."

"Maybe that was something that wasn't done back then?" But the tone of Elaine's voice made it clear she was stretching. Sure, they didn't do pregnancy photo shoots and all that stuff back then, but it wasn't like pregnancy was some shameful secret.

"Maybe," Jan said. "Then there's the fact that I'm an only child."

"Lots of people are," Elaine reminded her.

"I know. Maybe it means nothing. But why didn't they have any other kids? Was it because they didn't want to, or because they couldn't?"

"Did you ever ask your mom about it?"

"No. Well, I'm sure I complained about wanting someone to play with when I was young, but never as an adult. It seemed invasive to ask. Now I wish I had."

"There could be some very benign reason they never had more kids," Elaine said. "I'm sure you were quite the handful."

Jan smiled. "I was a perfect angel. Mostly."

"If you say so." Elaine smiled back. "Okay, I don't know if the only-child thing is evidence. But what else are you thinking about?"

"Well…" Jan took a moment to think this all through and make sure she had it all straight in her mind. "Just some off-hand remarks I overheard as a kid. Things that don't necessarily mean anything on their own, but always stuck with me."

"Like what?"

Jan took a deep breath. She realized she'd never told anyone this, not even Peter.

"One night when I was supposed to be in bed I got up to get a drink of water and I heard my parents talking. My dad was talking about how everything they'd done to get me had been worth it."

"That could have meant any number of things."

"I know. But the way he said it…I don't know. It struck me as strange, and I was just a kid."

"Okay." Elaine was listening, but the look on her face made it clear she wasn't convinced there was anything strange here. Well, she was probably right. Still, Jan went on.

"Another time, I came up to some friends of my mother's after church. They didn't know I was there, and I didn't tell them. But they were looking at my mom across the room and they were whispering about how they thought I might be adopted."

"What? Why in the world would they say that?"

"They said something about how no one had even known she was pregnant before she showed up one day with a baby."

"Some friends. Gossiping about her like that, and at church too!"

"I think we both know plenty of gossip happens at church." Jan shook her head. "Anyway, I never told my mom what I'd overheard, but it stuck with me. Her own friends hadn't known she was pregnant. How was that possible?"

"Things were different back then," Elaine said. "Maybe it wasn't something you talked about."

"It was the early sixties, not Victorian times," Jan said. "Even if you didn't talk about it, wouldn't it be pretty obvious when she was nine months pregnant? Even the best maternity clothes can't hide it at that point."

"I'm sure there could have been any number of reasons they didn't realize," Elaine said.

"Like what?"

Elaine thought for a moment. She looked up, as if hoping to find the answers floating in the air. "I don't know, but maybe there are some."

"Maybe." Jan finished adjusting the tins and leaned back against the counter. "And here's another thing I've always wondered. My parents lived in Augusta. Why was I born in Portland?"

"Isn't Portland where your grandparents lived?" Elaine asked.

"Yes. But why would that matter? Why would she go all the way up there to have the baby?"

"I don't know. I'm just asking."

"It makes no sense."

Elaine was quiet for a moment. Then, she took a deep breath. "But you're suggesting that it would make sense if you actually were born in Portland, but to different parents. And that you were stolen?"

Jan didn't answer right away. Was that what she was suggesting? She hadn't really admitted that, even to herself. But slowly, she found herself nodding. Something deep within her, some long-unspoken question, had been unearthed. Something she hadn't even really acknowledged to herself until just now.

"I guess so. I guess that is what I'm saying."

Elaine flipped through the sheets in the folder. "Okay. Let's say you are the baby that was kidnapped from the hospital that day," Elaine said slowly. "I think it's a pretty big stretch, at least given the evidence so far, but I suppose I can see how it's possible."

Jan felt some of the tension in her shoulders melt away. Elaine hadn't laughed out loud. Jan loved her for it.

"Let's say it is true. It's been over fifty years, and the police and the FBI were never able to solve the case. How would we go about finding out the truth?"

We. Jan's heart swelled at the sound of that word.

"I don't know." Jan hated to admit it. "But I'm sure we can figure it out together."

FROM THE
GUIDEPOSTS ARCHIVES

This story, by Rochelle Robinson of Lake Station,
Indiana, originally appeared in *Guideposts*.

Spring can get mighty rainy here in my little corner of Indiana. I was driving through town one gray March morning when the drizzle suddenly turned into a downpour.

I saw a woman carrying her baby, trying to keep the child dry underneath her coat. But they both got soaked, and looked completely miserable. I pulled over, rolled down the window and handed the woman my umbrella, figuring I would just buy myself a new one, which I did. The next week, I found myself giving that umbrella to a man at the bus stop. *I need more umbrellas!* I thought.

That gave me an idea. Now I buy a handful of umbrellas every time I go to the dollar store. Black, red, striped, polka dot, whatever I can find. I stash them in my car, and whenever I see someone on the street getting drenched in a storm, I pull over and hand them an umbrella then say, "God bless you."

In the past two years I've given out about fifty umbrellas. People don't seem to know how to react at first, but once they get that umbrella over their heads, their faces brighten.

Sign up for the
Guideposts Fiction Newsletter
and stay up-to-date on the books you love!

You'll get sneak peeks of new releases, recommendations from other Guideposts readers, and special offers just for you . . .
and it's FREE!

Just go to Guideposts.org/Newsletters
today to sign up.

Guideposts.®

**Visit Guideposts.org/Shop
or call (800) 932-2145**

Find more inspiring fiction in these best-loved Guideposts series!

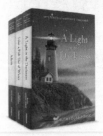

Mysteries of Martha's Vineyard

Come to the shores of this quaint and historic island and dig into a cozy mystery. When a recent widow inherits a lighthouse just off the coast of Massachusetts, she finds exciting adventures, new friends, and renewed hope.

Tearoom Mysteries

Mix one stately Victorian home, a charming lakeside town in Maine, and two adventurous cousins with a passion for tea and hospitality. Add a large scoop of intriguing mystery and sprinkle generously with faith, family, and friends, and you have the recipe for Tearoom Mysteries.

Sugarcreek Amish Mysteries

Be intrigued by the suspense and joyful "aha!" moments in these delightful stories. Each book in the series brings together two women of vastly different backgrounds and traditions, who realize there's much more to the "simple life" than meets the eye.

Mysteries of Silver Peak

Escape to the historic mining town of Silver Peak, Colorado, and discover how one woman's love of antiques helps her solve mysteries buried deep in the town's checkered past.

Patchwork Mysteries

Discover that life's little mysteries often have a common thread in a series where every novel contains an intriguing whodunit centered around a quilt located in a beautiful New England town.

To learn more about these books, visit Guideposts.org/Shop